DEAD
AGAINST
HER

ALSO BY MELINDA LEIGH

BREE TAGGERT NOVELS

Cross Her Heart

See Her Die

Drown Her Sorrows

Right Behind Her

"Her Second Death" (A Prequel Short Story)

MORGAN DANE NOVELS

Say You're Sorry

Her Last Goodbye

Bones Don't Lie

What I've Done

Secrets Never Die

Save Your Breath

SCARLET FALLS NOVELS

Hour of Need

Minutes to Kill

Seconds to Live

SHE CAN SERIES

She Can Run

She Can Tell

DEAD
AGAINST
HER

MELINDA
LEIGH

 Montlake

Published by Montlake, Seattle

www.apub.com

Amazon, the Amazon logo, and Montlake are trademarks of Amazon.com, Inc., or its affiliates.

ISBN-13: 9781542030625 (paperback)
ISBN-10: 1542030625 (paperback)

ISBN-13: 9781542030618 (hardcover)
ISBN-10: 1542030617 (hardcover)

Cover design by Shasti O'Leary Soudant

Printed in the United States of America

First edition

For Charlie, Annie, and Tom
You are everything

Chapter One

Hate is a living thing, a seed to be planted and watered. If adequately nourished, it blooms and grows. When the conditions are just right, it acts like an invasive species and takes over, obliterating the original plants, blocking their sunlight and oxygen.

Starving them.

Until they die.

I consider my own hate, carefully tended, fertilized with years of imagining this very moment. The hand holding the gun feels disconnected from my brain. The hate is possessing me.

Controlling me.

I study the two people securely tied to chairs before me. Ironically, beneath the intensity of my hatred, I feel oddly detached.

The man tugs at his binds, but they don't give. I know how to tie a fucking knot. His mouth quivers. He's trying to play it cool, but he can't pull it off. Sweat beads on his upper lip, and the wide whites of his eyes reveal his terror. Next to him, the old woman—his mother—is still. She's too frail to fight back. Her end is near, and she knows it. She's the smarter of the two.

I focus on him. After all, he's the reason I'm here.

He opens his mouth but emits only a croak. Panic is constricting his throat. I know the feeling well.

He swallows hard, then speaks. He's trying to conceal his fear, and his voice comes out too loud. "Don't do this. You're going to regret it."

Will I, though?

Regret is a funny emotion. By definition, you can't experience it until after the fact. So who knows?

What I'm doing is wrong. I know that. I enjoy his fear much more than I should. I breathe it in, like the scent of a meal I've been preparing for days and finally get to eat. Anticipation has whetted my appetite until I am ravenous. The pull of the trigger will be utterly satisfying. Deep in my bones, I suspect this could be the very deed that makes me whole again.

I cock my head. "I don't think so."

Tied to the chair next to him, the old woman whimpers. Tears pour down her cheeks. She's spent too much time in the sun. Her skin is as wrinkled as a paper bag and mottled with spots. While she isn't my primary target, she isn't exactly an innocent either. She's made selfish choices. She birthed and raised a monster. She enabled him. She knows what he is. She's always known, even if she prefers to ignore his innate viciousness. But is this really her fault? Unconditional love is a natural part of parenthood, but it should have limits. You should be able to love someone without ignoring the damage they inflict upon others.

Vaguely, I register that I should feel some kind of pity for her. He's put her in a tough position. Instead, I'm filled with a comfortable vacantness, as if my heart is as hollow as a dead tree.

"You can leave now, and we won't tell anyone," he begs.

I should have gagged him. I really don't want to have a conversation. Or do I? I don't need to explain my actions. He knows how we got to this place. He knows he's at fault. But maybe I need to revel in his pain. Did he take pleasure in mine?

Probably.

That's the kind of man he is. He's caused plenty of people distress in his lifetime. He's a bastard. A bully. A user.

A new thought pops into my head. Maybe he's the parasite, feeding on other people's suffering like a plant absorbs sunlight. He's an invasive vine that needs to be pulled from the garden by the root. Like poison ivy, eliminating him will leave a mark, but it must be done.

He licks his lips. "You don't know what you're doing. You've never killed anyone. It'll ruin you."

"I guess I'll find out." Tormenting him sends a rush of pleasure through me. The tables are finally turned in my favor. "How does it feel to be helpless? To know you're going to die?"

He clamps his mouth shut, and his face goes as pale as ice.

The old woman cries out, then begins mumbling a prayer. She repeats the words over and over. They prickle my nerves and stoke my hate higher. God didn't answer my prayers. He let me suffer. How dare she ask for His intervention now, when she's finally paying the price for her sins.

I point the gun at her. "Shut up."

But she moans.

Fury rushes through me and words burst out. "I am in charge!"

Control slides further away, and I don't bother to reach for it. I lunge forward, press the gun to her head, and pull the trigger. She slumps instantly. Her death is so fast, so abrupt, it's almost anticlimactic. But then, *her* death isn't my priority.

He flinches; then shock smooths all emotion from his face. His gaze shifts from his mother to me. His mouth opens, then closes again. He should cry out. He should be overwhelmed with grief and trauma. He isn't. He's calculating his next move. The bastard. But he is clearly speechless. Power floods me. I have waited a long time for my revenge.

I step back and compose myself, brush a stray hair off my forehead. "Didn't think I was serious, did you?"

He says nothing. He turns his head and stares at his mother. The details sink in. His face morphs into a mask of disbelief and horror. But I can't be sure if it's an act. Anyway, I want more. I want acknowledgment for my suffering. Anger rides my skin like fire ants. He owes me a response, damn it.

"Answer me!" I shout.

When he doesn't, I aim at his kneecap and fire. The gun bucks in my hand. Blood splatters. His body convulses, and he screams. He pulls hard at the binds around his wrists. The chair wobbles as he thrashes. He could overturn it if he keeps trying, but tipping over the chair won't free him. Those knots are solid. He isn't going anywhere.

I shoot him in the other knee. He screams again, the sound high-pitched, feral, and helpless. The smells of gunpowder and blood fill the air.

"Do you believe me now?" I yell.

He groans. Tears and snot run down his face. Pain makes his eyes wild.

"You're going to bleed to death, but it will take a long time." I think about this. I want to make him suffer. I want to watch him die. But I can't afford to stay here too long. The farm is isolated, but mail and packages are delivered regularly. Did she have any nosy neighbors?

I can't take the chance of being caught. I won't ruin the rest of my life. He's already taken too much time from me. I deserve a future. Also, I don't want to be forced to kill anyone who is truly innocent. I need to end this soon, before we are discovered. I point the gun at his shoulder and fire another shot.

His body jerks again, but this time he doesn't thrash. He's too weak. His head lolls. Blood runs from his wounds, blooms on the fabric of his clothing, drips to the floor in spreading puddles beneath the chair. The noises he makes no longer sound human. I've reduced him to an animal. The thought brings me nothing but satisfaction.

Am I evil?

Maybe.

I get close, right in his face. "Are. You. Sorry?"

He is. I can see it in his eyes even before he nods. He's given up. He's surrendered. I've won. But I need to hear his admission.

"Say it!" I scream.

"I'm sorry," he croaks, the words barely audible.

Finally.

I lean close to his ear. "So you're the one full of regret."

I straighten. His eyes roll back in his head. He's blacking out with the pain and blood loss. I raise the gun again and press it hard into his forehead. His lids flutter. Our gazes meet. He knows I've won. I focus on the moment. I want to remember every detail. Killing him must be deliberate, and he needs to know it's coming.

Maintaining eye contact, I pull the trigger.

Compared to the other shots, this one seems quiet. I see the light extinguish from his eyes. His body goes limp instantly. Silence falls on the room. I can hear the old clock on the wall ticking as its second hand chugs along. The peace that fills me is almost blissful. But I can't take the time to let it sink in.

I turn away from the bodies and walk out of the house, locking the back door before I pull it closed. I stand on the porch. Everything feels different. The night air is pleasantly cool and damp. The sky is clear, the stars bright pinpoints on its inky blackness.

I am reborn. I have a lifetime ahead of me. With his death, I can put the horrors of my past aside and move on.

Ironically, *I* feel no regret.

Only relief.

But even as I tell myself it is finally over, disagreement tugs at me. I peel the gloves from my hands. I've taken plenty of precautions. I've left no fingerprints. I contemplate leaving the murder weapon behind. It's his, after all. But I put it in my pocket with the balled-up gloves. I take no chances.

Just in case this isn't the end of my troubles, but the beginning.

Chapter Two

Sheriff Bree Taggert turned onto the rutted lane and stopped her vehicle in front of an old farmhouse. A neighbor had called for a wellness check. As Bree assessed the property through her windshield, she could see why. Weedy pastures and run-down structures painted a desolate landscape. The front-porch supports leaned to the right, as if a hundred years of relentless winds had battered them into submission. The land immediately around the house needed mowing, and the meadows beyond were waist high.

She reached for her radio to let dispatch know she was on scene. "Sheriff Taggert, code eleven."

Bree climbed out of her vehicle. The house stood on a slight rise, giving her a decent view of the farm. Up close, the structures looked even more neglected. Someone was clearly trying—but mostly failing—to keep the place going. Peeling paint, missing shingles, and broken fence boards evidenced age, hard use, and poor maintenance. The house might have been white once upon a time but had been stripped to a bare, forlorn gray.

A large barn sat behind the house. The weather-beaten exterior still showed faint traces of deep red. The fencing around two large pastures had mostly collapsed. A smaller grass enclosure next to the barn had been recently repaired. In it, a dozen goats milled around the muddy area near the gate. Bree didn't know much about goats, but the animals seemed restless. Chickens roamed freely. She spotted a few cats slinking around the barn door.

Something was off here. She could feel it—an undeniable wrongness hovering in the air between the agitated goats and the pecking chickens. According to tax and motor vehicle records, Camilla Brown, age seventy, owned the property and resided here, but the goats, chickens, and cats were the only signs of life. The place had a vacant feel, much like the abandoned farm down the road from Bree's.

Her gaze swept across the horizon. From an acreage standpoint, the farm was large, but the nearest neighbor was at least a half mile down the road. Did Ms. Brown live all alone out here? She was elderly. Was she no longer able to maintain the farm? Had she suffered an accident or medical emergency? Was she somewhere on the farm, hurt—or worse?

Bree called both the landline and cell number on record for Ms. Brown. When no one answered, she left messages.

The thought of finding Ms. Brown's body depressed Bree, and she almost wished she hadn't volunteered to take the call. But her deputies were always busy, it was near shift change, and the farm was on Bree's way home, so it had made sense for her to handle it. Plus, after an afternoon of negotiations over renovation and expansion plans for the sheriff's station, she'd wanted to escape the office like a prisoner newly granted parole. The plans were exciting. They were adding a locker room for her new female deputies, plus new holding cells and other sorely needed general updates throughout the station. But bureaucracy gave her a throbbing pain behind her eyes.

It was only Tuesday.

Bree turned at the sound of an approaching engine. A pickup truck rattled up the drive and parked next to her SUV. An elderly man climbed out, looking spry for his age, which she estimated to be at least seventy. Skinny and bowlegged, he dressed in jeans and a plaid shirt like an old-movie cowboy. His face was as wrinkled as a piece of foil that had been crumpled into a ball and smoothed back out.

"Sheriff." He touched the wide brim of his hat. "I'm Homer Johnson. I live on the next farm. I called you." He nodded toward the house. "Drove by the place earlier and saw the goats outside. Camilla usually brings them in by four. Chickens should be in by now too. She'd never leave them out past dark. They'll be coyote food. I tried calling her and banging on the door. She won't answer her phone, and her door is locked. She never locks up during the daytime." Homer seemed to have thought of everything.

"When did you see her last?"

Homer squinted at the setting sun. "I saw Camilla at church last Sunday. She never misses, and neither do I. This is the first time I've been by since then. But I'm worried. Camilla is a widow, and like me, she's getting up in years. She had one of those mini strokes last year. Had to sell off a bunch of her goats 'cause she couldn't keep up with the work." He sighed. "I feel for her. I'm struggling with the same thing. At least my boy is involved in the business and we still turn a decent profit."

"Do you have a key to her house?"

"No, ma'am. If I did, I wouldn't have called you."

"Let's see what's going on." Bree started toward the front walkway. Dead leaves crunched under her boots. Though early September was still warm, the leaves of a mature oak tree in the front yard had already begun to turn and fall. Winter was just around the corner in upstate New York.

Homer followed her. They went up the porch steps.

Bree stopped on a welcome mat and thumped on the door. "Ms. Brown? This is the sheriff. Please come to the door."

The house remained quiet. In the background, goats bleated.

"I already did that." Homer scowled. Worry deepened his crow's-feet into craters.

"We have procedure to follow." Bree couldn't just break into a house.

The front door was solid wood, with no glass panes and a dead bolt. Gaining entry here would require a battering ram.

As if reading her mind, Homer said, "No one uses the front door."

"Let's try the back." Bree descended the steps and started around the house, standing on her toes and peering in windows as she walked, but all the curtains were drawn. The most she could see were narrow slashes of dim rooms where the drapes didn't quite meet.

Homer strode at her side. They rounded the back corner of the house and turned to look at it. A rear porch spanned the back, mirroring the one in front.

"She never closes her curtains either." Homer propped his hands on his hips. "Leastways not the downstairs ones. The weather's been nice this week. The windows should be open. Mine are."

So were Bree's. She went up the back-porch steps and knocked. No one answered.

"I'm going to check the barn." She jogged down the wooden steps, a growing sense of urgency quickening her pace.

Homer kept up with her as she crossed the weedy backyard and passed an open chicken coop. The big birds squawked and scattered. The goats ran in circles, bleating and stomping, as Bree passed their pen.

She went to the heavy double doors and rolled one side open. The interior was less barn and more commercial milking operation and was better kept than the rest of the property. Milking machines were elevated on a raised platform. She peered through a doorway into another room that contained large stainless-steel tables and refrigerators. The equipment might be a little dinged up, but everything was immaculately clean.

"Hello?" Bree called. "Ms. Brown? This is Sheriff Taggert."

The goats bleated louder, as if trying to get her attention.

Bree turned away from the empty barn and inclined her head toward the goats. "Are they normally this agitated?"

"No, ma'am. I suspect they're hungry." He rubbed his white-stubbled chin. "Might be overdue for milking as well."

Bree scanned the pen. The muddy ground was heavily trampled. The pasture was mostly dirt, the grass having been chewed to the ground. "What does Ms. Brown do with the goats?"

"She sells goat cheese at the farmers market, along with free-range chicken eggs. There's a restaurant in town that buys her cheese as well. That's all the business she has left. It's a shame. This farm used to be a lot bigger."

Farmers cared for their livestock before themselves. Their animals were their livelihood.

"I could toss them some hay for now," Homer offered.

"Thank you. That would be helpful." And keep him occupied while Bree entered the home. Who knew what she would find?

"Yes, ma'am." He moved through the open barn door and toward some hay bales stacked on a raised pallet.

Bree turned toward the house. She retraced her steps to the back porch and examined the door. Unlike the front door, glass panes were set into the top half and she could see into the kitchen, which was empty. There was no dead bolt, just a simple doorknob lock that would take thirty seconds to breach.

Country living.

She shook her head, thinking of the state-of-the-art alarm system at her own farm. But then, Ms. Brown probably hadn't received the threats that Bree had.

She used her cell phone to update dispatch. "There's no response at the door and no sign of the homeowner. The livestock hasn't been fed. I'm concerned the homeowner could be ill or injured. I'm going in."

Not wanting to break a window or bust in the door unless it was absolutely necessary—the sheriff's department didn't need a lawsuit in the event Ms. Brown was fine and simply indisposed—Bree pulled a small tool kit from her pocket and deftly picked the lock. The lock was so old, she probably could have opened it with a credit card. She pushed the door open and the smell of rotting flesh hit her like a fist.

Decomposition.

Bree's gut twisted. Ms. Brown wasn't napping, nor was she in need of assistance.

No. That smell meant something—probably Ms. Brown—was dead.

CHAPTER THREE

Bree took a step back to regroup. Whatever was decomposing had probably been dead at least a day or so. Her stomach tangled, and she was grateful it was empty. Taking a deep breath of fresh air, she pushed the door wide open. Inside, the buzz of insects tightened the queasy knot in her belly.

The flies always found a way in.

With a last gulp of fresh air, Bree stepped into the house. The kitchen was dated but tidy, with wooden countertops worn smooth with decades of scrubbing. Her gaze swept over the room. A rectangular table sat in the middle. One end was set with two plates, two glasses, and two sets of utensils, catercorner to each other. Four chairs were tucked under the table. Empty spaces marked where two more would fit. An iconic CorningWare casserole dish sat on the stovetop. On the counter, a clear dome covered a cake on a pedestal. Flies buzzed around the glass lids, trying to get at the food. Bree moved through the kitchen, trying to block out the sound.

She hated flies.

The smell thickened as she approached the doorway to the living room. Breathing through her nose and clamping her mouth closed, Bree suppressed a quick, reflexive gag. At the threshold, surprise stopped her cold. She froze, her feet rooted to the worn linoleum as she took in the scene with disbelief.

She'd expected to find the homeowner dead of a fall, heart attack, or stroke, but the image in front of Bree was so unexpected, she couldn't move. Her brain didn't want to accept what it was seeing. She squeezed her eyes closed for a few seconds, then reopened them. Nothing had changed. The scene was still horrific.

Two bodies slumped, tied securely to straight-backed wooden chairs. The chairs had been placed side by side a few feet apart and turned in the same direction.

Like an audience facing a stage.

The first victim was an elderly woman, her head hanging sideways at an unnaturally relaxed angle. Ms. Brown, Bree guessed. A bullet hole marred the center of her forehead. Flies hovered around the wound, her eyes, nose, and mouth. Bree's throat went dry and she swallowed. She saw no other injuries on the old woman's pale blue cotton blouse or jeans. A cell phone poked out of the front pocket of her blouse. Bree made a note to have it bagged and tagged before the ME removed the bodies.

The second victim was male, and his body seemed younger. His head lolled forward, so Bree couldn't see his face. But he was clearly dead. Unlike the woman, he'd been shot multiple times. Patches of dark dried blood bloomed on his plain gray T-shirt and jeans. The blood had dripped to the floor and puddled under the chair. Bree noticed that the blood had had time to dry.

She closed her eyes. At the age of eight, Bree had hidden her two younger siblings under the back porch of their house while their father shot their mother and then turned the gun on himself. She hadn't seen their bodies. Had their deaths been this bloody?

A scraping sound brought Bree back to the present. She whipped her head around. Her hand automatically went to the butt of her weapon. Homer stood in the kitchen doorway, his tanned face as white as raw flour.

"Stop!" Bree commanded.

He didn't move, but she doubted he could hear her. His gaze was locked on the bodies, his eyes wide with disbelief and horror. Nothing short of physical intervention would break his shocked trance.

Bree stepped in front of the carnage, blocking his view. He blinked and stared at her, slowly returning to his senses. His mouth opened, then closed again, and he looked as if he might be sick. Not wanting the scene to be contaminated, Bree commanded, "Do not come into this room!"

He flinched.

Recognizing the harshness of her tone, Bree lowered her voice. "Back out of the house carefully. Do not touch anything. I'll be out shortly."

Homer's Adam's apple shifted as he swallowed hard, visibly composing himself. Then he followed her orders.

Bree drew her weapon. These deaths were clearly not fresh, but that didn't mean the killer couldn't still be here. She'd seen weirder things in her law enforcement career. Once, she'd arrested a man who'd killed his wife and lived with her dead body for two weeks, until the smell was so bad the neighbors called the cops.

She cleared a formal parlor and study in the front of the house, then went up the stairs to the second floor. She stopped on the landing and listened but heard nothing. Turning left, she went into the primary bedroom, clearly occupied by the old woman. Bree opened the closet. Church dresses and shoes were lined up on the left. Working clothes hung neatly on the right. Everything had been ironed, even the jeans. Bree stooped to check under the bed. In the attached bath, she pulled aside the shower curtain that hung around a huge claw-foot tub. Then she retreated from the main bedroom into the hallway.

Her heartbeat echoed in her ears as a floorboard creaked under her weight. One glance told her the hall bath was empty. The second bedroom held a twin bed and appeared to be unoccupied. In the third bedroom, suitcases, boxes, and masculine clothing indicated the male was in the process of moving either out or in. She looked in the closet and under his bed as well. But as she'd suspected, the killer was long gone. Easing her weapon back into its holster, she returned to the first floor. Passing the dead in the living room, she went through the kitchen and out the back door.

For a full minute, she stood on the porch and gulped fresh air.

Homer was doing the same, leaning forward, his hands on his thighs. "Who would do that to her?" His voice was weak and sad, but he no longer looked as if he were going to vomit.

"I don't know. It was definitely Ms. Brown?"

He replied with a single, tight nod.

"Do you know who the man is?" Bree tried to smell the grass and earth, but the foul of decomp clung to the insides of her nostrils, coated her throat, and overrode every competing odor.

"I couldn't see his face, but it could be her son." Homer's use of the present tense sent a spear of sorrow through Bree. "She said he was going to move in with her. I didn't know exactly when."

Throat dry, she nodded. Sadness and anger warred inside her as she pictured the table in the kitchen: the silverware in its proper place, the cloth napkins, the home-baked cake. The scene spoke of effort and care and love. Who had prepared dinner for the other? Ms. Brown or her son? It didn't matter.

Before they could enjoy their meal, someone had murdered them both.

Bree addressed Homer in a gentle but firm tone. "I want you to stay here but not touch anything. I also need to get a statement from you, but there are a few other things I must do first."

Homer nodded. "Yeah, OK."

"Also, I'm going to ask you not to make any calls. I don't want this news getting out before any next of kin is notified. Death is hard enough on a family without them hearing about it on TV."

"I understand." Homer's watery eyes locked on Bree. "She didn't have much family except for her boy. Just a brother in Scarlet Falls. A few nieces and nephews there too, but she wasn't real close to them. They live nearby, but they don't visit."

"I need to make a few calls."

Homer nodded toward the barn. "Camilla clearly didn't pass today."

Bree knew he used the word *pass* in respect for the dead, but the word scraped on her nerves. *Pass* was a gentle word, and Camilla's death had been anything but. She'd been violently murdered. She'd been tied up, tortured, and terrified. Had she been forced to watch her son being killed?

Bree had taken over raising her niece and nephew after her sister's murder in January. She'd been thrust into the role of parent only a short time, but she already understood that love for a child overrode all other emotions. Watching your child die would be the worst thing a parent could endure.

For Ms. Brown's sake, Bree hoped she'd died first.

Homer continued. "It might seem unimportant, but those goats need to be milked. They'll be mighty uncomfortable."

"Can you do that?"

"Sure. I've helped Camilla in the past. Just like she helped me."

Bree didn't want any part of the scene contaminated, but animals could not be left in distress. Plus, Homer had already been in the barn. "All right, but you'll have to wait until a deputy arrives to supervise. Until then, please wait by your truck."

"Yes, ma'am." He turned and walked away. His vigor had evaporated, and his posture slumped as if he'd aged ten years in the last twenty minutes.

Bree used her cell phone to report the murders to dispatch. She requested deputies be summoned and that they bring portable lights. Darkness would fall in the next hour. Then she informed the medical examiner and called for a county forensics team. She did all this via cell phone instead of using her radio. Local media listened to police radio broadcasts via scanner. Bree couldn't keep the news of the murders from the press, but she could delay their arrival and buy her investigation some time before media presence complicated the situation.

Next Bree called Matt Flynn, a criminal investigator she employed as a consultant on an as-needed basis. Budget constraints prevented her from hiring a full-time detective. Matt was a former sheriff's department investigator and K-9 handler. He'd retired from the force after being shot in the line of duty in a friendly-fire incident several years before. A bullet to the hand interfered with his ability to fire a handgun accurately and prevented Matt from being employed as a deputy. But the injury had never stopped him from doing his job, and he was a hell of a detective.

He was also, for lack of a better term, her boyfriend.

"Hey," he answered.

If she hadn't been standing in front of a murder scene, she would have appreciated the deep, sexy tone of his voice.

"Unfortunately, this is a business call," she said with regret.

His sigh was audible over the connection.

"Yeah. I've got a double homicide." Bree gave him the address. "It's ugly."

"Aren't they all? I'm on my way." Matt ended the call.

Bree slid her cell into her pocket. She returned to her vehicle for personal protective equipment. Homer leaned against his pickup, his arms crossed, his hat tipped down to cover his eyes. But his shoulders trembled as if he were crying and reminded Bree that the two victims inside had been real people, with hopes and dreams and loved ones who would mourn their passing.

But again, the term *passing* hardly applied to this situation.

Bree tamped down her fury. Two people had been violently ripped from their lives.

Grabbing her camera and a pair of booties from the back of her SUV, she returned to the house. She slipped the covers over her shoes on the back porch. On her way inside, she pulled a pair of gloves from her pocket and tugged them on. She went through the kitchen, trying to walk the path she'd previously used and minimize her impact on the scene.

Just inside the doorway, she snapped photos of the overall scene before moving closer and taking more pictures. After she'd captured the entire room, she approached the bodies.

She stopped next to the man, taking care not to step on any dried blood. A few smears at the edges of the blood pools suggested someone had already done so. She had to squat low and crane her head at an awkward angle to see his face. Three facts struck her simultaneously: One, like the female victim, he'd been finished off with a bullet to the forehead, execution style. Two, he'd been beaten. Three, Bree knew him. Even with bloated, bloodied, and bruised features, she recognized her former deputy, Eugene Oscar.

The man she'd recently forced out of the sheriff's department.

CHAPTER FOUR

The sunset glowed behind the treetops as Matt Flynn slowed his Suburban at the mailbox. His gaze swept over the worn and tired farm. At the top of the driveway, he left his Suburban next to the two sheriff's department patrol vehicles. Bree's SUV was parked up by the house, alongside a battered truck. A generator hummed and portable lights had been set up to illuminate the yard as twilight faded.

Matt walked up the drive and headed toward the house. One deputy was securing the perimeter around the yard with crime scene tape and sawhorse barriers. Another stood on the front walkway holding a clipboard. Matt paused next to the second deputy to have his name added to the crime scene log, a record of every person who entered the scene.

He spotted Bree in the side yard, conferring with her chief deputy, Todd Harvey. As always, even under the worst circumstances, his heart did a little skip at the sight of her. But a murder scene was all business.

Matt approached the pair. As usual, Bree looked like professional law enforcement. Not a single dark hair had escaped her neat bun. Her tactical cargoes and uniform shirt were relatively wrinkle-free for the end of the day, and her hazel eyes were locked in a flat cop stare. But something was off about her posture.

Todd stepped backward to make room for him in the conversation. Typically, the chief deputy was fairly unflappable. He was an excellent supervisor and leader, the type of man who would handle situations within his experience and seek advice for those that weren't. Tonight, his frame was as rigid as the giant old oak tree in the front yard.

Bree made eye contact. Her facade slipped for a second, and he could see more small signs that the scene inside that house had deeply disturbed her. Her eyes were too focused, and there was a barely decipherable unease in their depths. Before becoming sheriff of Randolph County the previous winter, Bree had been a homicide detective in Philadelphia. She was no stranger to murder. It took something truly shocking to disconcert her. Then she blinked, and the emotion was gone again.

She glanced around, as if to make sure there was no one within hearing range, then lowered her voice and dropped the bomb. "One of the victims is Oscar."

Shock flattened Matt like a steamroller. "As in former deputy Oscar?"

Grim-faced, Bree nodded. "The farm is owned by Camilla Brown. The neighbor confirmed the name of her son is Eugene Oscar. Camilla remarried after Oscar's father died."

Nodding, Todd hooked a thumb in the front of his duty belt. "We ran the plates of two vehicles parked in the shed. The pickup is registered to Ms. Brown. The Explorer belongs to Oscar."

"You want to see the bodies?" Bree asked.

"Yes." Matt didn't want any more information prior to viewing the scene with his own eyes. He preferred to have no preconceived ideas, even those from an experienced investigator like Bree. The same scene could leave varying impressions on different detectives. Matt wanted a clean slate when he viewed it for the first time.

"You're going to want to suit up." Bree sniffed her own shoulder and made a face. "The smell . . ."

The faint odor of decomp wafted from her. Matt returned to his vehicle and put on PPE coveralls to prevent his clothes from absorbing the smell. They walked toward the back door, which stood open.

Bree gestured to the rear of the house. "I initially made entry through the back door, as that lock seemed to be the easiest to breach without causing damage."

No one wanted to kick in a door for a well-being check and then discover the homeowner was on vacation or in the shower.

Todd trailed behind Matt and Bree.

At the back-porch steps, they all paused to don shoe covers and gloves, then went inside. The smell of decay washed over him. The lighting wasn't adequate for crime scene inspection. Matt pulled a flashlight from his pocket and turned it on.

Bree shut the door. As much as the closed space trapped odor, an incoming breeze could disturb evidence. Matt took in the kitchen, the flies, and the obvious signs of meal preparation. The normality under the horror disturbed him. He shoved aside the emotions threatening to rise. He could feel for these people later, after he'd brought their killer to justice.

He braced himself as he approached the doorway, then stopped just before entering the living room. The worn blue couch sat at an awkward angle, as if it had been pushed back to make room. Two victims were tied to chairs in the center of the large space. Nylon ropes bound the victims' ankles, wrists, and torsos to the high, straight backs. The female's death was relatively neat—a single shot to the forehead, like putting down a horse. The male's had been messy. The killer had taken his time with him.

"The chairs were brought from the kitchen," Matt noted. "There was too much preparation, and too much follow-through on those plans, for this to be a crime of passion or self-defense."

"Yes," Bree agreed. "This was straight-up murder."

They walked through the doorway. Todd took up a position near the wall. Bree and Matt walked a few steps closer.

Matt crouched and shone his light on the male's face. Yep. Definitely Oscar. "Killer beat the crap out of him and shot him four times. Must have been pissed off."

"Or trying to make a point," Bree added.

"There is something cold about the setup."

"That's the impression I got too."

"Oscar was what, late forties? And in decent shape. He wouldn't allow himself or his mother to be tied up and shot. He'd fight back."

"The killer was armed, and it's possible there was more than one of them."

Matt checked Oscar's belt. "He's not wearing a holster."

"I took his weapon and his badge when I suspended him." Bree's voice was tight and edged with just a touch of guilt.

"Yes, but he ended up retiring, right?"

"Right," Bree said. "It seemed best for the department to move on."

Originally, Oscar had been put on administrative leave for not following protocol on several occasions and for mishandling evidence in a big case. Though Matt and Bree suspected he'd done the latter on purpose at the request of a local politician, they hadn't been able to prove his intent. The prosecutor had been reluctant to pursue formal charges, and a deal had been struck. Retired law enforcement officers were allowed to carry guns per federal law, as long as they met a few guidelines. Oscar would have. If he'd been fired for cause, he'd have been treated like any other private citizen. Any charges brought against him would have affected his application for a concealed carry permit.

"Most cops have additional guns. Let's find out if any weapons were registered to Oscar." Matt straightened and glanced around the room. Lamps, knickknacks, and framed photos were arranged neatly on tables. Except for the staging of the scene with the chairs, the room looked normal. "I don't see any signs of a struggle here. How does the rest of the house look?"

"Same. Generally tidy. I found men's clothes, a few suitcases, and boxes in a secondary bedroom upstairs when I cleared the house."

A sick feeling swept over Matt at the image of Bree clearing the house alone. Rural policing was a bitch sometimes. Backup could be too far away to be immediately useful.

Todd spoke up. "This whole scene feels . . . elaborate. Why tie them up? Why not just shoot them?"

"All good questions." Matt shrugged. Potential motives rolled through his mind. "The woman died fast, but Oscar didn't. So maybe they didn't want to talk to her, but they could have wanted information from him."

"Or this was retribution." Bree stared hard at Oscar's body. "Punishment."

Matt added, "I don't see blood anywhere else in the room. Oscar's wounds bled. If he was shot and moved through the house before being restrained, there should be a blood trail. I think they were both tied up before the bleeding started."

"I can't see Oscar surrendering that easily." Bree frowned. "Even to an armed intruder."

"Unless the assailant grabbed his mother first," Matt suggested.

Bree's frown deepened. "Yes. A gun to his mother's head might have persuaded him to give up without a fight."

Matt envisioned someone aiming a gun at the old woman and giving Oscar instructions. "I can see that working."

Bree moved closer to examine the binds used to restrain both victims. "These knots are distinctive and identical on both victims, as if they were tied up by the same person."

"Can't tie someone up and hold a gun against their head at the same time," Todd said.

"Those knots will need to be preserved." Bree stepped back. "We'll consider both single and multiple assailants at this time. Maybe we'll get lucky and find prints."

But Matt doubted anyone who had orchestrated this crime would have left prints. The overall scene was too organized. This killer had successfully killed two people, one of them former law enforcement, with little fuss. He checked Oscar's hands. The fingers were purple and bloated, but Matt didn't see any scrapes on the knuckles that would indicate Oscar had fought back. The assailants had known what they were doing. Matt thought it likely they'd killed before.

He spotted a hole in the plaster wall. "There's one bullet."

"I see another down by the baseboard," Todd said. "Might have ricocheted after it hit one of his legs."

Bree's radio crackled and a voice said, "The medical examiner is here."

A few minutes later, Dr. Serena Jones appeared in the doorway. The tall African American woman wore scrubs and carried her kit. Her assistant followed, carrying an additional kit and standing aside to wait for the ME to complete her initial assessment. The group exchanged professional greetings, and then Dr. Jones paused to scan the overall scene before advancing closer to the bodies and giving them a cursory inspection using her own flashlight.

Dr. Jones drew back. "Is that Deputy Oscar?"

"Yes," Bree said. "The vehicle in the barn is registered to him, and the neighbor confirmed the older woman is his mother, Camilla Brown."

The ME nodded. "I recognize him, but given the obvious beating and the beginning of bloat, I'll confirm the IDs of both victims medically." The ME was all about dotting i's and crossing t's.

"Property records show the female has owned this property for twenty years," Bree said. "She should have local medical or dental records."

Matt knew Oscar had worked for the sheriff's office for more than two decades and had lived in the area his whole life. His health records should also be easy to obtain.

Dr. Jones continued. "Cause of death appears to be gunshot wounds, to be confirmed upon autopsy. Considering the amount of blood on the floor, it appears that the bullet wounds to the male's body bled considerably, indicating his heart was still beating. The head shot bled very little and was likely the fatal wound." Once a person was dead, their wounds didn't bleed much.

"Can you give us an approximate time of death?" Bree asked.

Avoiding the blood on the floor, the ME walked a slow circle around the victims. "The house isn't air-conditioned, and the weather has been moderate this week. I doubt temperature significantly affected the rate of decomposition."

Bodies exposed to exceptionally warm temperatures would decay faster. The opposite was true of bodies in cold atmospheres. But early September had been comfortable, with daily temps fluctuating between 65 and 75 degrees Fahrenheit.

Dr. Jones used two gloved hands to slightly turn the female victim's head. "Rigor mortis has come and gone, so we're probably beyond thirty-six hours postmortem."

Rigor mortis, or the chemical stiffening of the muscles after death, generally peaked around twelve hours after death, remained for twelve hours, and gradually released over the next twelve.

The ME pursed her lips. "Body temperature won't be helpful after this many hours. At room temperature, an average human body cools 1.5 degrees per hour. These two normal-weight, normally dressed bodies would have reached room temp by eighteen hours or so."

Dr. Jones lifted the hem of the female victim's blouse to examine the abdomen. "The first signs of decomp begin at that stage."

Matt saw green-tinted skin as well as a few green-and-black streaks known as marbling that marked the breaking down of blood vessels.

Dr. Jones pointed a gloved finger at the right side of the victim's abdomen. "See the discoloration in the right iliac fossa region? The intestines are loaded with bacteria and lie close to the surface. Early stages of putrefaction are usually evident here." She straightened and studied the body with a professional frown. "So, we have moderate fly activity, marbling, and some bloat in the torso." She paused, as if weighing all the factors. "At the moment, I estimate the postmortem interval is thirty-six to forty-eight hours. I might be able to narrow that window during autopsy."

Matt looked at his watch. Eight p.m. "So they were killed between eight p.m. Sunday and eight a.m. Monday."

"Yes," Dr. Jones agreed.

Bree nodded. "The neighbor last saw Camilla Sunday morning at church, so that fits."

Matt and Bree might be able to pinpoint the time since death more closely through their investigation, but it was a beginning.

"Let's get started." The ME signaled to her assistant, who stood by with a camera. The assistant began photographing the bodies in situ. Images would be taken from all angles, beginning at a distance and spiraling inward, before the bodies were removed from the scene.

Matt, Bree, and Todd walked out of the house to let the ME work. The wind shifted, bringing the scent of manure with it. Matt almost laughed. Any smell pungent enough to overpower the scent of decomp was welcome, even manure.

They walked around the house. The county CSI van was parking at the head of the driveway.

"Do we have any additional questions for Homer Johnson?" Todd asked. "He took care of the goats. Now he's just standing by."

Bree shook her head. "Send him home. We can follow up later. Ask him to keep the deaths to himself until we have a chance to notify next of kin."

"How long?" Todd asked. "In case he asks."

People were morbid, Matt knew. They couldn't help but talk about deaths, especially ones as violent as these murders. Plus, anyone driving past the farm would gossip about the law enforcement activity.

Bree faced Todd. "According to Homer, Ms. Brown's brother lives in Scarlet Falls. I'll drive down there tonight to do the death notification. I want you to start the paperwork. We need background checks for both victims, Ms. Brown's brother, Oscar's ex, and Homer." A judge had already signed the search warrant for the farm. "Warrants for Oscar's and Ms. Brown's phone and financial records are being requested." Thanks to modern technology, warrants could be approved electronically. She turned to Matt. "Let's search the house and see what we find."

They went inside, giving the ME and her assistant a wide berth. A thorough search of the parlor yielded nothing of interest. They moved on to the study, which clearly belonged to Camilla. Bree went to the desk. "We'll take the computer with us."

Matt focused on a row of wooden filing cabinets, where he waded through decades of farm records. It saddened him to see evidence of the business's decline. Over the past ten years, the livestock had been downsized and the planting of hay and other crops had ceased.

Bree held up a piece of paper. "The last business tax return shows she was barely making ends meet."

"Large operations have been pushing small farms out of the market."

"The dairy farm down the road from me went bankrupt over the summer. The bank is in the process of foreclosing. Maybe Camilla or Oscar borrowed money from the wrong person."

"And they were killed for the debt?" Matt shook his head. "I could see roughing them up. But killing your borrowers ensures you won't get paid."

"Thankfully, it seems Camilla kept excellent records, but we don't have time to read every document tonight. I want to interview the family. Their address in Scarlet Falls is only a twenty-minute drive from here, but it's already almost ten p.m." Bree walked out from behind the desk.

Matt thumbed through a file of legal documents and snapped a photo of an attorney's letterhead. "There are both family and business legal documents here prepared by the same attorney. Hopefully, he'll have copies of their wills if they made any."

"I'm betting Camilla had a will. She kept meticulous paperwork." Bree waited near the doorway. "Coming?"

"Yes." Just about to close the drawer, Matt spotted a hanging folder labeled WILL in block print. "She did have a will, and here's a copy." He pulled out the folder and skimmed through the legalese. "It's pretty simple. Oscar was the primary beneficiary. Camilla's brother, Bernard Crighton, is next in line."

"We'll have to get a valuation for the property."

They went upstairs. Bree veered toward the primary bedroom while Matt entered what was clearly a guest room that appeared unoccupied. A light coating of dust covered the dresser and nightstands. The closet was empty except for hangers. The next—and last—bedroom was slightly larger. Two closed suitcases were lined up against a wall. Another lay half-empty on the bed. The closet door stood open.

A man's wallet, a set of keys, a cell phone, a laptop, and an envelope sat on a writing desk. He tapped the phone. A passcode window appeared. The computer was also password protected. Matt opened the wallet. Oscar's driver's license photo stared back at him from the clear plastic window. Matt thumbed through the rest of the wallet: credit cards, health insurance card, gym ID, and $115 in small bills. He set down the wallet. The envelope wasn't sealed. Inside, he found a notarized letter from Oscar to his previous landlord breaking the lease on his apartment. His move-out date had been last Sunday.

The suitcases mostly contained clothes. Matt found nothing unusual in any of them. A few boxes held personal effects. He made a note to collect the laptop and cell phone as evidence. The techs in the lab would need to bypass the security on both.

Masculine toiletries filled the vanity drawers in the bathroom. Matt found only over-the- counter medications.

Bree emerged from the primary bedroom as Matt went into the hall. "Any luck?" she asked.

Matt told her about the letter.

"He was divorced, right?" Bree asked.

"Yes."

"Was it amicable?"

"I left the department right after they split up, but he seemed pretty bitter. I met his wife a few times at community or department events, but I don't really remember her. She was quiet. They didn't have any kids."

"Then we'll have to talk to the ex. Disgruntled former spouses love to vent."

"They do." Matt gestured toward the bedroom. "I found his laptop and cell on the dresser."

"Most people keep their phones in their pockets or at least close by. His mother did."

"Maybe he was upstairs when he was surprised by the shooter."

"Maybe." Bree waved toward the primary bedroom. "Camilla took blood pressure medication and loved to iron. She even ironed her jeans and pillowcases." Bree blew a piece of hair off her nose. "But other than an admirable dedication to housekeeping, I didn't find anything of note. There were a few pieces of jewelry in the dresser, so I doubt theft was the motive here."

Matt agreed. "I found cash in Oscar's wallet."

Bree nodded. "Let's interview her brother. We'll keep the house sealed for now, so we have the option of conducting another search. I'll have my deputies box the financial records and electronics." Items that didn't seem important now might become more interesting as the investigation proceeded.

They went downstairs. The ME and her assistant were bringing in body bags. One CSI tech in full PPE was taking samples of dried blood. Another was digging a bullet out of the wall. Bree stopped to confer with the CSI techs. Outside, Matt stripped off his coveralls. He went to his vehicle and opened the cargo hatch. After opening his war bag, he pulled out a package of wet wipes. He rubbed one over his face and hair. When he was finished, he leaned on his vehicle to wait for Bree to finish issuing instructions to her team.

She joined him, lifting her shoulder to sniff her uniform sleeve. "I need to change clothes."

No one wanted to perform a death notification while stinking of the rotting corpse of the family's loved one.

They dropped Matt's vehicle at his house and drove to the sheriff's station, where Bree took ten minutes to wash her face and put on a fresh uniform. She sprayed air freshener on her hair. Then Bree and Matt climbed into her SUV and headed for Scarlet Falls.

Officially, they would be performing the death notifications. But at this point, Bernard Crighton, as the beneficiary of Camilla's will, would also be interviewed as the first viable suspect.

CHAPTER FIVE

Bree drove south, her mind on the death notification. She ran a few initial sentences through her head. But the rest of the conversation would depend on the brother's potential reaction. Some people were too upset to speak. Others wanted to talk, to do anything they could to bring their loved one justice. Had Bernard Crighton been close to his sister? Was Bree about to rock his world?

She glanced at Matt in the passenger seat. The dashboard light highlighted his sharp cheekbones. His reddish-brown beard was closely trimmed, barely more than stubble. He would let it grow for a week or so, then shave it off. She wasn't normally a fan of facial hair, but it looked damned good on him. He was a physically intimidating man, standing a beefy six three, with broad shoulders, piercing blue eyes, and a chiseled Scandinavian bone structure models would kill for. In her mind, she often compared him to a Hollywood Viking. A battle-ax and iron helmet would have suited him.

Tonight, he wore tactical cargo pants and a black polo shirt bearing the sheriff's department logo. They'd been dating for several months, and she knew the body under those clothes did not disappoint. They'd gotten to know each other in the course of multiple murder investigations. Bree had resisted a personal relationship, concerned that their working one would suffer. But that hadn't happened. Instead, they'd become a comfortable, mutually respectful, and efficient team.

She could count on one hand the number of people she trusted, and Matt was one of them.

"Bernard teaches history at a small local college," Matt began, scrolling on her vehicle's dashboard computer. "He's been at the same job for more than twenty years. He has no criminal record. There's nothing more serious than a parking ticket on his motor vehicle history. He's lived in the same home for nearly fifty years. He drives a ten-year-old Mercedes." Matt typed on the keyboard. "Nothing even remotely scandalous comes up in an internet search."

It was nearly eleven thirty when she parked at the curb in front of Bernard Crighton's house. The neighborhood was well-established suburban, with tidy lots and mature trees. Tall, narrow houses were separated by skinny strips of grass. Some homes showed signs of remodeling. Others needed it.

Crighton's house fell in the middle of the spectrum. The shutters and garage door looked to have been recently replaced but the landscaping was tired, with shrubs that had surpassed their useful life and gone dead inside.

"Quiet neighborhood." Matt scanned the street.

Bree glanced at the house. The windows were dark. "We'll probably wake him."

"Can't be helped." Matt reached for his door handle. "We don't want him to find out when he turns on the news to catch the weather report with his morning coffee."

"No." Bree sighed.

News vans had arrived at the crime scene before Bree and Matt had left for Scarlet Falls. Bree had promised the reporters a statement in the morning. But the presence of the medical examiner's van would tell them someone had died, and they had the address. A quick public records search would tell them who lived there. Some would no doubt speculate, and Bree couldn't guarantee information wouldn't be leaked, not with so many people at the scene. The family of the victims needed to be informed ASAP.

But she hated this duty more than any other. She'd rather face a killer than bring grief to a family's doorstep.

She stepped out of the car and started up the cement walkway. With a deep breath she knocked on the door. The house remained quiet for a minute. Bree pressed the doorbell and heard the echo of the chimes inside the house. A light went on in an upstairs window. A face appeared behind the glass, peered down at them, and then withdrew. A few minutes later, the sound of footsteps approached the front door.

A man in his late sixties answered the door. He was tall and slim, in leather slippers and a navy-blue robe over old-fashioned pajamas. His face was narrow. He wore his silver hair on the long side and swept back from a high forehead in a dramatic wave. His eyes narrowed at them. "Can I help you?"

"Are you Bernard Crighton?" Bree asked.

"Yes," he said in an anxious tone.

Bree didn't want to give him the news on the doorstep. "May we come inside?"

His eyes were heavy with sleep. "Yes. Of course." He stepped back to give them room. The foyer was like its owner, dated but well kept. The wallpaper and dark-stained molding looked more antique than run-down.

"What's this about?" Mr. Crighton's tone was clipped.

Bree supposed the foyer was as far as she was going to get until she explained their visit. "I'm Sheriff Taggert from Randolph County." Bree introduced Matt. "I'm sorry to inform you that the bodies of Camilla Brown and Eugene Oscar were discovered this evening on Ms. Brown's farm. We're sorry for your loss."

Crighton didn't react for a few long seconds. Then realization dawned in his eyes and he pressed a hand to the V of his robe. "They're dead?"

"Yes, sir." Unfortunately, Bree had done enough death notifications to know it was best to deliver the news quickly and directly. Police did not arrive on a doorstep in the middle of the night to deliver good news. Anticipation only added stress. Euphemisms could confuse people, and confusion made everything worse. "Camilla was your sister?"

Instead of answering, he waved them inside, turned, and walked through a wide doorway. Bree and Matt followed him into a wood-paneled study. Crighton navigated the space in the dim light spilling in from the hall, but Matt went to the wall and flipped a switch, flooding the room with soft light from several lamps.

A large antique desk occupied half the space. A leather couch and chairs formed a conversation area on the other side. Overflowing bookshelves lined the wall behind the desk. Additional volumes were stacked on the desk and floor. The decor had the potential to be stuffy, but the furnishings were just worn enough to make it a comfortable, well-used working room.

Crighton went to a sideboard and poured what appeared to be whiskey from a decanter into a tumbler. After a sip, he turned to face them, leaning on the front of the desk. His hands were shaky. "I assume you won't accept any?"

"That's correct." As the daughter of a raging alcoholic, Bree wasn't much of a drinker, and she would never imbibe on duty. "I know this is a shock, but I need to ask you a few questions."

Crighton took another small sip of his whiskey. "Was it an accident? I told Camilla the farm was too much for her, but she refused to leave it."

The statement felt odd. Farm accidents happened, but typically they involved heavy equipment or large animals. A dozen goats and a few chickens didn't seem particularly dangerous to Bree, especially when two people had been killed, one of them a healthy, younger man. She supposed a single individual could have fallen, but both? Seemed unlikely. Fire was more likely in old buildings.

She shook her head. "No, sir. I'm afraid Ms. Brown and her son were shot."

Crighton froze, his glass halfway to his lips. "Shot?"

"Yes." Bree waited while he absorbed the news.

Crighton moved to sit on a leather couch. Bree and Matt eased into the wing chairs facing it. Bree pulled her notepad and pen from her shirt pocket.

"Was it suicide?" Crighton asked, his head tipped down.

Bree evaded the question. "Was either Camilla or Eugene suicidal?"

"I'm no psychiatrist, but they were both struggling. Eugene was struggling with the recent end of his career, and he was still bitter about his divorce, though that happened a couple of years ago." Crighton stared at his whiskey. "Camilla hasn't been the same since her second husband died."

"When was that?" Leaning forward, Matt rested his clasped hands between his knees.

Crighton jerked a shoulder. "Seven, eight years ago, I think. She bounced back after her first husband's death. He was killed in a car accident when Eugene was young. Back then, she had a son to finish raising, so that forced her to keep moving forward. But after Husband Number Two had his heart attack, she seemed to withdraw from life." A huge sigh shuddered through him. "I suspect she was depressed. I probably should have gone to see her more often. I should have helped her."

Bree wrote a note. She thought anyone close to their sister would refer to her late husbands by their names, not their numbers. But then, she was hardly one to judge a person for not maintaining family ties. She had let down her own siblings for years and hadn't pursued a real relationship with her brother until after their sister had been murdered. If guilt was consuming Crighton tonight, Bree could understand.

On the other hand, Crighton would inherit the farm, so maybe he was acting.

"Families are complicated," she empathized, hoping he'd open up more. "When did you see your sister last?"

"About a month ago, my daughters and I went to the farm for Camilla's birthday. We took my grandchildren to see the goats." Crighton's eyes misted, but he willed away any tears before they escaped. He blinked, then turned drier eyes on Bree. "You didn't answer my question about suicide." He shook his head as if to clear it. "Wait. Camilla could have considered suicide, but she *never* would have killed her son. Eugene was everything to her. Did he do it?"

Bree shook her head. "We don't believe they died by suicide."

Realization and shock widened Crighton's eyes further. "They were murdered."

Shot didn't leave any other options.

Bree nodded. "Yes."

He fell backward, his shoulders hitting the couch with enough force to rock it. "I can't believe it. Who would kill an old woman running a small goat farm? Was anything stolen?"

"We didn't see any evidence that robbery was the motive," Bree said. "I need to ask you where you were between Sunday at eight p.m. and Monday at eight a.m."

"I was here." He circled a hand. "The family left around seven thirty. I read for a few hours and went to bed."

Bree made a note. "Can anyone attest to your presence here?"

"No," he said.

"Did Camilla have any enemies?" Bree asked.

"No." Crighton didn't hesitate. "She'd become more and more introverted over the years. The only places she ever mentioned going were the tractor supply store and church."

"She had no friends that you know of?" Matt pressed.

"She never mentioned anyone." Crighton gave them a slow shake of his head. "There was a neighbor who helped her a few times. But she never talked about him in a way that led me to believe their relationship was anything more than neighborly."

Bree lifted her pen. "Do you remember his name?"

Crighton looked at the ceiling as if searching for an answer. "It's an old-fashioned name. He lives down the road from my sister's place. Henry?" He snapped his fingers. "No, Homer. That's it."

"What about other family members?" Bree asked.

Crighton sighed. "Camilla and I are the last of our generation. My girls and I visited the farm often when my children were young, but now that they're adults . . ." He paused, his brow furrowing as if he was thinking about his response. "My wife died of cancer when they were teenagers. I thought my sister could be a mother figure for them, but they never bonded. You can't make people form attachments, can you? They make the annual trip to the farm at my request, but they're not close to my sister."

"How many children do you have?" Bree lifted her pen and shifted to a casual question. Hammering away on a single topic could put him on the defensive. Developing a rapport took time but yielded more evidence.

"I have two daughters," he said.

Matt leaned back. "They live close by?"

"Yes." Pride softened Crighton's features. "Shannon is an elementary school teacher. She's married with three children. Stephanie is a lawyer. They all still come to Sunday dinner whenever they can."

"You cook for all those people?" Matt asked.

"Sometimes." Bernard winced. "Admittedly, if I have too many term papers to grade, we order pizza, but it's the getting together that matters."

Bree noted the names and professions of his daughters. She could research them later. "You said your kids weren't close to Camilla. Do you know why?"

"No." Crighton sighed. "Camilla withdrew from us over the years. When I'd call her, she never seemed happy to hear from me. She took no interest in the girls' lives." He lifted a shoulder.

"Was there anyone else in your sister's life?" Matt asked. "A man?"

Crighton turned up a palm. "I don't think so, but then again, I only know what she shared with me."

"When was the last time you saw Eugene?" Bree asked.

Crighton's hand dropped to his lap. "He was there when we visited last month. It was the first time I'd seen him in years. Camilla talked about him moving in with her, but I could tell she was glossing over her disappointment."

"Disappointment?" Bree asked.

"She desperately wanted grandchildren." Crighton's gaze shifted to the ceiling. "I remember when Eugene married. That was about fifteen years ago. Camilla was so excited. Then the years passed with no grandkids, and she gradually stopped talking about it. When he divorced without any kids, she was . . ." His forehead wrinkled as he searched for the right word. "Almost bitter, like her son's failure to reproduce was just one more letdown in a long life full of them. Nothing had worked out the way Camilla had planned. At times, she seemed almost jealous of me and my family life."

A few heartbeats of silence passed.

Then Matt shifted forward an inch. "How well did you know Eugene's ex-wife?"

"Heather? Not well at all." Crighton shrugged. "We only met her at weddings, funerals, and other large events. She didn't talk much."

Matt asked, "Did your sister like her?"

Crighton shook his head. "While they were married, Camilla pitied her inability to have a child. After the divorce, my sister's opinion changed. Apparently, Heather took Eugene for everything. He complained the alimony was killing him."

"We'll get his ex's number," Bree said. "You visited Camilla last month. When was the last time you spoke with her or Eugene?"

"I called Camilla a few weeks ago. She was getting ready for Eugene to move in." Crighton's face pinched like he was sniffing sulfur.

"You didn't approve?" Matt asked.

Crighton shrugged. "She needed help on the farm. Her health was deteriorating, and my nephew was going through a rough patch. The arrangement was practical."

Bree didn't say a word. Neither did Matt. They'd interviewed enough suspects together to work in sync. They both waited for Crighton to fill the silence.

Which he did, in less than a minute. "I'm old-fashioned. I expect an adult man to be able to support himself."

"And you're a professor, Mr. Crighton?" Bree asked.

Crighton lifted his chin and made eye contact. "Yes. I teach medieval history." He set down his empty glass and spread his upturned hands. "Camilla told me Eugene retired, but I saw the scandal on the news when he left the sheriff's department. I'm pretty sure he did something to get himself fired. Maybe whatever he did also got him killed."

"Why do you say that?"

"I don't know. Just a feeling. I hate to say this about my own nephew, but something about Eugene always seemed a little sketchy." Crighton's head tilted as if he'd just come to a conclusion he should have seen before. "Wait a minute. You're the sheriff. He worked for *you*. You should know more about him—and what he did—than I do."

Something shifted in his attitude. He didn't elaborate, but Bree sensed the dynamics of their interview had changed in a way that left her inexplicably uneasy.

Crighton's gaze became less grief-stricken and more wary. His eyes sharpened as if he were sizing up Bree with fresh eyes, as if he were finally waking up and making connections he should have made earlier.

Bree hated to appear as if she were running away from his scrutiny. She asked one final question: "Do you know who inherits the farm?"

Crighton's head drew back, and his eyes became shuttered. A muscle twitched in his cheek. He didn't like the question, and he answered it through clenched molars. "Yes. I do."

He appeared financially comfortable, but appearances could be intentionally deceiving.

Matt went for the direct question. "Do you know what the farm is worth?"

"No, and I don't care." Crighton crossed his arms. "I can't imagine it would be much. It's in rough shape, and there's plenty of land for sale upstate. There's nothing special about the property that makes it valuable."

She stood. "Thank you for answering our questions. Again, we're sorry for your loss. I'll need your phone number. We might be in touch with additional questions." She handed him a business card. "Please call me if you think of anything that might help solve your sister's and nephew's murders."

He slid the card into the pocket of his robe, then walked them to the door. "Don't worry. I'll be in touch." His tone sounded . . . ominous?

Bree and Matt left the house and returned to their vehicle. She slid behind the wheel.

Matt closed his vehicle door. "That got weird."

"He seemed to grow . . ." Bree tapped a finger on the steering wheel. "Almost hostile at the end of the interview?"

Matt gazed at the house. "He suggested the reason Oscar lost his job might be related to his death."

"That was almost two months ago." Bree slid out her notepad and jotted down a few bullet points from the interview while the details were fresh in her mind.

"Why was Oscar so broke?"

"Good question. He didn't make a ton of money, but after more than two decades in the department, he was at the top of the pay grade. Initially, he was on paid administrative leave." Bree had wanted to fire him, but there had been an official process that had needed to play out. "Then he retired. He shouldn't have gone without pay at all."

"We need to find out how much alimony he was paying."

"His financial statements should be interesting." Bree put the SUV into gear.

Matt checked his watch. "Tomorrow?"

"Yes. But send Todd an email. I want him to add warrants to obtain phone and financial records for Bernard Crighton and Oscar's ex to the list." She glanced in the rearview mirror as she pulled away from the curb. Bernard Crighton still stood in his open doorway, watching them leave. He raised his hand to his ear, as if making a call. As she drove back toward Grey's Hollow, she couldn't shake the feeling of foreboding.

CHAPTER SIX

Bree drove to Matt's house and parked outside. Exhaustion dragged at her like ankle weights. "Would you mind if I slept here for a few hours? I'll just wake the family if I go home now."

"You don't have to ask. I always want you to sleep over." He leaned across the console and placed a soft kiss on her mouth. As he pulled away, Bree hooked a hand around the back of his neck. Holding him in place, she kissed him back, then pressed her forehead to his. "Thanks."

"For what?"

"For being there. And being you." She released him and stepped out of the SUV. She opened the back and grabbed her gym bag. They went inside. She heard the scrape of dog nails on hardwood. Hearing but not seeing the dark-coated dogs, Bree tensed. She'd made great strides with her fear of dogs, but having one rush at her in the dark was intimidating.

Matt flipped on a light switch, illuminating the kitchen. Two German Shepherds came down the hallway from the bedroom toward the kitchen. In the lead, Greta, a solid black dog, streaked toward them. A traditional black-and-tan shepherd followed her. Older and wiser, Brody took his time. He had once been Matt's K-9 partner.

Matt commanded Greta to sit in German, and she slid to a stop. But she could barely contain her excitement, and her butt bounced on the floor. Bree reached out and scratched behind her ears. Greta lasted for about a minute, then bounded away.

Brody ambled down the hall and sat obediently, waiting to be petted.

Bree stroked his head. "Always the gentleman."

He gave the younger dog a serious side-eye.

Matt let both dogs into the yard for a minute. Then they all went into the bedroom. Bree and Matt showered together. The night had been long and depressing. She was too tired for sex, but she appreciated the companionship. She towel-dried her hair, used the toothbrush she kept there, and borrowed a T-shirt from Matt's drawer. Soft and worn, it hung to midthigh.

Matt came up behind her. "This is a big bathroom. There's plenty of room. You could keep more than a toothbrush here."

Bree watched in the mirror as he wrapped his arms around her and drew her against his body. Leaning back against the solid warmth of him, she gestured toward the drawer. "I also brought moisturizer and deodorant. I don't have that much more in my own bathroom."

"You are low maintenance in the cosmetics department," he agreed.

Bree wasn't sure if she was low maintenance or just too lazy to bother with much makeup. Either way, she saved time and money.

"There's space in the closet too. I'm not exactly a fashion icon." He nodded toward her duffel bag, which sat on the vanity. "You could keep a change of clothes here."

She turned and looped her arms around his neck. "Maybe I will."

She'd been spending at least one night a week at his place, so it made sense. But taking up space in his house with her belongings felt like a next step. She waited for apprehension, but it didn't come. Instead, the idea pleased her.

"Maybe you don't always need to rush out before dawn either. It would be nice to eat breakfast together." He kissed her temple.

"It would."

"People have seen us date. We've had dinner together in town several times now."

"This is true," she said. Taking their relationship into the public arena had been a big step for her, but it felt like the right move.

"You are entitled to a personal life."

"I agree." Bree was no longer determined to keep their relationship a secret, but she didn't feel the urge to make a media announcement about it either. "I go home early because of the kids."

"The kids know we're together."

Bree nodded. "I'm not sure how to handle my nights out with them yet. This parenting thing is all new to me."

Nights out implied sex—at least to Luke now and Kayla when she was a bit older, whether or not sex was happening. On one hand, she wanted them to know that sex was a natural part of an adult relationship. On the other, they weren't adults, and she didn't want to set the wrong example. There was so much to consider when raising kids, things that had never occurred to Bree in her past life.

Matt kissed her. "OK. I can understand that."

"I want to be honest with them, and I want them to have healthy attitudes toward sex, but they also need to respect themselves and not rush into it."

"We did *not* rush into sex." Matt grinned. "I waited forever." He dragged out the last word in a teasing tone. He turned to the black dog and pointed to a large dog crate. "Greta, kennel."

The shepherd obediently entered the crate and Matt closed it. Then he used an extra clip on the lever.

"What's that for?" Bree asked.

"She keeps letting herself out of the crate. She's too smart for her own good."

"Collins is going to have fun with her." Bree had chosen Deputy Laurie Collins to be Greta's handler.

"She'll settle down once she's working. She's bored." Matt had been training the dog to get her ready for the academy. Boredom indicated she was ready.

Taking Matt's hand, Bree led him toward the bed. They climbed in, and she fell asleep in his arms.

When she woke, pain shot through her leg. Her foot was asleep, and her legs hooked at an unnatural angle around a large object. She opened her eyes. While they'd slept, Brody had stretched out on Bree's side, leaving little room for her.

Matt rolled over. "Is there a bed bigger than a California king?"

"Not that I'm aware of." Bree extricated her legs from around the big dog. His brown eyes opened. She patted him and whispered, "You're a good boy."

His tail thumped.

Matt groaned. "What time is it?"

She checked the time on her phone. "Five o'clock. Go back to sleep. I have to go. Luke will be up soon."

Her nephew always fed the horses in the morning. And high school started at ridiculous o'clock. Still bone-weary, Bree got out of bed, pulled her gym clothes from her bag, and dressed. She walked around the bed to kiss Matt goodbye before leaving. Brody rolled into the space Bree had vacated.

She drove to her farm in the darkness. A mile from home, she passed her neighbor's abandoned farm. The place had been empty for only a few months, but a tree had fallen on the porch roof, partially caving it in. Without a homeowner to maintain it, would Camilla Brown's farm decay that quickly? Bree found the thought depressing.

She arrived home at five fifteen. She stepped out of the SUV and stood at the edge of the grass, breathing in the country air. The barn and meadow stretched out behind the house, and Bree reveled in the sheer span of space around her. Nine months ago, she'd lived in Philadelphia. Now, she couldn't imagine returning to the city.

So much had changed in a short period of time.

As exhausted as she was, Bree detoured to the barn. Three horses blinked at her as she walked down the aisle. She stopped to pat the nose of her niece's sturdy little horse and her nephew's bay gelding before slipping into Cowboy's stall. The paint gelding had been her sister's mount, rescued from the kill buyer at the livestock auction. Bree stepped close and leaned her head against his neck. The scents of hay and horse comforted her.

Cowboy wrapped his neck around her and nibbled at her pocket.

"I don't have any carrots. Sorry." She straightened and scratched under his mane. He bobbed his head in approval.

With a sigh, Bree gave him a final pat, left the stall, and locked up the barn. She crossed the backyard and went into the house, quietly easing the door closed and resetting the alarm. The light over the stove glowed, and Bree found a note on the counter. *Dinner is in the fridge—Dana.*

Bree's former partner and best friend, Dana Romano, had retired and moved to Grey's Hollow to help Bree raise her nephew and niece. Luke, at sixteen, would be at home for only another two years, but Kayla was still in grammar school.

Nails scratched on hardwood, and Ladybug trotted into the kitchen. She didn't have Greta's energy—or her coordination—and slid straight into Bree's knees. The dog weighed sixty pounds, and Bree braced herself against the wall to keep from being knocked down. Bree crouched to give the slobbery dog a big hug. While Greta might still be a little threatening, there was nothing even remotely intimidating about Ladybug. She was squishy and soft and had never met anyone she didn't consider her best friend. Her stump of a tail spun in a crazy-fast circle. The dog always greeted her as if they'd been apart for years instead of hours. Bree was grateful that Matt had tricked her into adopting the chubby pointer mix.

Bree's black cat, Vader, sauntered into the kitchen and jumped up onto the counter. He stared down at the dog in disgust.

Bree rubbed behind the dog's ear. "Don't mind him. He's a snob." She straightened and gave the cat a scratch on her way to the fridge.

Unconcerned with the cat's opinion, the dog stretched out on the floor and watched Bree grab a bowl of pasta from the refrigerator. Standing in front of the sink, Bree ate a forkful of cold ziti. Nine months ago, eating cold leftovers alone would have been normal. But this morning, loneliness hit her hard. She'd learned to like coming home to a rowdy family dinner, with Luke shoveling an unbelievable amount of food into his mouth at a rate that gave Bree indigestion and Kayla telling terrible jokes and giggling so hard she could hardly eat.

The light turned on, and Dana stood in the doorway. An early riser, she was already dressed in shorts and a T-shirt. Her short gray-and-blonde-streaked hair was fashionably tousled compared to Bree's typical working bun or day-off ponytail. Though she'd passed her fiftieth birthday, regular spin classes and good genes kept Dana long and lean. "Are you OK?"

"Yeah. It was so late, I stayed at Matt's."

"Good." Dana walked into the kitchen. She took the bowl from Bree and waved her toward the table. "Sit. I'll make you breakfast."

"The pasta is fine."

"Are you sure? I'm making french toast for Luke." At Bree's nod, Dana shrugged. "It should at least be warm." She put the food in the microwave.

While the appliance hummed, Bree slid into a chair. She propped her elbows on the table and dropped her head into her hands.

A minute later, Dana set the bowl on the table in front of her. "Eat." She chuckled. "And I have officially become my Italian grandmother."

Bree lifted her head. The pasta smelled better warm, and Dana had topped it with fresh Parmesan.

Bree dug in. Footsteps thundered on the steps.

Luke loped through the kitchen. "Morning," he said without pausing. The back door slammed as he went out to feed the horses.

"I take it he's still annoyed with me?" Bree asked.

"Yep, but you did the right thing. A weekend camping trip with his friend's college-age brother as the sole chaperone is a recipe for trouble."

"I know. What I don't understand is why I feel guilty." Would Bree ever feel confident about her parenting skills?

"Why did you say no?"

"Because a twenty-two-year-old who we don't know is not adequate supervision for a dozen teenage boys. Luke might make good decisions, but his friends might not. *And* there's no guarantee even a good kid will make the right choice when faced with enormous peer pressure."

Dana added, "How many accidents did you respond to in your patrol days involving teenagers and alcohol and/or drugs?"

"Too many." Bree vividly remembered several. Photographing dead kids was almost as horrible as notifying their parents. "I know I had all the right reasons to tell Luke no. I still feel bad. I want to reward him for working hard and making good choices. Instead, I feel like I'm admitting I don't trust him." She held up a hand. "I know. This has nothing to do with trust. It's about skills and maturity he and his friends don't have yet, and it's about the lack of control he'll have in the situation."

"He'll get over it. Your job is to raise him, not be his friend. You're going to make decisions that he doesn't like."

"You're right."

Dana grabbed eggs and milk from the fridge. "Are you sure you don't want french toast?"

"I'm sure." Bree ate a forkful of pasta.

Still wearing her pajamas, Kayla walked in and slid onto a chair. She wasn't a morning person.

Bree rose and poured her a glass of orange juice. "How was school yesterday?"

"I made two new friends at lunch." She smiled and took a sip of juice. She described the event in detail while Dana whipped up french toast. Kayla topped her slices with butter.

Bree looked down, surprised that her bowl was empty. Considering yesterday's horrific discovery, she was equally surprised that her heart was full. Just a short time with her family brought her unexpected peace, a needed respite from the stress of her job. She used to be a complete loner, but she thought that was because she hadn't known how nice it was to have people to share her life.

Now she did, and sometimes it still made her uncomfortable, as if she were somehow putting them out by allowing them to reciprocate in the relationship. But she couldn't imagine living alone again.

Luke came through the back door, which slammed shut behind him.

"How are your classes?" Bree asked.

"I hate pre-cal." He filled a glass with milk.

Dana slid a loaded plate in front of him. "Does anyone *love* pre-cal?"

Bree laughed. "I'm sure *someone* does."

"That someone wasn't me." Dana sat down with her own plate.

"How about the rest of your classes?" Bree asked him.

"Fine." He shrugged and shoveled food into his mouth without answering. Finally, he pushed his plate forward. "Johnny's brother, Mateo, is very mature."

"That's great," Bree said.

"So, can I go on the trip?" Luke asked, his chin lifted in defiance.

Bree sighed. "No."

"You're not being fair." His voice turned sullen. "You haven't even met him. Mateo wanted to come over last night, but you weren't here because you were working. Whenever you have a big case, we barely see you."

The comment stung. "I'm sure he's a nice young man, but my answer is still no." Bree kept her voice level and calm. Inside, her gut was twisting. "One college student isn't enough supervision for twelve high schoolers."

Luke didn't speak again as he grabbed his backpack and headed out the back door. Bree took a deep breath and made a mental note to ask her brother, Adam, to spend some time with Luke. An artist, Adam was nervous about a new painting he'd delivered to the gallery. Time together would benefit them both.

"Luke's being a jerk," Kayla said.

Bree pressed her lips flat to suppress a grin. "Mind your own business. Luke will be fine." She wished she actually felt the confidence she was projecting. "Someday, I might make a decision for you that you don't like."

"Well, I still won't be a jerk to you," Kayla said around a mouthful of food.

But Bree feared teenage Kayla wouldn't be as amenable as grade-school Kayla. "I really hope that's true."

Dana started her fancy coffee machine.

Kayla carried her empty plate to the sink. "Can you drive me to school, Aunt Bree?"

Bree checked her watch. She wanted to get to the office early, but her niece loved having Bree's attention all to herself now and then. For Kayla, Bree would wait. "Yes."

"Yay!" Kayla raced from the table. Her feet thumped up the stairs.

Dana set two cups of cappuccino on the table. "Rough night?"

"Yeah."

"I saw a news report about a shooting and assumed that's what you were working on. Do you want to talk about it?"

Bree pushed away the empty bowl and reached for the mug with two hands. The kitchen wasn't cold, but remembering the scene, she appreciated the warmth that seeped into her fingers through the ceramic. "Double homicide, execution style. One of the victims is Eugene Oscar."

Dana's mouth dropped open for a few seconds. "As in your former deputy Oscar?"

"Yep."

"Fuuuuuuck."

"Exactly." Bree sipped the cappuccino. "We notified next of kin, so his identity will be on the news. I need to schedule a press conference for sometime today."

"The reporter said there were two victims."

"Oscar's mother." Bree sighed, then gave a brief description of the murders.

"When you suspended him, you strongly suspected he was involved in some shady business. I suspect you'll find several people with motive."

"The prosecutor decided not to charge him. The physical evidence just wasn't there. My suspicions were irrelevant if I couldn't prove the shadiness."

Dana gave her a look. She had a long, distinguished career as a homicide detective. Her ability to slice through evidence to the heart of the matter made her a great sounding board.

"I know," Bree agreed. "His death closely follows his forced retirement. Those two events could be related. Then again, he might also be involved in sketchy business unrelated to the sheriff's department."

Dana's forehead wrinkled. "Too many possibilities this early in the investigation."

"We have his electronics." Bree's mind whirled. "I'm hoping the techs find something on his computer or phone."

Dana crossed her fingers in support. "Go get dressed. I'll make more cappuccino."

"I need a gallon." Bree rose and set her bowl in the sink.

"Done."

Upstairs, she showered, dressed in a clean uniform, and contained her messy hair into a knot at the nape of her neck. Then she stopped in the kitchen for a second cappuccino and took it into her home office to check her work email while she waited for Kayla.

It was far too soon to receive any information from the medical examiner or forensics. Most of the emails were routine paperwork. She opened a message from one of the county supervisors bitching about the latest quote for the sheriff station renovations. Scanning the rest of the email, she rolled her eyes even though she was alone.

The supervisor was asking if they really needed two holding cells. Seriously. Bree resisted answering. Her current mood did not allow for the necessary diplomacy. She moved to the next message and froze at the embedded close-up of an erect penis. She scanned the text above the image. You're going to choke on my cock . . . The message deteriorated into a stomach-turning rape fantasy.

Not again.

Before she could stop it, a mental image of violent assault popped into her head. Bree had more than a decade of criminal investigations under her professional belt. She'd seen enough violence to be able to fill in all the nasty details. Queasy sweat gathered under her arms, and bile rose in her throat. Shame and anger bubbled up. The feelings of vulnerability and humiliation were exactly what he wanted. He was assaulting her mind, her sense of safety, and her personal privacy without even getting close to her.

And she couldn't stop it, which aggravated her even more.

Damn him.

"More cappuccino?" Dana asked from the doorway. She studied her for a second, then her brows dropped with concern. "What is it?"

Bree waved a hand at her computer. "Why is a dick pic even a thing?"

Dana rounded the desk and looked over Bree's shoulder. "It's just another way to harass you." She frowned. "Did it come to your professional or personal account?"

"It's the work email."

"How many have you gotten now?"

"I don't know. I've received the occasional threatening or insulting message since I took the job, but there are a half dozen or so with the same voice. Even though they come from different email accounts, we suspect they're written by the same person. These are different, beyond ordinary hate mail, and I can't put my finger on why."

Dana gestured toward the screen. "These seem like personal attacks—and the violence in the threats is escalating."

"Exactly." Bree forwarded it to the county forensic computer specialist, Rory MacIniss, with a brief message: Here's another one.

"Has the tech had any luck locating the sender?"

Bree shook her head. "Not yet. Rory says the sender knows what he's doing. He's spoofing IP addresses to make it appear as if the emails are originating from other accounts, and he's using a different disposable email account with each message so I can't block them." Bree closed her email and shut down the computer. "But there isn't anything I can do about it. As long as it's just emails, I have more important problems to worry about."

Dana gave the closed computer a troubled look that conveyed her worry. "I know how capable you are, but those threats imply too much violence for my liking."

"I can't disagree."

"You need to watch your back."

"I will." Bree did not appreciate feeling like a target. Her instincts told her that this hater wouldn't stop at mere threats.

CHAPTER SEVEN

The mattress shifted, and a cold, wet nose bumped Matt's face. Even half-asleep, he knew what it was. He opened his eyes. Greta stared at him from approximately two inches away. There was no sign of light behind the window blinds, but Matt had no doubt it was five thirty. The dog had an impressive internal clock. She hadn't budged when Bree had left thirty minutes before. But now it was time to get up.

When his eyes met hers and he didn't immediately rise, Greta shifted her position to plant both paws in the middle of his chest. She was not small, and her weight pressed the air from his lungs.

Matt reached up to pat her head, then pushed her off his lungs. "Good morning, Greta."

Her tail began a slow wag, and she licked his face.

An irritated canine groan sounded from the foot of the bed. Matt looked beyond the young black dog. Brody opened one eye. If the older shepherd could have rolled it, he would have.

Matt sat up and lifted his phone from the nightstand. Five thirty-two.

"You're good," he said to Greta.

Her head cocked, and the arrogance in her face made him laugh. The dog had a huge ego.

Brody looked like he wanted to put his head under the covers.

"Sorry, buddy." Matt patted a hind leg. "Just a few more weeks. If everything goes to plan, she'll be off to the academy by the end of the month."

Like Matt, the older dog would likely have mixed feelings after Greta left. Matt had been fostering her for his sister's dog rescue. Greta had been adopted and returned. Matt had quickly recognized her potential. She was too smart, too driven to make a good house pet. But that same pain-in-the-butt disposition would make her a great police K-9. She was fearless, and in the months he'd been training her, she was never happier than when she was working.

She jumped off the bed and barked at him, prancing with excitement. She did not have Brody's patience. His ability and willingness to think through a situation was uncanny. Matt had never met a dog that was his equal. Hell, he didn't know many people as smart or as trustworthy as Brody.

"OK, OK." Matt surrendered. "How did you get out of the kennel anyway?"

The clip lay on the floor, and Greta looked pleased with herself. The dog was Houdini.

He pulled on shorts and a T-shirt and went to the kitchen, Greta right on his heels, urging him on with bumps from her nose.

"Brody!" he called as he opened the back door. Greta raced into the fenced yard and zoomed around the perimeter three times before stopping to pee. Barking sounded from the kennel on the other side of the fence. Greta ran back into the kitchen. Matt laced up his running shoes. He ducked back into the bedroom, where Brody ignored him.

"OK, then. We'll be back soon."

Brody squeezed his eyes closed, settled deeper into the comforter, and snored. Since his retirement, he no longer approved of dark-o'clock runs. Plus, he'd been shot in the same career-ending incident as Matt, and the dog had lingering shoulder issues. The vet had said he shouldn't overdo the physical activity. Brody had taken the vet's instructions to heart.

Matt snapped the leash onto Greta's collar, and they set out at a brisk jog, increasing their pace over the next few miles. They covered five miles at a good clip, returning to the house as the coming dawn brightened the sky. Back in the house, Matt showered. Brody finally got out of bed. After a long, full-body stretch, he ambled into the kitchen for breakfast. Matt served up the dogs' kibble, then took Brody outside to do his business without being accosted by Greta. Matt scrambled eggs for himself, then left the shepherds settled in for their early-morning nap. He didn't bother to crate Greta. What was the point?

Outside, the sun had barely broken the horizon as his sister's minivan turned into his driveway and parked in front of the kennel. After he'd left the sheriff's department, Matt had intended to train K-9s, but his sister had filled the runs with rescues before he could get started. Since discovering Greta among the discarded dogs, Matt had changed his business plan. Now, he intended to actively search animal shelters for dogs that might make suitable K-9s.

Sometimes you choose your path in life. Other times, it chooses you.

Or your sister chooses it for you, Matt corrected himself with a chuckle.

Cady stepped out of her vehicle and opened the rear cargo hatch. A dog crate occupied the back of her van.

"New rescue?" he asked.

"Pulled him from the shelter." She nodded. "Owner surrender." She opened the crate, crouched, and dropped a slip lead over the dog's head.

Matt stepped back to give the animal space. Most rescues were timid.

"No need." Cady laughed. "This guy is not shy."

A lean black dog bounded out of the crate and jumped on Cady's legs, wagging and licking. She gently pushed his paws off her thighs. "Feet on the ground, lover."

Seeing Matt, the dog shifted his excitement and leaped toward him. Cady redirected him. "According to the surrender forms, they got him as a puppy for the kids, didn't bother to train or exercise him, then wondered why he's destructive and hard to control."

"So same old, same old. At least he looks like he's in good health." Matt eyed the dog and played Guess That Breed. "Lab and pit?"

"Probably." Cady led him toward the kennel. "I'll let him settle in. Maybe you could work with him?"

"Sure."

They went inside, and the kennel erupted in barking. He and Cady didn't bother trying to talk as she put the newcomer in a run. Several dogs jumped on the kennel doors for attention. Others cringed at the backs of their runs. Matt helped his sister feed the dogs. Finally, the barking subsided into the scraping of stainless-steel bowls being pushed around the concrete runs.

"Do you have plans today?" Cady asked, fastening the door latch on the last kennel. "I need to talk to you and Bree about the fundraiser, and I'm picking up two dogs from a hoarding situation."

"Sorry. I'm working on a case." Matt hated to say no to his sister. "Please don't go alone."

"No worries. I won't." Cady was neither helpless nor foolish. She wouldn't intentionally put herself in dangerous situations. But she would take a calculated risk to help an animal in need. "I'll get another volunteer to go with me. Are you on the case of the murdered goat farmer?"

"Did it make the news already?"

Cady began filling water bowls. "I heard the story on the way here. It sounded terrible."

"It was." Matt pictured the scene and his scrambled eggs rolled over.

Cady frowned. "Be careful."

"You too." Matt turned back toward the house.

"We still need to talk about the fundraiser!" Cady yelled at his back. "I have totals and last-minute catering decisions."

Cady was organizing a black-tie event to fund training and equipment necessary for Greta to join the sheriff's department as a K-9.

"I'll text you," Matt called over his shoulder. He grabbed his keys and headed for the sheriff's office.

Bree's vehicle was already in the lot when he arrived. Inside, the station was unusually quiet.

Matt passed the reception counter, where Bree's admin looked up from her computer. Marge was about sixty, with the dyed brown hair and sensible shoes of a grandma but the tenacity of a pit bull.

"Morning, Marge," he said.

She smiled over her half glasses. "Coffee is fresh in the break room. The sheriff is in her office with the chief deputy."

Matt passed through the mostly empty squad room and approached Bree's office. Her door was open. Behind her huge desk, Bree was all polished professional. Her uniform looked crisp and her dark hair was bundled in a neat coil at the nape of her neck, but shadows of their long night underscored her hazel eyes.

Matt knocked on her doorframe. "Where is everybody?"

Todd sat in a guest chair facing Bree's desk. "Handling a multivehicle fender bender in the grocery store parking lot and rounding up loose alpaca on Highway 9."

Bree waved Matt in. "I was just giving Todd a summary of our interview with Bernard Crighton."

Todd balanced a pocket-size notepad on one uniformed knee. "The warrants for phone and financial records are waiting on the judge's approval. I expect they'll be ready first thing this morning."

"Start the murder book." Bree slid a printout across the desk. "Here's my written report on the interview."

When did she type those?

Todd collected the pages.

"Do we know if Oscar owned guns?" Bree asked.

"He did." Todd skimmed a finger down a sheet of paper. "There was a Glock 19 registered to him."

"We didn't find a handgun at the house," Matt said. *Was Oscar killed with his own gun?*

Bree nodded. "Matt and I are interviewing Oscar's ex-wife this morning."

Todd made a note. "I'll review personal information as it comes in."

"The ME should finish the autopsies by early afternoon," Bree added. "They were on her schedule for this morning."

Each autopsy took approximately four hours, but the ME liked to get an early start to her day.

Matt said, "And hopefully, the techs will make some progress with Oscar's phone and laptop today as well."

"We'll meet back here and review the case later today. I'll have Marge schedule a press con for then as well." Bree powered down her desktop computer, stood, and faced Matt. "Let's go talk to Oscar's ex."

They left the station. Matt stopped at his Suburban, retrieved his body-armor vest, and tossed it into the back seat of Bree's vehicle. They'd learned the hard way that he always needed to be prepared for violence. Then they headed across town. Bree was quiet—too quiet—as she focused on the road.

"You have something on your mind?"

"I received another email." At a stop sign, Bree opened an email and handed him her phone before crossing the intersection.

Matt read the message.

Anger burned like an oil fire in his chest. "You need to take these threats seriously."

"I am." Bree released her grip on the steering wheel and flexed her fingers, as if she'd been holding it too tightly, and while her face was set in its neutral mask, a muscle in her cheek twitched. The threatening email had disturbed her more than she was admitting.

"I'm not kidding." He fumed. "How many threats have you gotten now?"

"Most aren't threats, just people spewing hate." She tried to evade his question.

"How many?"

Bree shrugged. "More than I can count. Some weeks more than others. If I'm in the news, the hate mail pours in. It's picked up some since the incident in July."

"The one with Oscar?"

"Yes. Not everyone was on my side. Since the prosecutor refused to bring charges against him for lack of evidence, there are people who believe I forced him out of the department for political reasons."

"He was a sloppy, crooked cop," Matt said.

Oscar had failed to follow procedures on several occasions. Bree had issued him multiple warnings. Finally, he'd mislabeled evidence in a major case, rendering that evidence inadmissible. Suspecting he'd intentionally contaminated the evidence to protect a buddy, Bree had put him on leave, but the prosecutor hadn't wanted to pursue formal charges. By mutual agreement, Oscar had retired.

Bree shrugged. "We can't prove the crooked part. For some, refusing to follow procedure is 'fucking technical bullshit.'" Her fingers curled into air quotes. "Quite a few of my critics say he was set up and fired because he refused to 'cave to political correctness.' I've been blasted for hiring female deputies and expecting the taxpayers to foot the bill for a separate locker room." Bree shook her head. "I still have a hard time believing the department didn't employ a single female deputy until after I took office."

But Matt believed it. Easily. "Is forensics having any luck tracking the senders?"

"No. I've only sent Rory the worst ones, which we believe are from one individual. I don't have the resources to track down every insult from a disgruntled jerk with an anonymous email account."

"I guess not." But Matt wanted to.

"And if I did, I'd be accused of trying to silence my critics." Her lips flattened. "Sheriff is an elected office. I'm tried in the court of public opinion."

It was very difficult to get rid of an elected official, which was why the former sheriff had been able to get away with so much corruption for decades. His popularity had soared with every accusation of excessive use of force. Even after his crimes were made public, not everyone believed he'd been guilty. They insisted he'd been set up.

"I don't like it either, but I don't have the skill set to find him. I have to trust Rory to do his job." Bree glanced at Matt. "Look, I've been dealing with sexists my whole professional life, and this is not the first time I've been threatened in my law enforcement career. I'm hoping this jerk just wants to vent."

Matt gestured at her phone. "I don't think *this* is venting." He had a very bad feeling. "*This* is a deliberate, specific threat."

And it was disturbing as hell.

"Agreed, but we have a murder to solve. We'll have to worry about dick pics and nasty messages later."

"And the direct threat of violence to you?"

Her mouth flattened into a grim line. "Still takes a back seat to murder. Forensics is on it. I don't have the manpower to do more. My house and family are well secured, and I'll take extra care with myself. None of the haters have ever followed through."

Yet.

Chapter Eight

Matt conceded her point with a single nod, but he would never accept that threats of violence were simply part of Bree's job.

She blew a hair off her forehead. "Now, what do we know about Oscar's ex-wife?"

Matt used the dashboard computer. He began with motor vehicle records and expanded from there. "Heather Oscar is forty-seven years old. She drives a 2012 Honda Accord. As far as I can tell from a cursory search, she is squeaky clean. I don't even see a single traffic ticket."

"Does she work?"

"She's a librarian, and she's been employed by the county for twenty years."

Matt plugged Oscar's ex-wife's address into the GPS. He glanced at the dashboard clock. It was nine o'clock. "Hopefully, she didn't already leave for work."

"And didn't watch the news this morning," Bree added.

Technically, the ex-wife wasn't official next of kin, so waking her in the middle of the night hadn't been warranted. But Matt wanted to observe her when she learned of Oscar's death. He wanted to see her respond to the news before she had time to think about the ramifications. Before she had time to mentally prepare for their visit or rehearse her response.

Ten minutes later, they stepped out of the vehicle and walked onto the cracked concrete sidewalk of a small apartment complex. Matt scanned the area. Most of the vehicles were inexpensive or older models. Four plain brick buildings were arranged around a rectangular patch of weedy grass.

"Crighton said Oscar complained about excessive alimony." Bree frowned. "Whatever Heather was doing with all that money, she wasn't spending it on rent."

"These are not luxury units," Matt agreed.

They walked up the path. Heather lived on the ground floor, and her unit opened directly onto the walkway. Bree and Matt flanked the steel security door, and Bree knocked. A few minutes later, light footsteps quickly approached the door. Bree and Matt stepped back to be fully visible through the peephole. The door was flung open by a woman dressed in yoga pants and sneakers. She was much more attractive than Matt had expected with short blonde hair, smooth skin, and a Marilyn Monroe–like figure.

She eyed Bree's uniform. "What's wrong?"

"Are you Heather Oscar?" Bree asked.

Heather nodded. "Yes. What happened?"

Bree glanced around. "May we come inside?"

"Yes, of course." Heather gently shooed a striped orange cat away from the door. "Get back, Tiger."

Matt and Bree stepped over the threshold. Matt closed the door behind them. The foyer was a square of tile adjoining the living room. The apartment was well kept, with freshly vacuumed cream-colored carpet and a low gray couch and matching chair.

"What happened?" Heather repeated.

"Eugene Oscar is your ex-husband?" Bree verified.

Heather nodded.

Bree continued. "Eugene's body was found last night. We're sorry for your loss."

Heather didn't react for a few heartbeats, then asked, "He's dead?"

"Yes, ma'am," Bree confirmed with one short nod.

Heather raised one hand to cover her mouth. She wrapped the other around her waist. A minute later, she lowered the hand on her mouth to hug her waist. "This is going to sound cold, but why are you here? Eugene and I aren't married anymore."

Bree lied without missing a beat. "You're still listed in his personnel file."

Technically, Matt thought it probably wasn't a *lie*. Heather's name *was* probably buried somewhere in Oscar's file. But it wasn't the reason for their visit.

Heather seemed to accept the statement. "How did it happen?"

"He was shot," Bree said.

Heather blinked in surprise. Her head shifted backward. "Was it in the line of duty?"

"No." Bree's head tilted. "Eugene retired from the sheriff's department recently."

Heather's eyebrows shot up. "Retired?"

"You didn't know?" Matt asked.

Heather shook her head. "No. I haven't seen Eugene in ages."

"He retired after a big case over the summer." Bree gave no details.

Matt added, "It was on the news."

Heather sighed. "I've been too busy with work to watch much news lately. I work at the Cross Street Branch of the county library. We had a major water leak back in June. Between the budget, permits, and approvals, county bureaucracy has made the repairs a never-ending nightmare." She adjusted her ponytail. "I'm supposed to be off today, but we'll see."

"Can you be more specific about when you last saw or spoke with Oscar?" Bree pulled out her notepad.

"Not off the top of my head," Heather said.

Tiger rubbed against Matt's ankles. He stooped to scratch it behind the ears, and the cat purred loudly. "Nice cat."

Heather smiled sadly. "I adopted him after the divorce. He's good company." The tabby returned to his owner, who scooped him into her arms. His purring grew louder as she held him against her neck. "If Eugene didn't die at work, then how did it happen?"

"We don't know." Matt straightened. "He was killed at his mother's farm. She was also a victim."

Heather gasped. "Camilla? Oh, my God. Why would anyone hurt her? She was a little weird, but she had very little interaction with anyone besides Eugene."

"Did you know Eugene had moved in with her?" Matt asked.

Heather scratched the cat's head. "No. The last time I spoke with him, he was renting a place over near the railroad. But as I said before, that was quite a while ago."

Bree made a note. "Did your lawyer handle your alimony?"

"Alimony?" Heather's brow furrowed. "I never received any alimony from Eugene. Did he say I did?"

"Not to me," Bree clarified. "But other people said he complained about paying alimony."

"I shouldn't be surprised. He was a very good liar." Heather shook her head. "I didn't want a nickel from him. I just wanted him gone."

Bree lifted her pen. "Then why did the divorce take so long?"

"Because he didn't want to give it to me." Heather's mouth tightened.

"Why did you want a divorce?" Matt couldn't imagine anyone wanted to be in a relationship with Oscar, but Heather had married him once.

"He lied." She closed her eyes for a few seconds. When she opened them, they were misty and filled with bitterness, betrayal, and hurt. "All I wanted was a child. I did everything I could to get pregnant from the day we married, but it didn't happen. After a couple of years,

I started to get concerned. I went to a specialist, but they couldn't find anything wrong with me. Oscar refused to participate in any sort of fertility testing or treatment." She looked away, her eyes bright with angry, unshed tears. She bowed her head. "At first, I thought it was just pride. But eventually, I found out the real reason. I was cleaning out a filing cabinet and found some old medical records. Oscar had gotten a vasectomy a few months before our wedding. We had a huge argument and he admitted he'd never wanted children, and he lied about it for our entire marriage."

"That's an unbelievably horrible thing to do." Bree's tone implied *even for Oscar*.

Heather's head snapped up. "I can prove it." She rushed from the room. Matt heard a drawer opening and closing. A machine hummed and it sounded as if she was printing something. She returned a couple of minutes later and thrust a paper at Bree. "Here's a copy of the vasectomy receipt."

Bree took it and scanned the paper. "Thank you. You must have been angry."

"You're damned right I was angry." Heather's eyes flashed. "I kicked him out the same day. All those years he allowed me to hope, to plan, to try, when he knew it was all pointless. When he'd made sure it was pointless. How dare he do that to me? How could he be so cruel? Why did he marry me at all?"

Matt almost suggested Oscar had loved her and wanted her despite their differences, but you didn't lie to the person you loved. Oscar's behavior illustrated a complete disregard for her feelings.

"I'm sorry." Bree's voice rang with empathy. "Did he say why he did it?"

"He admitted that he hated kids, but he still wanted me." Heather bit off the bitter words. "He knew how I felt long before we married. He even pretended to be sad when I couldn't conceive."

Matt wanted to commiserate but kept quiet. Heather might not want a male opinion on the matter.

"Can I copy this?" Bree held up the receipt.

"You can keep it," Heather said.

"Thank you." Bree folded the paper discreetly.

Heather sniffed and blinked. A single tear tracked down her face. She brushed it away with an angry gesture. "I promised myself I'd put it behind me, that I would never cry over it again, but some days . . . Some days I still feel the ache of what he stole from me. I'm too old to start again. I'm too old to find another husband and try to have kids. He took away any opportunity for me to have a family. I can't get that back."

"How did he handle the divorce?" Matt asked.

"He was mad." Heather wiped another tear from her cheek. "For months, I was pulled over by other deputies at least once a week."

"What excuse did they give?" Bree's jaw tightened.

"Rolling through a stop sign. Speeding. Swerving. Erratic driving." She shrugged. "None of it was true. My commute is only a couple of miles, and after the first two times, I was extra careful not to break any rules. They just wanted to harass me." Her eyes narrowed. "They would all wear this smug smirk on their faces."

Matt could picture it. The old sheriff had heartily approved of bullying. "Do you know of anyone else that had reason to be angry with Oscar?"

"No." Heather plucked a tissue from a box on the end table. She blotted her eyes. "But I didn't really know him at all, did I?"

Had anyone?

"I need to ask you where you were between eight p.m. Sunday and eight a.m. Monday," Bree said.

"Here." Heather looked around her living room. "The library is closed on Sundays, and I don't really socialize much. I've tried to date a few times, but I just don't trust anyone enough to get beyond the first meet." She sighed. "I don't know that I ever will."

A few seconds of silence passed before Bree collected Heather's cell number. "Thank you for your help." She and Matt let themselves out.

Back in the SUV, he fastened his seat belt. His mind still whirled from Heather's revelation. "He kept a big secret from his wife. I worked with Oscar for a decade, but it seems I didn't really know anything about him either."

"What he did went beyond keeping a secret. It was heartless, cruel, and selfish."

"I wonder what other lies we'll uncover as we dig into his life."

Bree started the engine. "I have a feeling there will be more. But his isn't the only life I want to dig into. Let's find out everything we can about Heather. She claims to be putting his deception aside, but it's clear she's still plenty mad. She's had years for that anger to stew."

"Maybe she was angry enough to kill him."

Bree agreed. "We have two potential suspects, and neither of them has an alibi."

CHAPTER NINE

Bree mulled over the interview as she drove out of the parking lot. Oscar's ex, Heather, had seemed controlled, but Bree had the sense that Oscar's betrayal had burrowed deep. His lies had affected her whole life, had robbed her of the one thing she'd wanted.

And he'd done it purposefully.

Why? Why did he marry Heather? Their entire relationship had been built on a lie.

Would Heather be able to recover? Or would her rage be the kind that fed itself over time?

"Where to?" Matt asked.

"The ME's office. I'd like to catch part of Oscar's autopsy."

"Would you really?" Matt's tone suggested he didn't concur.

"Yes." Bree felt as if attending autopsies gave her a better understanding of a murder. Not all detectives agreed.

"It feels wrong because we knew Oscar, like we're invading his privacy."

"Unfortunately, solving his murder requires us to do just that." Before the case was solved, they would know everything there was to know about Eugene Oscar. But were they too close to the victim?

"Fine." Matt sighed. "But I'm not sure what we're going to learn in this case that we couldn't learn from a phone call. The cause of death seemed pretty evident, and we're on the clock."

Bree headed for the municipal complex. He was right. Their time was valuable. The first forty-eight hours of any investigation were typically the most fruitful.

Admittedly, her preference for attending autopsies was partially emotional. In order to stand for the dead, she felt obligated to view the damage caused by their killers, to understand what they suffered in a personal way that couldn't be conveyed through medical terms written in a clinical report. She needed to see what they'd endured with her own eyes.

While Matt thought viewing Oscar's autopsy was an intrusion, Bree thought skipping it would be disrespectful, as if she weren't giving his case 100 percent.

Every truth was in the eyes of the beholder.

They parked and went inside. They checked in with the receptionist, who buzzed them into the back rooms. In the antechamber, they donned gowns, gloves, masks, booties, and face shields before entering the autopsy suite.

Oscar lay on a stainless-steel table, his chest splayed open. The scale next to the body looked like it could have come from the produce section of the grocery store. It was currently weighing Oscar's heart.

The sharp scent of formalin accompanied the stink of decomp.

Dr. Jones looked up, both hands still buried in Oscar's chest cavity. "There you are."

Bree approached the table. Oscar had been beaten and shot four times. He had suffered. No doubt about that. She allowed herself a minute of pity, then shifted into detective mode. Regardless of her personal conflicts with Oscar, he hadn't deserved this. She would bring him justice. "Anything notable?"

"Victim's ID has been confirmed with dental records, though we all knew this is former Deputy Oscar." The ME paused for a breath. "He was a healthy, middle-age male of normal weight with good muscle tone. He took care of himself. I've found no sign of disease." Dr. Jones lifted her hands and pointed a bloody glove toward discolorations on the lower half of the body. "Livor mortis is fixed and seems concentrated in the lower body, as expected in a seated victim. Therefore, the victim was likely in the same position as when he was killed."

When the heart stopped beating, gravity made the blood pool in the lowest areas. The result was purple discoloration of the skin.

"So he wasn't moved after death," Bree confirmed.

"Correct." The ME nodded toward Oscar's legs. "As you can see, his kneecaps were both destroyed by bullets, and he was shot in the shoulder."

Bree could see the shoulder wound just above the Y-incision.

The ME continued. "None of these wounds would have been immediately fatal. They bled heavily but were survivable. Without treatment, though, he would have bled out over time."

"But he didn't have the chance," Matt said.

"No," the ME said. "I haven't gotten to the skull yet, but there's little doubt that the bullet to the forehead was the fatal shot. The body wounds have a slight downward trajectory, so the killer was standing in front of the victim when they pulled the trigger. I was able to recover the bullet from the shoulder wound." She motioned toward a shallow stainless-steel dish. The bloody bullet in the dish was in good condition, only slightly misshapen from its path through Oscar's shoulder. If they found the murder weapon, they should be able to make a ballistics match. "It's a 9mm."

Oscar's personal handgun had been a 9mm, Bree remembered.

Dr. Jones continued. "I estimate the body shots were midrange, fired from several feet away, but the head shot is a contact wound."

Bree focused on the hole in Oscar's forehead. The skin around it was blackened, charred.

"You can see the seared skin and soot around the wound." Dr. Jones hesitated. "When a gun is pressed hard against the skin when it's fired, all the materials—gases, soot, et cetera—discharged from the weapon become embedded in the skin."

"So the killer didn't just put the gun to his head," Matt said. "They pressed on it, hard."

"Yes," Dr. Jones agreed. "From a cursory look at the second victim's head wound, it also appears to be a contact wound. I'll let you know if his mother's autopsy yields any additional evidence." She turned back to her work.

"What about the ropes used to bind the victims?" Matt asked.

"Removed intact and collected by forensics." The ME reached for the electric saw that would cut through Oscar's skull. "Check with Rory in forensics. He's more than a computer tech. He knows all about knots too."

In a rural county, anyone who could do double duty was especially useful.

"Thank you." Bree turned to leave the suite as the sound of the saw changed as it cut through bone.

They pushed through the swinging door. As soon as they hit the antechamber, they stripped off their PPE and tossed it in the appropriate bins. For absolutely no reason—she'd been wearing gloves—Bree washed her hands.

"The Glock registered to Oscar is a 9mm, and we didn't find it in the house," Matt noted. "It's possible he could have been killed with his own weapon."

"He wasn't wearing a holster. Either he had it in his hand or whoever shot him knew where he kept it."

"We didn't find a gun safe in the house either."

"9mm is a very common caliber, though," Bree said. "It could be coincidence."

"Then where's Oscar's weapon?" Matt asked.

Bree didn't have an answer.

"Also, pressing the gun hard to Oscar's head and pulling the trigger makes me think the killer was angry. That could make the motive personal."

"It's possible," Bree said. "But the ME said the kill shot to Camilla was the same. Maybe the killer was just angry in general."

"They weren't messing around," Matt said.

Bree pictured a faceless killer approaching two bound victims. She saw the killer walk close, press the muzzle into Oscar's forehead, and pull the trigger. "I see a second option for the deliberation: cold-bloodedness."

"Ironically, that's on the other end of the emotional spectrum," Matt said. "Let's check ViCAP and NCIC for similar crimes in case the killer has done this before." The Violent Criminal Apprehension Program and National Crime Information Center were crime databases available to law enforcement.

"Yes," Bree said. "Also, Oscar was tortured, which could mean someone was trying to extract information."

"Or they were just really pissed off," Matt finished. "And punishing him."

"All possibilities," Bree said. "Let's go see Rory."

The county forensics lab was in the same building as the medical examiner's office. They made their way down a maze of corridors to the lab, which was almost as cold as the autopsy suite. They found the tech in a large room lined with stainless-steel tables. He was bent over a laptop that appeared to be the one taken from Oscar's room. He looked up as they entered.

Rory was tall and thin. Bree estimated him to be close to thirty years old, but at first glance he could have passed for much younger. He needed a shave, but the patches of stubble on his chin were as sparse as an adolescent's.

Bree gestured to Matt. "This is my criminal investigator, Matt Flynn. Dr. Jones said you had some information about the knots used in the Oscar case." Bree pointed to a table where the ropes were laid out on white sheets.

Rory swallowed as if nervous. "I was going to call you today."

"We were in the building," Bree explained. "About those knots . . ."

"Yes." Rory cleared his throat and stepped away from the computer. "The binds were tied off with what's called a ground-line hitch. It's not an uncommon knot, but it does require specialized knowledge. The hitches used are all nearly identical, which tells me the individual who tied them had practice."

"Who would use that knot?" Bree asked.

"Boaters, climbers, campers, scouts," Rory said.

Matt stroked his beard. "So, the killer is likely to be someone who participates in outdoor activities."

"Probably, yes." Rory rubbed his hands together. "I can also tell the person who tied them was right-handed due to the way the ropes pass over each other. We are also testing the ropes and hitches for DNA. The rope itself is one-eighth-inch black nylon paracord. You can buy it almost anywhere: Amazon, Walmart, Home Depot, marine stores . . . This rope looks new."

"So maybe our killer bought it for this purpose," Bree said. "But then again, maybe not."

Tracking the sale through local retailers would be a lot of legwork, but they could check suspects' credit card records for recent purchases. You never knew what piece of evidence would lead to the killer, and all evidence added up when it came time to go to trial.

"We also found three dried flower petals caught under the leg of the chair Oscar was tied to." Rory indicated another table, where three small flower petals were lined up on a piece of brown paper. The edges of the petals were stained with dried blood. "We're consulting a botanist to find out what plant these flowers originated from, but we found no matching flowers anywhere on the property."

"Did you find anything interesting on Camilla's or Oscar's cell phones?" Bree asked.

"Camilla didn't use her phone much. Her recent calls and texts were mostly to her son, the church, and some local businesses." Rory paused. "But Oscar had quite a few calls to numbers that were only active for a short time."

Matt frowned. "Burners."

"Yep," Rory agreed. "All calls. No texts."

"So content is unknown," Bree said.

"Um." Rory blushed bright red. "Sheriff, I have something else to show you." He moved back to the laptop he'd been examining when they'd walked into the room. "We found some pictures on Oscar's laptop."

Curious, Bree bent closer. "What kind of pictures? Anything like the one I received last night?"

"No, ma'am," Rory said. "These are different."

Oscar couldn't have sent that one anyway, thought Bree. He'd already been killed.

Matt stood behind her, looking over her shoulder.

Rory tapped the keyboard, waking up the laptop. The screen brightened to show a grid of photos. They were all pictures of a naked woman—with Bree's face on them.

Shock snapped Bree to full attention. "What are those?"

"It's not you," Rory blurted out. "I could tell the images had been edited immediately. Someone combined pornography with publicly available photos of you."

"I know it's not me." Bree fell back a step, as if trying to put distance between herself and the images on the computer screen. "But it doesn't matter, does it? People will believe that it is." She paused. "I receive so many nasty messages. I thought I'd seen it all." But nothing could have prepared Bree for seeing her face on another woman's nude body.

"Have you received anything like this before?" Matt asked. "The dick pic was bad enough, but this . . ."

"Not exactly." Bree waved a hand toward the screen. "I've received pictures of me with my face X-ed out. Others have insults written on the images. Some are just words. They range in mood from *God will strike you down* to *you're a whore.* Did you find any of those previous images on Oscar's computer?"

"No, ma'am," Rory said. "I checked. When I saw the fake pictures, I immediately wondered if Oscar had been the one harassing you."

"Oscar couldn't have sent the one from last night," Bree said. "He was already dead."

Matt frowned, his expression cold as he turned back to Rory. "Can you see what else he did with the photos? Seems to be a lot of work just to embarrass Sheriff Taggert."

"We're still digging through his email, but we know he uploaded the photos directly to some social media sites." Rory jabbed a finger toward the computer. "I'm sorry to say it gets even worse. He shared a deepfake video that replaced a porn star's face with yours."

Bree's heart sank and chilled like it had hit an iceberg.

"Most deepfake videos are pornographic," Rory said. "In fact, the huge majority are celebrity faces mapped over porn stars'. Ma'am"—his voice sounded apologetic—"a few days ago, he sent that video to porn sites all over the internet."

As if to punctuate his point, Rory clicked on a button. A video played. Shame heated Bree's face. She had no reason to be embarrassed. The video wasn't her, which anyone close to her would know. But it didn't matter. She felt exposed anyway. It felt real.

"Did Oscar make that video?" Bree asked.

"Not on this machine." Rory tapped on the screen. "There's no sign of the software or working files. But we can tell it's a manipulated video. For one, she doesn't blink, and that's because most photographs are taken with people's eyes open. The software that was used isn't good enough to simulate blinking. Also, the skin tones are patchy. The lips don't sync with the sounds, and you can see some flickering around the edges of your face. But whoever did this was smart enough to use the same porn actress in all the fake photos and the video. She's about your size and superficially believable."

Oscar hadn't chosen an actress with H-size breasts or some other glaring physical feature that would clearly indicate she wasn't Bree.

Rory clicked on "Stop" and the video froze. He closed the laptop.

"We'll need a list of all the specific websites where Oscar sent the video." Matt turned to Bree. "You'll need to send out takedown orders to each individual site."

The ramifications of what Oscar had done speared Bree like an arrow. "Did he have fake videos and images of anyone else?"

Rory touched the laptop. "Not on this computer."

So it was revenge solely directed against Bree.

"I'll send you that list of sites." Rory wrote on a sticky note. "But"—his shrug conveyed pointlessness—"the files get shared over and over. Copies multiply like viruses. The chances of getting rid of them all . . ."

Bree finished his thought. "Once something is on the web, it's nearly impossible to completely purge it."

Rory nodded. "You should get a lawyer and sue the ever-loving crap out of everyone who knowingly posts it. Deepfakes and revenge porn are on the rise. The overwhelming majority of it is directed against women. It's appallingly effective at ruining their lives."

Matt collected some information from Rory while Bree stood still, processing the video. She was numb. They thanked Rory and left the lab. Bree walked the corridors in a daze. The video felt like more of a violation than when she'd been shot.

Her bullet wound had healed. She might never recover from this.

Behind the wheel of her SUV, she turned to Matt. "Oscar and I clashed. He didn't like me from the beginning. But to go through all this trouble to punish me . . . that's a whole new level of hate."

"What he did was horrible. I never liked him, but I didn't know the extent of his cruel streak."

She could tell people the photos and video were fake until she turned blue. Who would believe her? Oscar's hoax could be the end of Bree's career.

CHAPTER TEN

Matt seethed. He wanted to punch Oscar in the face for what he'd done to Bree. Too bad he was already dead.

Bree started the engine, her face pale. "The fakes were Oscar's version of revenge porn, right? He wanted to humiliate me and maybe even make sure I don't get reelected."

Matt thought she was right about Oscar's motive. "Before you came along, he did whatever he liked, including enlisting his fellow deputies to harass his ex. You took him down."

"Let's not get off track. The fake porn is bad, but it seems to be directed only at me. So, there's no evidence that it's related to his murder." Bree paused. "Are any of the deputies still close to Oscar?"

Matt shook his head. "No. The deputies who were part of the old guard left."

"Do you know where they are now?"

"No. They haven't kept in touch. I was never really *in* the boys' club." Matt had long suspected the former sheriff had intentionally put him in the way of friendly fire for that very reason.

"What about Jim Rogers?" Bree asked. "Was he one of *the boys*?"

"He was."

"He's been out on disability, but he worked with Oscar for a long time. He might know something relevant about his life."

Rogers was a former deputy who had been shot in the line of duty back in the spring. He'd recovered from his injuries, but continuing issues with post-traumatic stress prevented him from returning to work. Rogers had also been one of the men who'd accidentally shot Matt in the friendly fire incident, and that incident had scarred them both. Rogers had apologized to Matt, but there was still awkwardness between them.

"Have you seen him recently?" She glanced at him.

"I ran into him about a month ago in town. We didn't say much more than hi. How about you?"

Bree shook her head. "I get official notifications on his disability status. That's it, but then, I don't know him very well. He didn't work for me for long before he was shot."

"Do you want to call him into the station or talk to him at his home?" Matt asked.

Bree's brow furrowed. "At his home, I think. He'll talk more where he's comfortable."

"He's north of town." Matt looked up the address and entered it in the GPS.

Fifteen minutes later, as they approached the property, Matt spotted a driveway marked by a red mailbox shaped like a barn. "There it is."

"I don't want to push Rogers too hard, but we need answers. You've known him longer than I have. I'll follow your lead on that."

Bree slowed and turned down a narrow gravel lane that cut through the trees. The isolation of the property didn't surprise Matt. Rogers was an avid hunter and had been the best tracker in the department. He liked space. The lane opened into a large, neat clearing. The front lawn was thick, green, and free of fallen leaves. The one-story home was more cabin than house. Made of natural wood, it looked as if it had grown there.

As they parked, the front door opened, and Jim Rogers walked out onto the small front porch. A yellow lab pup raced past his legs to the grass as Matt and Bree climbed out of the vehicle. The pup stopped in a sprawl of uncoordinated limbs, then attacked Matt's foot.

"How old?" Matt crouched and disentangled the pup's teeth from his bootlace.

"Four months. She's a holy terror." But Rogers's smile was full of affection.

Waving paws far too large for her body, the puppy rolled over for a belly rub.

Bree stopped next to Matt. She leaned over to give the dog a pat. "I can see she's vicious."

Rogers shrugged and walked toward them. "She's a lab. They're generally friendly if people don't ruin them."

Matt straightened and studied Rogers. The former deputy looked rough. An outdoorsman, Rogers was normally fit and lean. He'd lost weight from a frame that couldn't spare any. His cheeks were gaunt, and his eyes hollow. In the past, Matt had seen Rogers track a suspect all day long through the woods without tiring. Now, his steps dragged with exhaustion.

A month ago, when Matt had run into him, Rogers hadn't looked this bad. Something had changed.

The puppy peed in the grass.

Rogers praised her. "Good girl." He held out a hand to Matt. "Nice to see you."

Matt, then Bree, shook it.

The puppy romped after a butterfly. Rogers turned back toward the cabin and started across the grass. As he went up the porch steps, he whistled. The dog bolted toward him. She stumbled up the steps, slid to a sloppy stop, and nearly crashed into the wall.

"I assume you're here on business." Rogers opened the front door and gestured for Bree and Matt to follow him inside.

"Yes." Bree stepped across the threshold. "Unfortunately, this isn't a social call."

Matt entered the house. Based on the plain front facade, he hadn't expected the open floor plan or modern kitchen. Two sets of french doors opened onto a huge deck. Beyond that, sunlight gleamed off a small lake. The puppy scampered into the kitchen and stuck her whole head into a bowl. More water sloshed onto the floor than went into the dog.

"Nice place," Matt said.

The pup flopped into a patch of sunshine and closed her eyes.

"Thanks." Rogers mopped up the water with a microfiber towel. He tossed it over the back of a chrome-and-leather stool tucked under the island overhang, as if he knew he'd need the towel again soon. "I needed a project over the summer, so I did the kitchen reno myself." He gestured toward a doorway. "The bathrooms are still all 1970s. It isn't pretty, but I don't want to demo rooms with an avid chewer on hand." He gestured toward the sleeping puppy. "I need to focus on Goldie's training for the next couple of months."

"Back to hunting then?" Matt asked.

"Maybe." Rogers went into the kitchen and busied himself with a fancy coffee machine. "Cappuccino?" He gestured toward the stools on the other side of the island.

Matt recognized the island for what it really was—a barrier Rogers had placed between them. "Sure," he said.

"I never say no to caffeine. Thank you." Bree slid into a stool. With Rogers's back to them, Matt and Bree shared a worried look.

"What are you planning to do with Goldie?" Matt asked.

Rogers shrugged but didn't face them. "Maybe I'll train her for search and rescue. I haven't decided yet. I'll start with basic obedience, then start her on nose work."

Matt didn't ask about Rogers's plans for himself. Neither did Bree.

"Labs are good scent dogs." Matt sat on the stool next to Bree. He sensed Rogers had something to say but was working up the nerve or gathering his thoughts.

"Yeah, they are." Rogers took cups and saucers from a cabinet. The coffee machine hissed and gurgled. A few minutes of awkward silence followed as Rogers worked the machine like a professional. He served up white cups of cappuccino topped with foam and a dusting of cinnamon.

Bree sipped hers. "I'm impressed."

Rogers stayed on the other side of the island. He spun his cup on the saucer for a few seconds, then looked up and met Bree's gaze. "I'm not coming back to the department."

"OK." Bree didn't sound surprised.

"I won't stay on disability either." Rogers motioned toward his leg. "The leg healed well, but . . ." He paused, embarrassment flooding his cheeks. "I can't shoot a gun. Hell, I can't even hear a gunshot without breaking into a cold sweat. I doubt I'll ever hunt again."

"Most cops never draw their gun in the line of duty. You were in *two* shootings. PTSD is a valid illness." Bree set down the cup. "You're entitled to disability for as long as you need it. You don't have to make up your mind right at this moment."

"I've been trying to recondition myself to the sound, but even if I eventually do . . ." Rogers shuddered. "I'm never going to be the same. I need to find another career."

"OK, then." Bree nodded. "I respect your decision. You're entitled to disability retirement. That'll give you time to figure out what's next."

Rogers's gaze dropped. His hands shook, rattling his cup in its saucer. He lifted his fingers off the handle and gripped the edge of the counter. "There are things you don't know."

"Do you want to tell us?" Matt leaned his forearms on the island.

Rogers said nothing, but his eyes were haunted.

By what?

Bree looked to Matt with questioning eyes.

"This isn't about my shooting, is it?" Matt asked. "Because we've covered that. It wasn't your fault."

Rogers shook his head. "It's not about that."

Bree pressed. "Do you want to talk about it?"

Rogers shook his head again, harder.

"OK." Bree's voice softened. "We didn't come here to talk about your return to work anyway."

"You came here to ask about Oscar." There was no question in Rogers's voice.

"You saw the news," Matt said.

Rogers didn't move or respond for a few seconds. "He came to see me a few weeks ago." He paused, as if remembering. A huge sigh rolled through him. "I know it's not cool to speak ill of the dead, but Oscar was a bastard." Rogers was working his way toward revealing something, and it felt big. He stared down into his cup. "I'm not proud of the things I've done either."

After a few seconds of silence, Matt prompted him in a gentle voice. "Why did he visit you?"

Rogers rubbed the bridge of his nose. "It's a long story. I have to start at the beginning." He began to pace the narrow strip of tile on the other side of the kitchen island. "About two and a half years ago, I was on patrol. Oscar was out that night too. I backed up him and another deputy, Brian Dylan, on a traffic stop. You know how it is—you pull somebody over in the middle of the night, you want someone to have your back. It was a ways out of town on Route 57, out past the tractor supply store." He pivoted. "When I got there, Oscar was at the driver's-side door looking at the driver's documents. There were no passengers, just a lone driver. Oscar asked the driver if he'd been drinking. The guy said no. Then Oscar asked him to step out of the vehicle." Rogers stopped for a breath.

Matt didn't move for fear of breaking Rogers's flow.

"The driver's name was Kenny McPherson. Big guy. Said he was on his way home from work as a warehouse forklift driver. He seemed normal, maybe a little nervous, but nothing out of the ordinary. Most folks are a little spooked when they're pulled over. Oscar put him through a road sobriety test and said he was wobbly. I didn't see it. The guy looked steady to me. That's when I started to get a little uncomfortable." Rogers rubbed a hand over his mouth.

Without moving his head, Matt looked sideways at Bree. She was rock still, almost as if holding her breath.

Rogers rubbed his jaw and continued. "Dylan asked McPherson if he could look in his car, and the guy said yes."

Most people did because they saw no reason not to. They didn't expect cops to break the law. Mostly, criminals knew to say no.

Rogers continued. "So Oscar asked me to keep an eye on the guy while he and Dylan did a quick search of the vehicle. Dylan shines his light under the driver's seat and comes out with a baggie full of pills. McPherson freaks out, yelling, 'Those aren't mine,' but Dylan just gives him that nasty smirk of his. He and Oscar were practically laughing by this point."

Matt could picture it all too well.

Rogers's gaze became vacant, as if he were seeing the scene. "Dylan brought the pills to the guy, shakes the bag in front of his face, and starts listing all the charges he's facing. McPherson yelled back, saying Oscar and Dylan were setting him up. Then Oscar stumbled backward a step and accuses the guy of pushing him. Dylan starts yelling that McPherson assaulted an officer. They throw the guy over the hood of his car and handcuff him. The guy was raging as they put him in the back of the patrol car. He knew they were fucking him over." Rogers stopped pacing and faced Matt. "I pulled Dylan aside and told him I hadn't seen the guy do anything. I asked him point-blank if he'd planted the drugs. He said no, but I could tell he was lying. Oscar and Dylan faced off against me. My word against both of theirs." He shifted his gaze to Bree. "Oscar was driving an old car that night. It didn't have a dashboard cam." Rogers stood in the middle of the kitchen, looking lost.

"What happened to McPherson?" she asked.

"They piled on the charges, and he went to prison for a couple of years. Oscar came to see me to let me know that McPherson was out. Oscar wanted to set him up for another crime. He asked if I still had any friends in the department who could *take care of it.*"

Bree's back snapped straight, but she kept her tone even. "Do you?"

Rogers snorted. "No. That whole gang is gone, and I'm glad."

"Do you know why Oscar and Dylan targeted McPherson?" To Matt, it felt like a lot of effort.

Rogers shook his head. "No. I'd say they liked to fuck with people, but this seemed personal."

"Are you worried about McPherson?" Bree asked.

Rogers lifted a shoulder. "Whatever happens, I deserve it."

"Could you have proven Dylan planted the drugs or Oscar faked being pushed?" Bree asked.

"No." Rogers shook his head. "But I know both Dylan and Oscar, and why would McPherson have agreed to a vehicle search if he was carrying drugs under the seat of his car?"

He wouldn't have.

Silence settled over the kitchen.

Rogers sighed. "If I had contradicted Oscar's or Dylan's statements in any way, the defense attorney would have pounced, and the DA would probably have dropped the charges."

The local DA liked his win record and didn't prosecute cases with questionable evidence.

"But my career would have been over." Rogers looked at Matt. "Unlike you, I made the choice to play along. I prioritized myself and allowed them to send an innocent man to prison. But I got a call last week from a lawyer representing Kenny McPherson."

"What does he want?" Bree asked.

Rogers's cheeks reddened. "I don't know. I didn't call him back."

Lawyers were usually persistent. He'd be back. Then Rogers would have to decide if he was going to come clean about the past or not.

And if not, could he live with the shame Matt was pretty sure he was feeling right now?

"Do you know if Oscar still kept in touch with Dylan?" Matt asked.

Rogers nodded. "They stayed tight."

Bree asked, "Do you know where we can find Dylan?"

Rogers looked away for a second, then returned his gaze to Bree's. "He went to the Scarlet Falls PD when he left the sheriff's department."

"Have you seen or talked to Dylan recently?" she asked.

"No." Rogers crossed his arms over his chest. His lips mashed together, as if he was thinking about something but didn't want to share.

Technically in Randolph County and part of Bree's jurisdiction, Scarlet Falls had its own police department. The sheriff mostly provided backup to their officers.

Rogers leaned a hip on the counter, as if his confession had burned off all his energy and he needed the support. "The worst part is, I'd forgotten all about that case until Oscar called me." His eyes went bleak. "How could I have forgotten about ruining a man's life?"

CHAPTER ELEVEN

An hour later, Bree faced a small mirror in the restroom of the sheriff's station. She smoothed a few wrinkles from her uniform shirt and tucked a hair back into her bun. Her stomach grumbled, reminding her she'd skipped lunch. But she had no time—or appetite. The press conference would start in ten minutes.

The door opened and Marge walked in, tsking.

"I hope you're not going on camera like that." In her hand, she held the cosmetics bag from Bree's desk in her hand.

Bree sighed. "I was. Are you here to tart me up?"

Marge shook her head and opened the bag. "At least put on some concealer and powder."

"I'm investigating a real murder, not filming an episode of *CSI*."

"I'm not suggesting you wear stilettos," Marge deadpanned, crossing her arms. "But you're shiny, and somehow also pale. You want to look cool and collected."

Bree turned back to the mirror. She *was* shiny and pale. "I hate worrying about appearances when I should be focused on the case."

"You're a public figure. You need to do both." Marge handed her a tube of liquid concealer and a compact. "Appearances matter."

Knowing Marge was right, Bree dabbed concealer under her eyes and applied a light layer of powder. "OK?"

Marge's scrutiny felt like a spotlight. "Almost." She held out a tube of lipstick.

"Really?" Bree sighed. "I don't like lipstick. It's gummy and sticky. When I wear it, all I can see in the mirror is *lips*."

"This color is subtle." Marge took back the concealer and powder. "Trust me."

Bree did, but she applied the lipstick sparingly. It was barely a color, but the combination of cosmetics made her look less pasty.

Marge eyed her face. "You're passable."

"Gee, thanks." Bree closed the lipstick.

Marge took it from her hand and put it back in the bag. "Go."

Bree left the restroom, then waved to Matt and Todd for them to follow her outside. She wanted their presence to show that the department was devoting resources to the murders. With the men behind her on either side, she stepped up to the microphone that had been set up on the sidewalk in front of the station. She faced the parking lot, where news crews and reporters jockeyed for position. After seven months as sheriff, she knew a number of reporters on sight.

"Yesterday, we responded to a call for a well-being check," Bree began. "We discovered two bodies, both dead from gunshot wounds. The victims have been officially identified as Eugene Oscar and his mother, Camilla Brown. Their deaths are currently being investigated as a double homicide." She gestured behind her. "Investigator Matt Flynn and Chief Deputy Todd Harvey are assisting with the investigation with the support of the entire sheriff's department."

A reporter shoved a mic at Bree. "They were murdered?"

Bree nodded. "Yes."

"Is this the same Eugene Oscar you fired two months ago?" a reporter yelled. Bree recognized the voice and zeroed in on Nick West from WSNY News.

Bree chose her words carefully. "Eugene Oscar recently retired from the sheriff's department."

"But wasn't he originally fired for cause?" Nick West asked. Today, his killer smile looked a little too cocky.

"No. He was on administrative leave, and then he retired," Bree repeated, but her discomfort gathered. Nick wouldn't let the subject go entirely. He was young—in his late twenties—but he had the instincts of a good journalist. She'd have to deal with him later. She signaled for a tall redhead to speak.

"When were they killed?" the redhead asked.

Bree leaned closer to the microphone. "According to the medical examiner, they died between eight p.m. Sunday and eight a.m. Monday."

A blonde woman raised her hand. She had huge fake eyelashes and thick eyeliner. "Paris Vickers with the *Daily Grind*. Who found the bodies?"

"I did," Bree answered. "While conducting the well-being check for a concerned neighbor."

A gray-haired man called out, "Is it normal for you to go out on routine calls?"

"When we're busy, yes." Bree looked for the next question.

Paris Vickers raised her microphone. "Do you have any suspects yet?"

"I can't comment on the details of an active investigation," Bree answered and turned to another reporter.

Before he could speak, Paris persisted. "Should the residents of Grey's Hollow be worried that there's a killer on the loose?"

Bree shook her head. "At this time, we have no reason to think the killer represents a danger to the community at large." Again, Bree attempted to steer away from Paris, but she just kept talking.

"But you don't know the motivation behind the killing?" Paris's tone sounded more like a statement than a question.

Bree fell back to her standby answer. "I can't comment on an active investigation."

Paris smirked. "If you can't comment on the case, maybe you'd like to comment on the nude pictures of you that are all over the internet?"

Bree froze. Her throat constricted until she doubted she could croak out any answer at all, not that she had one. She wanted to kick herself. She should have expected this. But Rory had said the videos and pics had been uploaded to porn sites. Had they really gone viral that quickly? Or had her email harasser tipped off the reporter? She hadn't even had a chance to file takedown orders.

Hell, she hadn't even contacted an attorney yet.

Excitement buzzed and reporters murmured to each other. Bree didn't look behind her, but she heard Todd's shoes scuffle on the concrete. Without seeing Matt, she knew he would be stone-faced.

Paris's mouth curved in a satisfied smile.

Bree swallowed and tried to sound cool, but her cheeks were hot. Knowing she had to respond, she said, "Those pictures are obvious fakes," in a *subject closed* tone.

But Paris wasn't finished. "Have you ever modeled nude, Sheriff?"

"No," Bree snapped, then breathed and replied in a calm voice, "I've never modeled, period. As I already stated, those images aren't real."

"I saw them. They looked real to me." Paris gave her a look of disbelief. "Have you ever starred in a pornographic video? Because there's one of those with your image circulating as well." Bedlam broke out as other reporters started yelling out questions. Some opened their phones, clearly searching for the images. Paris's smile deepened, as if she was very pleased with herself.

Bree tried to answer no, but no one heard her over the yelling. "May I have your attention." Sweat dampened Bree's forehead and gathered under her arms. It dripped under her body armor and soaked her shirt at the base of her spine. She needed to take back control. Finally, she barked a commanding "Quiet!" into the microphone.

A hush slowly settled over the crowd.

Bree pushed aside her embarrassment. She needed to spin this story. *Not spin,* she corrected herself. She was only telling the truth, but she needed to change her emotional response. Fear and humiliation made her look weak. She summoned indignation and anger in their place. She let her voice rise just enough to sound strong but not defensive. "The images circulating on the internet are edited. They are deepfakes that were manufactured to embarrass me. They aren't real."

Someone snickered, "Prove it."

"Her tits look real!" someone yelled.

Bree looked for the speaker, but no one met her gaze. She scanned the news crews, making eye contact with reporters and cameras as she panned the crowd. She needed to speak to viewers as much as the journalists in front of her. "All it takes is a simple piece of software to superimpose one person's face over another person's body. It could happen to anyone. I find that very disturbing." Bree stared at Paris. "If you examine the images carefully, the editing is very obvious." Bree let her tone rather than her words imply *shame on you.*

Paris squirmed, but her lips pursed in annoyance. She wasn't embarrassed.

"Now"—Bree spoke in a *getting back to real business* tone—"I need to return to my murder investigation. Thank you for your time." She stepped away from the microphone and turned back toward the station. She kept her strides even and calm. It couldn't appear as if she was running away, even though that was exactly what she wanted to do.

Inside, she made a beeline for her office. Marge, Todd, and Matt followed and clustered around her desk.

Bree's butt hit her chair hard. She propped her elbows on the desk and dropped her face into her hands. After a few seconds, she lifted her head. "Was that as big of a disaster as I think?"

As expected, Matt looked pissed. Todd tugged at his collar, as if acutely uncomfortable.

Marge said, "Yes."

Bree could always count on her for honesty. "What do we know about Paris Vickers?"

Marge's lips pressed into a flat line. "She's a bitch?"

Bree couldn't suppress a quick snort. "Besides that."

"The *Daily Grind* is a tabloid blog," Marge said. "No one takes it seriously."

"Doesn't matter." The scope of the disaster was just beginning to swarm like panicked ants in Bree's belly. "Now that Paris brought the deepfakes to light, everyone will go looking for them."

"I'll make sure the press has cleared out." Marge headed for the door.

Todd glanced at his phone. "I need to take care of something."

"Do you need me?" Bree asked.

"No. One of the patrol vehicles was hit in the Wendy's parking lot. The deputy wasn't inside. No big deal. I'll handle it."

Bree nodded. "When you're done, I'd like you to talk to the neighbor, Homer. He's been Camilla's neighbor for decades. He must know something about the family history."

Todd brightened. "Anything specific you want to know?"

"I'm interested in property values. Does he have any idea what the farm might be worth? Also, how far any family conflicts go back," Bree said. "Hopefully, he'll know some dirty details that aren't in any official documents."

"Let's hope." Todd closed the door behind him on the way out, as if sensing that Bree needed a moment alone with Matt.

When he was gone, Matt perched on the corner of her desk. "Are there any pictures of you in a tank top or shorts on the internet?"

"I don't think so." Bree didn't have personal social media accounts. As a detective in Philly, she'd been on the news a few times, but she'd always dressed in business attire. Before making detective, she'd been in uniform. Now as sheriff, she usually wore a uniform when she was on duty, jeans and a T-shirt when off. "Why?"

"Because the easiest way to prove those images are false is to show your tattoos," Matt said. "There would be no question the images aren't really you."

"I don't show my tattoos in public." Bree pressed a hand to an ache in her forehead. "I can't strip off my uniform shirt in front of the press."

Matt crossed his arms and frowned. "How ironic that your only defense to prove nude pictures are fake is to take off your clothes."

"They're private," she objected, even though the protest felt childish and prudish. It wasn't as if she'd be showing any parts of her body that were truly intimate. As a five-year-old, Bree had been mauled by her father's dog. For most of her life, she'd concealed the horrific scars on her shoulder and ankle. As an adult, she'd covered those scars with tattoos, but she remained reluctant to put them on display. In her mind, the tattoos were for *her*, not anyone else.

"I know." Matt's eyes softened. "If Oscar weren't dead, I'd beat the hell out of him for you."

"Thanks, but he is dead, which means I can't haul him into court and sue him."

New York State had new laws against revenge porn and deepfake pornography.

"You need a lawyer. If the *Daily Grind* shares or republishes those images, you can go after them."

"Who should I hire?" Bree had no time to interview attorneys.

"Morgan Dane."

"She's a defense attorney."

Matt nodded. "But I bet she'd take your case anyway. High-profile cases are good for business. You need someone really good with managing the press, and that's definitely one of her strengths."

Bree would rather break up a bar fight than deal with the media. Publicity and diplomacy were two of the most difficult aspects of being an elected official. Being sheriff wasn't just about being a good cop. Bree had to think like a politician.

"I'll make an appointment with her," she said. "But for now, we need to get back to the investigation." Bree wanted to forget about the deepfakes and focus on her case. Give her a killer to hunt down any day . . . "Let's go talk to Kenny McPherson. If Jim Rogers was correct, Kenny had plenty of motive to kill Oscar."

"I also want to know why Oscar would plant drugs and falsify charges against him."

"Let's get background info on Kenny. Then we'll go see him." Bree's phone vibrated with a call from one of the county supervisors. "I have to take this call. It's probably about the renovations. You can use a computer in the squad room."

Matt stepped out of her office.

Bree answered the call. "Sheriff Taggert."

"Sheriff, this is Madeline Jager." Madeline Jager was a county supervisor who'd been recently elevated to administrator. Bree sensed the promotion had gone to her head.

Bree waited. She didn't have any small talk in her.

"I saw the press conference."

Bree's belly cramped. "And?"

"And the board wants to meet to discuss the photos and video."

"What photos and video?"

"The ones of you," Jager stammered.

"They're fake."

"So you say," Jager snapped.

Anger heated Bree's blood. "I'm in the middle of an investigation, Ms. Jager. I don't have time for this."

"You'd better make time, Sheriff. This story is snowballing."

The line went dead. Bree set down her phone. She wanted to throw it through the window. How was she responsible for someone else making a fake video of her? She hated feeling helpless or vulnerable, and that's exactly how Oscar had made her feel. He would be thrilled to know he was still inflicting damage on her from the grave.

She called Morgan Dane. The attorney's voice mail answered. Bree hesitated. She didn't want to leave any specific information on the recording. She went with a vague, "This is Sheriff Taggert. I'd like to speak with you at your earliest convenience." Bree left her number and hung up.

She sat back in her chair, swiveling from side to side, thinking—and fuming.

Deep down, she wished that if she solved the murders—if she did her job exceptionally well—no one would care about edited nude pictures or deepfake pornography, but she knew that wouldn't happen. People—and the press—seemed more interested in a fake scandal than a real murder.

Chapter Twelve

Todd dealt with the dented patrol vehicle, then drove out into the countryside. Matt's house was only a few miles out of his way. Cady might be there. He needed to check in with her about the fundraiser. The event had sold out early, but she'd managed to add a few more seats. Todd had sold every ticket she'd given him.

He could tell her in a phone call.

But he really wanted to see her. Besides, it would take only a few minutes to stop now. If she wasn't working in the kennel, then he'd call her.

He made the turn onto Matt's road. When he caught sight of Cady's minivan in the driveway, it sent a ridiculous quiver of excitement through his belly. He parked and got out of his vehicle. A dozen dogs barked as he walked into the kennel. He watched her heft a fifty-pound sack of dog food over one shoulder like it was a bag of flour.

The Flynns weren't small people. The whole family looked like they stepped out of an episode of *Vikings*. Like a strawberry-blonde Lagertha, Cady stood nearly six feet tall. A former collegiate rower and current kickboxing instructor, she had plenty of muscles on broad shoulders. Her biceps popped below the short sleeve of her ratty gray T-shirt. Worn jeans showcased legs that were long and strong.

"Let me get that for you." Taking the bag from her felt a little stupid.

Though she was having no difficulty with the weight or size, she let him have it anyway. "Thanks."

He carried it to a plastic bin and dumped the contents inside. "I sold those extra tickets." He stepped back, rolling up the empty bag and stuffing it into a garbage can.

"That's great!" Securing the lid to the bin, she glanced over her shoulder. "I'd love to order K-9 body armor for Greta."

"You planned a fantastic event. They were an easy sell." Todd loved that she stood eye to eye with him. He loved everything about her. Beyond her looks, she was kind, loyal, generous, and fierce. She trained with her older brother, Nolan, a former MMA fighter. He had no doubt she was capable of delivering an ass whooping, but she chose to deescalate. She excelled at talking people into giving up neglected animals.

"Dogs are an easy sell." Her cheeks flushed. "Everyone supports a K-9 for the sheriff's department."

Todd dug into his pocket for his notepad. He tore out the list. "Here are the names."

"You didn't have to bring those personally. You could have emailed me." Cady accepted the paper. Their fingers brushed.

Suddenly hot, Todd cleared his throat. "I was driving by."

"Well, thanks." She adjusted her ponytail. "How's your IRONMAN training going?"

"OK." Todd swallowed a stammer and forced coherent words out of his mouth. "I've done shorter triathlons. I don't mind the running and road biking, but the swimming . . ." He exhaled. "I hate the swimming. So many laps." Plus, Todd was lean and had no buoyancy. If he stopped stroking, he sank like a stone.

"You're training in a pool?"

"I try to swim in the river now and then if I can find a training partner."

"Can I help?"

"How?"

"Does your training partner need to be in the water?" Even the smudge of dirt on her freckled nose was adorable. "I can row next to you. Make it less boring. Ensure you don't drown."

"Always good." Todd brightened. Spending time with Cady would certainly make the swimming portion of his workouts less painful.

"The offer is open. I love to row."

"That would be great," was all he managed to spit out.

A few seconds of silence ticked by.

Cady smiled. "Text me about the training. I'm serious."

"Thanks. I will. You let me know if you need anything else for the fundraiser."

"OK." She smiled with her whole face. Her cheeks scrunched, and her eyes crinkled up at the corners.

Was he really just going to leave? *Ask her out for coffee, you dope.*

But that smile made his tongue stick to the roof of his mouth. He swallowed. "Bye."

You are a fucking coward.

He climbed back into his vehicle and stared at the kennel through the windshield.

His own divorce had been low-key, but he recognized in hindsight that it had left a mark. He'd been depressed for years afterward. He'd thrown himself into work but had been unmotivated to improve his personal life. Until he'd met Cady last winter.

He'd wanted to ask her out in the spring, but she'd nearly died at the hands of a killer. He'd decided to wait until she'd recovered. But the waiting had backfired, and he feared he'd been friend-zoned. Now, he didn't know how to move forward, and his tongue froze every time he saw her.

He started the engine and pulled away. He'd be swimming a lot more, that was for sure. By the time the IRONMAN ran next summer, he'd be Aquaman.

Until then, back to work.

He passed Camilla's place and turned at the mailbox that read JOHNSON. Homer's farm was in better repair than Camilla's. The house was large, white, and freshly painted. A half dozen outbuildings clustered behind a gigantic brown barn. Horses grazed in multiple pastures.

The battered pickup truck sitting in front of the barn told him Homer was at home. Todd parked. No one answered his knock on the front door, so he wandered around the house.

The barn doors stood wide open. He stepped into the cool interior and spied Homer through the back door, hosing the leg of a big bay horse. As Todd approached, the horse startled. The big animal flew backward. Homer tried to hold on to the lead rope but couldn't control twelve hundred pounds of wild-eyed horse. The bay whirled and thundered down the aisle—directly at Todd.

His heart stuttered.

"Get out of the way!" Homer shouted.

But if the horse made it out the front door of the barn, it was a straight, open lane to the road. Todd didn't want it to get hurt. He was the one who'd scared it. He balanced on the balls of his feet, poised to dive out of the way at the last minute, just in case.

Then he raised his arms as the horse galloped toward him. "Whoa there. Whoa." He prepared to leap sideways, but the horse slid to a stop a dozen feet short of him, snorting and pawing at the dirt aisle.

"There's a good boy," he murmured in a soft voice.

The horse arched its neck and snorted like a dragon.

"You are a beauty." He walked up to it and picked up the lead rope.

Homer hustled up the aisle and took the rope from him. "Thanks." He turned to the horse, which looked not at all sorry. "You're a big dope," Homer said, but his voice was filled with affection. "You'd better not have busted your stitches."

"I'm sorry I startled him." Todd moved out of the way.

"You act like you know horses."

"I grew up out here in the country. My best friend's family had horses. We rode all the time. Fell off as much as we stayed on. Can't decide if we were brave or stupid."

"Probably a bit of both." Homer crouched to examine the horse's front leg. A row of stitches closed a cut in the muscle just above the knee. "He's OK. He's not spooky. He's just fired up from being cooped up in his stall for the past few days. Normally, my son works the vinegar out of him every day. Stall rest is a bitch with a horse that has more energy than sense."

"He's gorgeous." Todd stroked the animal's neck and swore it preened at the compliments. He introduced himself.

The old man gave him a nod and motioned toward the horse. "This is Speed, which is short for Mr. Lightspeed Pilot."

"Dad! Are you OK?" a voice called from the entrance.

"I'm fine." Homer rubbed the horse's forehead. "This big idiot was just looking for another way to hurt himself." He gestured toward the younger man hurrying down the aisle toward them. "And that is my son, Evan."

Evan slowed his steps as he approached. "I told you a stud was too much for you to handle."

Homer gave his son a look. "I breed and train horses. It's what I do. It's what I've always done. If I don't do that, I'm nothing. In that case, you can take me out back and shoot me."

"I told you I'd take care of his leg when I got here." Evan sounded tired.

"My horse. My responsibility." Homer huffed.

Evan massaged the back of his neck. "When are you going to trust me to handle the business?"

"When I'm dead." Homer spit in the dirt. "The only way I'm leaving this place is in a pine box."

Evan sighed. He was fortysomething, with the tanned skin and deep crow's-feet of a man who spent his days outdoors. "Stubborn old man."

"You know it." Homer nodded.

The words were heated, but Todd sensed concern and affection, not anger, behind them. He turned to Homer. "I need to ask you a few questions about your neighbor, Camilla."

Homer grimaced, then with a huge sigh, handed the lead rope to his son. "His leg needs another ten minutes of hosing before being rebandaged."

"Dad, I've got this." Evan took the rope. "You'd think he'd trust me after all these years of working together."

Matt suspected Homer wasn't afraid of his son not being capable of handling operations, but instead feared not being needed.

Evan led the horse back toward the rear of the barn.

Watching them, Homer crossed his arms over his chest. "He's not limping." He dropped his hands. "I don't know why I worry so much. Speed is retired. All he has to do is court the ladies now."

"How long have you had him?" Todd asked.

"I snagged his mama at an auction fifteen years ago. It's almost unbelievable that a horse with her pedigree was this close to being shipped off to slaughter." Homer pinched his fingers in the air. "I didn't know she was in foal for another month. I watched Speed come into this world. This guy won quite a few races in his day," Homer said with pride. "Now, what did you come here to ask me?"

"I was curious about the value of Camilla's farm and thought you might have some information on that."

Homer scratched his chin. "A few months ago, a developer was sniffing around here, trying to buy up the land for a development of fancy mini estates." He said *estates* as if the word were distasteful. "The offer for my place was decent, but I'm still making money. I was surprised Camilla didn't consider selling. She was barely paying the bills. But then, she's never lived anywhere else. I don't know where she'd go."

"Tax records show Camilla owned the farm for twenty years."

Homer nodded. "That's when her daddy passed and left the place to her." He whistled. "Her brother was so mad, he sued the estate to challenge the will in court." Disapproval dragged the corners of his mouth down. "The old man had the right to leave his farm to whoever he pleased, especially since Camilla was the one who took care of him. Bernard moved to Scarlet Falls and raised his family there. Camilla stayed on the farm with hers, but Bernard still thought he was entitled to his share anyway."

"I assume he lost the court battle?" Todd asked.

"Yep." Homer gave him a tight-lipped nod. "The court had no time for his nonsense. Camilla earned that farm the hard way."

"So there was tension between Camilla and Bernard?"

"There was," Homer answered. "Recently, it seemed Bernard was trying to mend fences. He came up for Camilla's birthday last month. Brought his girls and grandkids too. Camilla was excited about it. She loved those kids." Homer frowned again.

Todd sensed an impending *but* the size of an eighteen-wheeler.

"But it turned out they all showed up just to ask her for money." Homer shook his head. "Camilla laughed when she told me because she didn't have any money. All she had was the farm. They suggested she sell it. Said her life would be easier if she downsized. But she refused to give up her home. It's been her whole life. What would she do without it?" He pondered his own question for a few seconds, clearly comparing Camilla's predicament to his own.

Todd prompted, "Was Camilla angry?"

Homer considered the question. "No. Not angry." His brow furrowed into a thousand wrinkles. "She *was* disappointed, and maybe a little bitter."

"Was her brother angry she said no?"

Homer nodded. "He's always been a selfish prick. When the old man was sick and Camilla was taking care of him, the brother hardly ever came over to help. It's not like he lives across the country. He's in the next town."

"Did she say why they wanted money?"

Homer shook his head. "No. Just that they only bothered with her when they wanted something. I don't think she was surprised Bernard was being an ass. He's always been a selfish, entitled snob. But Camilla thought the girls were better than that."

"Is there anything else you can tell us about the family?"

Homer shook his head. "I don't think so."

"Then thank you for your time." Todd left the barn and returned to his vehicle.

Interesting.

Todd headed back to the station to do more research on Camilla's family. Their history was clearly more complicated than Bernard pretended.

Chapter Thirteen

In the passenger seat of the SUV, Matt entered Kenny's address into the GPS. Kenny lived in Grey's Hollow, so the drive was short.

Behind the wheel, Bree made a left. "What do we know about Kenny?"

Matt relayed the background info he'd found on Kenny earlier. "Other than Oscar's charges, Kenny's record is clean. Before that incident, he had no priors and a steady employment history."

"The sentence seemed harsh for a first offense."

"Yeah. He refused to plea-bargain and maintained his innocence all the way to trial. The judge gave him the maximum, probably as punishment."

Over 90 percent of cases were plea-bargained to save the court time and money. Arrestees were encouraged to accept deals. Some judges resented criminals insisting on trials for small offenses and issued harsh penalties as a lesson to the offender and as a signal to others: *exercise your legal rights, and we'll throw the book at you.*

"So much for the right to a trial by your peers," Bree said.

"The system has its problems," Matt agreed. "Kenny is fifty-one, single, and currently works the night shift at a warehouse as a forklift operator. He has six months left on parole. There's really nothing else to say about him. His prison record showed one altercation with another inmate. That incident was used to deny parole at his first hearing, but it was granted a few months later. According to his parole officer, he's complied with all the requirements of his release. He has no social media accounts and no real online presence."

Less than ten minutes later, Bree pulled up to the curb in front of a tiny house a few blocks from the small business district of Grey's Hollow, and they walked to the front door.

The elderly woman who answered their knock was the size of a ten-year-old. The top of her head barely reached Matt's ribs. At least seventy-five years old, she was dressed smartly in a navy-blue track suit and bright white sneakers. She looked exceptionally fit for her age, moving with a youthful bounce in her step. Blonde streaks artfully highlighted short gray hair. Despite her vigor, her age couldn't be denied. She squinted through thick bifocal glasses, and Matt could see a flesh-colored hearing aid in one ear.

She checked her watch and eyed Bree's uniform with suspicion. "I just finished my workout, and I need to shower before my bridge game. If you're here to beg for my vote or a donation, you can just move right along. I'm not interested."

Bree introduced herself and Matt. "We're looking for Kenny McPherson."

"Why?" The woman's tone turned suspicious, as if she was protecting Kenny.

"We're investigating a murder," Bree said, clearly hoping her answer would be shocking enough that the older woman would give up Kenny.

But the woman's eyes narrowed. "Then you're looking in the wrong place. Kenny's a good boy. I've known him since he was this big." She held a hand out about two feet over the floor.

Bree didn't comment. "Can I have your name, ma'am?"

"Phyllis Weir," she snapped. "Kenny was never a druggie. Those charges were bullshit."

Matt gave her a reassuring smile. "We're not here about the old charges."

Not exactly.

"You know the blood test didn't show any drugs in Kenny's system." Mrs. Weir was not swayed by his charms. She cocked her head, crossed her arms, and shifted her posture into outright defiance. "He mows my lawn. He's been fixing up the house. He drives me everywhere. I'm telling you, he's a good man."

Matt tried a different approach. "How do you know him?"

"His mother—God rest her soul"—Mrs. Weir crossed herself—"was my best friend. She died while Kenny was in prison. Her heart was broken." She glared at Bree. "Do you have a warrant? I don't have to tell you shit if you don't have a warrant."

Matt tried to sound casual but firm. "Ma'am, we just want to talk to him."

Mrs. Weir blew an irritated breath out of her nose, then jerked a thumb over her shoulder. "He rents the apartment over the garage behind the house." Before Bree could say *thank you*, the woman shut the door in their faces.

"Not a fan of law enforcement," Matt said.

"Clearly not." Bree turned away from the door. "I'll bet she's calling Kenny to warn him right now."

They quickened their pace.

Matt gestured to the driveway that ran along the side of the house. "You go up the driveway. I'll cover this side in case he decides to run."

They split up. Bree headed for the driveway on the left while Matt hustled across the grass and around the right side of the house. A detached single-car garage dominated the rear yard. Matt peered in the high windows and saw a twenty-year-old Buick Century parked inside. A set of wooden steps led up to the apartment over the garage. Matt caught a quick flash of movement at the rear corner of the yard. A bald man in a short-sleeved gray T-shirt and jeans disappeared behind the building.

"Halt. Sheriff's office!" Matt shouted, then he turned and yelled for Bree. "This way. He's running." From her perspective, she wouldn't see the fleeing man.

Matt raced after him. Ahead, the man leaped over the four-foot chain-link fence into the rear neighbor's backyard. Twenty-five feet behind him, Matt ran faster. At the fence, Matt grabbed the top and vaulted over it, barely breaking stride. He sprinted across the grass, quickly gaining ground.

The man glanced back over his shoulder as he ran past the neighbor's detached garage. Though he'd shaved his head since his original arrest, Matt recognized Kenny from his mug shot. He clutched a cell phone in one hand. Mrs. Weir had definitely warned him. Matt had to appreciate her loyalty.

At the front corner of the garage, Kenny paused and spun, grabbing the handle of a recycling receptacle and upending it into Matt's path. Bottles broke and cans spilled out across the concrete. Matt slowed, but he couldn't avoid a patch of broken glass. His foot slipped, and he went down on one knee and one hand.

Swearing, he pushed himself to his feet and continued the chase. Kenny reached the street and turned right. He should have headed across the yards, where he could use more objects to slow down Matt. Out in the open, there was no way that bastard was getting away. Matt turned on the speed. He was at least six inches taller than Kenny. And while the other man had clearly spent time lifting weights in prison—his lean frame looked solid—Matt ran every day and had considered training for an IRONMAN.

Kenny's next glance backward was filled with panic. Matt caught up with him in a dozen strides. He reached for Kenny's shoulder and shoved. The fleeing man tumbled face-first onto the pavement. The cell phone in his hand skittered in the road. As soon as he'd stopped sliding, Matt was on him. He flattened Kenny onto his belly and planted a knee firmly into the small of his back.

"Get off me!" Kenny screamed. "I didn't do anything wrong."

Matt had been so focused on the chase, he hadn't realized Bree was right behind them. She jogged to a halt next to him. Breathing hard, she handed Matt a set of handcuffs. Matt worked Kenny's hands behind his back. Kenny thrashed, resisting as Matt snapped on the cuffs. Once secured, the man stopped fighting. Out of breath, Kenny wheezed, and his chest heaved.

Leaning her hands on her thighs, Bree asked, "Kenny McPherson?"

Kenny flailed. "Fuck off."

Matt rolled him onto his back. "What the hell? We just want to talk. Stop fighting. Are you Kenny?"

"Yeah." Kenny frowned at them. Sweat shone on his bald head and soaked his T-shirt. Distrust tightened his face. "If you think I'm going to talk to you, you're wrong. I learned my lesson the last time. I won't cooperate so you can arrest me for something else I didn't do. Get a fucking warrant."

"I'm Sheriff Taggert." Bree gestured to Matt. "And this is Criminal Investigator Matt Flynn. You're on parole. You know we don't need a warrant. All I need to do is call your parole officer." Parolees were technically still serving out their prison sentences.

"Fuck me," Kenny said.

Bree gestured. "Let's get out of the street." She reached down, picked up Kenny's phone, and shoved it in her pocket.

Matt grabbed Kenny's elbow and hauled him to his feet. Then he steered him back to Mrs. Weir's yard.

"Do you want to talk in your place"—Bree motioned toward the apartment—"or at the station?"

Kenny frowned, indecision all over his face. "If I let you in, you're liable to plant evidence."

"We can take you to the station and search your place anyway," Matt said. If Kenny *had* been set up, Matt empathized with him. But the falsified charges were also the motivation that made him a potential murder suspect.

Bree stopped at the base of the staircase that led to Kenny's apartment. "I'm going to give you the choice. Where do you want to talk?"

"Fine. Here then." Kenny started up the steps. "Fucking cops." At the top of the stairs, a still-handcuffed Kenny stepped aside and nodded. "You'll have to get the door."

She opened it and walked inside. Matt followed Bree and Kenny into a studio apartment smaller than the average hotel room. In the main area, sheets were neatly folded on the arm of a futon. A small TV sat on the floor facing the futon. There was no table or chairs. The kitchenette consisted of a sink, a mini fridge, and a narrow electric range, separated by two feet of counter space. Matt spied one open door on the other side of the room. He could see a pedestal sink, a toilet, and a shower stall the size of a phone booth.

Kenny stopped in the middle of the living area. "I'm not talking unless you record the interview. I won't have you putting words in my mouth."

That was a first. Matt had never had a suspect request they record the interview.

Bree drew out her phone, tapped the screen, then set it on the wooden arm of the futon. "OK. I'm recording."

Kenny relaxed.

"Do you live alone?" Matt asked.

Kenny nodded toward his futon. "Are you serious? You think I could squeeze a roommate in here? I barely fit. Not that I'm complaining about Mrs. Weir. I appreciate everything she's done for me."

Matt had seen much worse. "I've seen plenty of felons stuck in rooming houses, so this isn't bad."

"Not bad?" Kenny mashed his lips. His face reddened as if his blood pressure were rising. "I went to prison on bogus charges. I never did drugs. I never hit anyone. Those deputies faked it all. It was a setup. I was innocent." He heaved a huge sigh. "Can you take these cuffs off?"

"You're not going to try to run?" Bree asked.

Kenny rolled his eyes at Matt. "What would be the point? I'd never get past Hercules here."

Matt circled a hand in the air. "I understand your previous experiences with law enforcement might not have been positive, but Sheriff Taggert will be fair."

Kenny turned around, and Matt removed the cuffs.

"Why did you run?" Bree began.

Kenny rubbed his wrists. "The last time I didn't run from the sheriff's department, they set me up for a crime I didn't commit and sent me to prison."

Bree gave him a respectful nod. "*Did* you resist arrest?"

"No." Kenny flushed. "I mean, I got mad and yelled. Who wouldn't? They planted a bag of drugs in my car. But I never hit or shoved either one of them."

"If that's true, then we're not unsympathetic," Bree said. "But we still have a job to do. It'll be easier for all of us if you cooperate."

"Whatever." Kenny snorted, a resigned sound. "Once the cops get hold of you, you're helpless. I learned that the hard way." He brushed a hand across his skull. "But I was lucky in some ways. People stood by me. My employer believed me from the beginning. When I got out, he gave me my old job back right away." He gestured to the window at the front of the studio. "My landlady is an old friend of my mom's. She knows I never did anything too. This place isn't much, but it's a hell of a lot better than a rooming house full of ex-cons. Plus, she only charges me enough to cover the electric bill. If she wasn't on a fixed income, she wouldn't charge me anything. I need to put away some money before I can get a place of my own." Bitterness narrowed his eyes. "I used to have a nice little house. It wasn't fancy, but it was mine."

"Didn't the parole board make you admit your guilt?" Bree asked.

"The whole system is a scam." Kenny crossed his arms. "I would have said anything to get out of prison. Trust me, so would you."

Matt didn't doubt it. Survival took a back seat to pride. "Why would the deputies have faked charges against you?"

"I don't know." Kenny rubbed his scalp. "I could never figure it out."

"If they set you up, they went to a lot of effort to do so," Matt pointed out.

"Right?" Kenny agreed. "Why would they do that? I didn't know any of them."

"They ruined your life," Bree said. "You have every reason to be angry with them."

Clearly, Kenny wasn't the brightest bulb on the light string, but he finally asked, "Why are you here?"

"Because one of those deputies"—Bree paused for effect—"retired Deputy Oscar, was murdered."

"Shit." Kenny paled.

"You didn't know?" Matt asked.

"How would I know?" Kenny's voice rose in protest.

"It was on the news," Matt explained.

"I don't have time to watch the news." Kenny's eyes were shifting around, as if his brain were playing catch-up. "When did he die?"

Bree said, "Between eight p.m. Sunday night and eight a.m. Monday morning."

"Figures." Kenny's head shook in disbelief. "The one frigging night I wasn't at work."

"Where were you?" Bree pulled a notebook from her pocket.

"Here." Sweat rings broke out under Kenny's arms. "Watching TV. If I had known I would need an alibi, I would've made plans." His voice thickened with sarcasm.

Matt thought of the old Buick in the garage under the apartment. "Do you own a vehicle?"

"No." Kenny closed both fists at his sides.

"How do you get to work?" Matt pressed.

"Mrs. Weir lets me use her car. She doesn't like to drive anymore. Her eyesight is going. So, I do her shopping for her and take her where she needs to go."

"That's nice of you," Bree said.

"I *am* nice," Kenny insisted. "Why is that so hard to believe?"

"You got into fights in prison." Bree tilted her head.

"One fight." Kenny's temper snapped. "And I didn't really have a choice. The other guy came after me. Either I defended myself or I'd be a target for the rest of my time."

He had a point, thought Matt. "Do you have any proof that you were here all night?"

"How the hell would I prove that?" Kenny's forehead furrowed, then his eyebrows shot up with an idea. "The GPS on my phone?"

"That would only show that your phone was here," Matt said.

"Damn." Kenny looked toward the door. "The driveway goes right by Mrs. Weir's bedroom. She would have seen me if I took the car out."

"But her eyesight is terrible," Bree repeated Kenny's own words. "And she wears a hearing aid. I assume she takes it out when she's sleeping."

Kenny threw up his hands. Anger raised a vein in the side of his neck. "Then I don't fucking know." He lowered his hands. "Wait. *You* have to prove I *wasn't* here. If you want to falsify evidence, we all know you can, but I won't make it easy for you."

Bree ignored the suggestion and changed topics. "When was the last time you spoke to Deputy Oscar?"

"He testified at the trial and at my parole hearing. It was his fault I was denied early release the first time. He didn't show for the second. I guess he had something else to do." Kenny punched one hand hard with the other, his frustration clearly building. "How'd he die?"

Matt noted that Kenny said *he*, not *they*. If he was lying, he was consistent.

"Both Oscar and his mother were shot," Bree said.

"His mother?" Kenny fell back a step. "His mother was shot too?"

"Yes." Matt tapped his forehead. "She was shot in the head."

Kenny held up both hands. He looked stricken. "What the fuck? She had to be old. Who kills an old lady? I would never do that. That's a really shitty thing to do."

Matt agreed, but was Kenny protesting too much? "Do you know where Oscar lived?"

Kenny shook his head.

"You were never tempted to find him after you got out of prison?" Matt let his question sound skeptical. "You never wanted to get even?"

"Why would I go looking for trouble?" Kenny asked.

"If you're really innocent," Bree said, "then he took years from your life. He hurt you financially. You lost your house, right? Your car. Your dignity. He took your future from you. You will never get that life back to the way it was."

Kenny's chin came up. "I don't want to give him the chance to ruin the rest of it. I have a new lawyer who says he's found a pattern of behavior with those two dudes. We're going to sue the hell out of the county. My plan is to get some money and move far away from this place. Then I can start over somewhere else. I never want to see him—or Grey's Hollow—again."

Matt shot him a knowing look. "Well, now you won't have to worry about Deputy Oscar's testimony. That's convenient."

Kenny shut down. "That's it. I'm done. I tried to cooperate with you, but you're clearly going to try and screw me over again. If you want to ask me any more questions, I want my lawyer present."

Bree pulled a business card out of her pocket and handed it to Kenny. "If you need to reach me for any reason, here are my numbers."

Kenny took the card and tossed it onto the futon. "I don't know anything. Are you going to arrest me?"

"No, but we're going to search your apartment," Bree said.

Matt glanced around. Wouldn't take long.

"Fine." Kenny huffed. "There's nothing I can do about it."

"Nope," Matt said.

Bree nodded to Matt. "You keep an eye on him. I'll search." She stopped the recording and fished Kenny's cell phone out of her pocket. "Your passcode?"

Frowning, he gave it to her. Bree scrolled. "Who's Quentin?"

"My boss," he said in a flat voice.

She nodded, then handed him his phone and turned to survey the room.

Taking the phone, Kenny went stiff as steel, and he seemed to be holding his breath.

She began with a small chest of drawers, checked the single kitchen cabinet, then the bathroom. Dropping to her knees, she used a flashlight to look under the futon. Straightening, she lifted each cushion and examined the seams. The floor was a solid sheet of vinyl. None of the baseboards seemed loose. The entire search took ten minutes.

Bree brushed her hands on her cargo pants. "OK, Kenny. I'm going to give you the benefit of the doubt and ignore the fact that you ran away."

Kenny exhaled and relaxed.

She stepped closer. "But if we come back to ask you follow-up questions, don't run."

Kenny nodded but said nothing as they backed away.

Matt and Bree returned to the car. Bree sat in the driver's seat, staring out the windshield. "His apartment was clean. No weapon. His phone showed very little activity over the last two weeks, just a few texts and calls with Mrs. Weir and his boss. What do you think?"

Matt considered Kenny's reactions. "Oscar's death seemed to take him by surprise."

Bree put the vehicle into gear. "And he was really thrown by Camilla's."

"Is he smart enough to successfully pull off a double homicide?"

"Maybe he's a good actor, and he's playing dumb." Bree glanced at the house in the rearview mirror. "He has no alibi, great motive, and a quick temper. He ran the instant Mrs. Weir warned him we were here. He barely kept his cool with us and we didn't even push him that hard."

"Let's assume for a minute that Oscar faked those charges. Why did he do it? It took work to pull that off. Oscar was lazy. He must have had a reason to go through all that effort."

"Good question. Maybe Brian Dylan can give us an answer," Bree said. "It's also possible that Kenny ran because he's guilty."

CHAPTER FOURTEEN

Behind the wheel of her SUV, Bree listened in as Matt called a buddy who still worked for the Scarlet Falls PD.

After a brief conversation, he lowered the phone. "Brian Dylan worked for the SFPD until a few weeks ago, when he was fired after arresting a teenage girl. The girl claimed he slapped her. Dylan said the girl was resisting arrest, but since he'd turned off his body camera, it was his word against hers."

"Body cameras are mandated by the SFPD." Bree had included cameras for all her deputies in her budget proposal. Thankfully, no one was objecting to them, because they were one of Bree's nonnegotiable items.

"That's right, and Dylan turned his off. The police chief in Scarlet Falls doesn't put up with that sort of behavior. The charges against the girl were dropped, and Dylan was fired."

"Sounds like I should be glad Dylan left the sheriff's department."

"Definitely."

"Do you know his address?" Bree asked.

Matt nodded. "He's on the edge of the county, out near the national forest." He plugged the address into the GPS. The automated voice told them to head west on the highway. "My buddy said Dylan was furious at being let go."

"He quit the sheriff's department just before I took over, so I've never met him." Bree pulled up to a stop sign, then made a left. "You worked with him?"

"I did. I never *saw* him do anything, but there were always rumors of him behaving inappropriately. I remember him being very tight with the old sheriff. Dylan's father was a deputy, killed in the line of duty when Dylan was a kid. There's a plaque in the hallway."

Bree felt bad she didn't remember the man's name. "That sucks."

"Yes, but it made him kind of a legacy in the department. I was surprised when he quit. Todd will know more."

"Let's call him. I didn't have a chance to ask him earlier." Bree made the call to her chief deputy with her hands-free connection. After he'd answered, she asked, "Tell me about Brian Dylan."

Todd's sigh was audible over the Bluetooth speakers. "I was glad to see his back when he quit."

"Did he have complaints in his personnel file?" Bree asked.

"No, but he should have," Todd said. "He was one of the old sheriff's favorites."

Bree asked, "Because of his father?"

"Yes, but people he arrested ended up with unexplained bruises."

"Let me guess," Bree said. "A lot of people resisted arrest when Dylan took them into custody."

"You know it," Todd said with disgust. "The old sheriff approved of heavy-handed tactics."

"Do you know why he quit the sheriff's department?" she asked.

"He didn't want to work for a female," Todd said.

He hadn't been the only one. Though she'd had to scramble to hire replacements, Bree wasn't sorry to be rid of anyone who would quit for that reason.

Bree asked, "Everything work out with the patrol vehicle?"

"It's fine," Todd said. "Just a dented fender. The body shop will fix it this week."

"Great. Talk to you later." Bree ended the call. The GPS prompted her to turn off the highway onto a narrow country road. Meadows gave way to forested slopes.

Matt scrolled on his phone. "According to his social media accounts, he's into conspiracy theories."

"What kind of posts?" Bree asked.

Matt scrolled on his smartphone. "How to keep the government and big business from tracking your every movement. Best antisurveillance technology. How to build a Faraday cage and why you want one."

"I almost want to read that one." Bree made a left. "That's not too unusual. I've read about potential electromagnetic-pulse attacks on the power grid. A Faraday cage blocks those EMPs, right?"

"Right, but there's more." Matt whistled. "The government adds subliminal mind control to TV advertisements. Secret high-altitude government planes are spraying chemicals into the atmosphere to reduce fertility. The queen of England is either a vampire or a cannibal. Seems he can't make up his mind which one. Finland is a fake country."

"OK. Now he's wading into aluminum-foil-hat territory."

"He also belongs to a survivalist group called the Hudson Footmen. They're preparing for a digital apocalypse. There's no overt anarchy on their page, but they skirt just short of violence." Matt reached into the back of the SUV and pulled out his body-armor vest. He donned it and tightened the Velcro strap with a firm tug. Bree wore a vest under her uniform shirt.

The SUV climbed as they entered the foothills of the Adirondacks. Along with the increase in elevation, boulders and rocky outcroppings appeared on the sides of the road. To the left, the landscape sloped upward. On the right side of the road, the grade dropped steeply.

A few miles later, the GPS announced they'd reached their destination. Bree slowed the vehicle but saw nothing but weeds and woods. "Do you see a mailbox or driveway?"

Matt was scanning the shoulder of the road. "No. I've never been to Dylan's house, but I heard him say that he liked being off the grid when he wasn't working." A few minutes later, he pointed. "There. See that reflector on the tree trunk?"

Bree barely saw the glint of sunlight on red plastic. She hit the brakes and made the turn onto a dirt and gravel road. The vehicle bounced across several deep ruts before she guided the tires out of the existing vehicle tracks. She drove a full mile before the lane curved and widened into a large clearing.

In the center, a multilevel home was painted an ugly army green, blending into the landscape. Decks on all sides provided a commanding view of the surroundings. Multiple satellite dishes were mounted on the roof, and Bree spotted high-tech cameras mounted under the eaves. A large shed stood behind the house, adorned with yet another satellite dish and more cameras.

They were being watched and probably recorded.

Bree parked next to a detached garage. The overhead doors were rolled up. Inside, a tractor shared space with a dual-wheel pickup truck, a dirt bike, and several long benches filled with tools.

"We're definitely off the beaten path." She reached for her radio mic and reported their location to dispatch. "But there's a significant amount of tech here."

Matt scanned the property. "Those electronics look new and expensive."

"Makes you wonder how he paid for them with no job." Bree noted the house stood on a slight rise, with a good view for home defense.

"Savings?"

They stepped out of the vehicle. Water rushed in the background. The Scarlet Creek ran behind the house. Farther south, the creek meandered into the Scarlet River. The deck on the back of the house would have a water view.

Bree felt eyes on her. The hairs on the back of her neck quivered. She glanced at Matt. "Do you feel that?"

"Someone watching us? Yep."

The uneasy feeling intensified as Bree scanned the surroundings. There were too many places for someone to hide. And with all those cameras, anyone could be surveilling them right now.

They rounded the front end of the vehicle, and someone yelled, "Stop right there!"

Bree bristled as she tracked the voice to the open garage door. She could barely see the outline of a man in the shadowy interior. "Brian Dylan?"

He took one step closer and sneered at her. "You're that new bitch sheriff." It wasn't a question.

"I'm Sheriff Taggert." Bree ignored the *bitch* label. "You're Brian Dylan?"

"This is private property. Who I am is none of your business."

"That's him," Matt said in a low voice.

"Mr. Dylan." Bree didn't like not being able to see him more clearly, but she resisted the urge to pull her weapon. "We'd like to talk to you."

Dylan yelled, "About what?"

"Eugene Oscar," Bree said. "We just want to ask you a few questions."

"I know my rights. I don't have to talk to you." Dylan inched forward. "I'm surprised you're working for this whore, Flynn. I hear you're still a big pussy who's afraid to carry a handgun." Dylan's tone turned mocking. "Did you finally man up?"

"I haven't changed." Matt seemed unperturbed by the insult.

Dylan snorted.

What an ass.

He was right about one thing, though. Bree couldn't make him talk. She didn't have the authority to force him to do anything. But she wanted answers. She glanced around the property. The place was outfitted like a high-tech military camp. Squinting into the dimness of the garage, she could see a cooler and other camping gear piled on the garage floor next to the pickup. Had he been away, or was he preparing to leave town? She spotted several skeins of nylon paracord in different sizes and colors hanging on the wall.

To get his attention, Bree went for shock. "Did you know that Oscar was dead?"

Dylan said nothing, but his posture stiffened.

"We found his body yesterday," Matt said. "He was murdered."

Dylan stepped into view. He wore full camo, complete with both a knife and gun strapped to his belt. "I didn't kill him. What's this have to do with me?"

Bree said, "Oscar's mother was also killed. Did you see the news?"

"Can't believe the media." Dylan didn't directly answer her question.

"You can easily verify the story," Bree said.

Dylan cocked his head. "So why are you here?"

Had he known about Oscar's death? Bree couldn't tell. "We're trying to solve Oscar's murder. We'd like some information."

"You have three minutes." Dylan hooked a thumb in his belt.

"When did you last see Oscar?" Bree asked.

"I don't recall the exact date," he said in a snotty tone.

Bree swallowed her frustration. "How about an approximation? A month ago? A week? Last year?"

"A few weeks, but I wouldn't testify to that. Everything I say can and will be used against me in a court of law, right?" Dylan asked.

Questioning cops was the worst. They knew every interview trap and how to avoid them. Dylan wasn't the best liar, but he knew which subjects to evade.

"We're not arresting you," Bree said.

"You wouldn't be here if I wasn't a suspect." Dylan lifted one hand. "I'll tell you right now. I didn't kill him."

Bree took a deep breath. "Do you remember Kenny McPherson?"

Dylan's mouth tightened, the tiny reaction giving him away. He remembered Kenny all right. Then Dylan's eyes shifted away for a split second, a clear indication he was going to lie, before steadying on Bree's gaze again. "The name might sound a little familiar."

"You and Oscar arrested him for drug possession." Bree reminded him of the basic facts of the arrest. "Kenny went to prison."

He shrugged. "Cops send people to prison. It's their job."

Bree changed course. "Oscar didn't tell you Kenny was out of prison?" She waited. The silence dragged out for a few heartbeats, but Dylan didn't answer.

She phrased her next question carefully. "Did Kenny have any reason to hold a grudge against Oscar?"

"You just told me that Oscar put him in jail, so I would think so." Dylan tried to sound casual, but he couldn't quite pull it off. "But you should ask him. I thought you were some kind of big-city detective. Did you get *that* job because you were a female too? The governor appointed you. Wait until you actually have to run for office. No one will actually vote for you."

Bree didn't let him change the subject. She got to the point. "Did you plant those drugs in Kenny's car?"

Dylan's posture snapped straight. "Fuck off."

No denial. Lots of anger. *So that's a straight-up yes.*

Matt shifted his weight, as if he'd also lost patience with the lies and evasion. "Did Kenny really shove Oscar? Or did Oscar make that up?"

Dylan said nothing. He just glared back at them, hatred simmering in his eyes.

"Oscar is dead, Dylan," Matt said. "He can't get into trouble."

But Dylan can, thought Bree. Dylan had testified at Kenny's trial. He'd knowingly sent a man to prison on fake charges. He could be prosecuted for perjury and falsifying evidence. Kenny said his lawyer was trying to establish a pattern with Dylan and Oscar. Kenny could sue in civil court. Dylan and Oscar had ruined his life.

"I won't let you ruin his reputation or mine." Dylan leaned forward, his chin jutting out, his chest puffed. He was trying to look arrogant and self-righteous, but it was all naked bluster.

Bree tossed out her final question. "What do you know about the Hudson Footmen?"

Dylan snapped, "If you don't have a warrant, get the fuck off my property, both of you."

"I'd like your contact information in case I have any more questions. Can I have your cell number?" she asked.

He shook his head. "Don't have one. Why would I have a device that lets the government track my every move? Now get out of here and don't come back or I'll sue you for harassment."

With no real options, Bree and Matt walked back to the SUV. On her way back, she caught a glimpse of movement in the window of the house. The silhouette was female. With daylight reflecting off the glass, Bree couldn't make out her features. The figure backed away from the window.

Bree slid behind the wheel. "Someone's watching."

Matt closed the passenger door. "I saw her."

"Could you get a description?" She started the engine.

"No. Too dark."

Bree shifted into reverse. "Definitely a woman, though?"

"Yes."

As she began turning the vehicle around, she glanced through the windshield. Dylan hadn't moved. Bree's gaze went to the window. No sign of the woman. "Do you think he was lying?"

"Yes." Matt scoffed. "About so many things."

"He knew who Kenny was."

"Absolutely," Matt agreed. "He was also lying when he said Oscar hadn't contacted him recently."

"Yep, and when he denied having a cell phone."

"He probably uses burners," Matt said. "He's definitely part of the Hudson Footmen, but he doesn't want to talk about them."

"Interesting that was the final straw for him. Maybe there's some fear there."

"Maybe. I wouldn't trust anything Dylan said. Everything he said felt like a lie."

CHAPTER FIFTEEN

Matt's stomach rumbled as they neared the station. He spotted a fast-food place. "Can you go through the drive-through? We need food."

"I'm not hungry." Bree turned into the parking lot.

"I'm starving, and you need food whether or not you want it."

"Fine." She pulled into the drive-through and lowered the window. The smell of french fries wafted into the vehicle.

Matt heard Bree's stomach audibly gurgle. He ordered two grilled chicken wraps for himself. Bree went for a burger, fries, and a vanilla milkshake. She passed him the bag, and he handed over her food. She ate the burger in a half dozen bites, then made quick work of the fries.

"It's a shame you weren't hungry." Matt dug into his second wrap.

"OK. I admit that was really good." Bree crumpled the burger wrapper into a ball and stuffed it into the empty bag. Grabbing her shake from the cup holder, she drank. "The sugar will keep me from going into a grease-and-fat coma."

"Interesting theory."

"I'll eat a salad tomorrow."

"You won't."

"Probably not," she admitted. Bree called home to let them know she'd be late. After ending the call, she said, "At least I had breakfast with the kids. I hate when I can't put them first."

"You always put them first," Matt corrected. "But some days, they don't have pressing needs, and the job does. When was the last time you missed dinner?"

"Yesterday," Bree said.

"Before yesterday." He knew she struggled with balancing work and family.

"It's been a while," she said. "The last couple of months have been nice and boring."

Cops typically spent more time on paperwork than working homicide cases.

"You're doing a great job with the kids."

Bree sighed. "With Kayla, I don't have to juggle her desire for independence with parenting yet. As a teen, Luke is more challenging. He's annoyed with me for not allowing him to go camping with his friends." Bree described the proposed trip.

"On the bright side, he's acting like a normal teenager," Matt said. "He's secure enough in your relationship to get mad at you."

"I guess. But he's right. When an important case comes up, I do work too much. Sometimes I think I'm setting the exact wrong example when I work these crazy long hours. I hate choosing between the job and the family. I always feel like I'm letting someone down."

"You're teaching them about working hard, following through on responsibilities, and being passionate about their work."

"I hope their passions don't involve dead bodies."

They arrived at the sheriff's station. Twenty minutes later, Matt carried a mug of coffee and a notepad into the conference room and sat at the table. Bree was already inside, opening her laptop at the head of the table. Todd hustled in, carrying a computer, the murder book, and some loose files.

Bree tapped on her keyboard. "We don't have the forensics report yet, but it hasn't even been twenty-four hours since they finished processing the scene. So far, we have the following persons of interest:

Bernard Crighton, Heather Oscar, Kenny McPherson, and Brian Dylan. Todd, where are you in reviewing their personal information?"

"Can we start with Bernard Crighton?" The light in Todd's eyes suggested he'd found something.

Bree rolled a hand in the air. "Sure."

Matt checked his notes. "Bernard doesn't have an alibi."

"Any recent purchases of black nylon paracord?" Bree asked.

Todd opened a file. "Not on his credit card statements."

"Motive?" Bree asked.

Todd opened his laptop and scrolled. "Money. He says he doesn't need any, but he's not exactly rolling in cash. His house is mortgaged, and he took out a second mortgage to send his youngest daughter to law school. Plus, the neighbor, Homer, said Bernard asked Camilla for money recently and she turned him down."

Bree looked thoughtful. "I saw no sign of extravagance in his home. Where does he spend his money?"

"For the last few months, he's paid two large sums of money to his son-in-law, Leonard Holmes," Todd said. "Leonard is married to Bernard's oldest daughter, Shannon."

Matt leaned back in his chair. "Do we know what the money was for?"

"No." Todd checked his papers. "The payments are significant. Over two hundred thousand in total. He depleted what was left of his savings."

Bree frowned. "We need more information."

"Does Bernard have any handguns registered to him?" Matt asked.

"No," Todd said.

Bree added, "But as a family member, he might know where Oscar kept his personal firearm."

"There's more." Todd tapped a paper.

Matt straightened.

Todd gestured toward Bree. "Your interview report said Bernard claimed to have last talked to his sister a few weeks ago. But his cell phone records show he called Camilla four days before the murders." He held up a hand. "*Annnnnd* Oscar's traffic app shows Bernard's house as the last address entered, three days before the murders."

"Bernard is quite the liar," Matt said.

"Lying puts him on the top of my suspect list," Bree said. "I wonder if he knew about the offer on Camilla's farm. We need to talk to him again."

Matt stroked his stubbled jaw. "I'd like to search his house. Oscar's gun is still missing."

Bree flattened a palm on the table. "Let's try to get a search warrant ASAP. We can bring him in for questioning while we serve it."

Todd nodded. "Here's one more interesting bit of info. Oscar's financial records also show he paid a large sum of money to Leonard Holmes last year."

"That's where his money went?" Bree asked.

"Yes." Todd shuffled his pages. "I researched Leonard Holmes. The SEC froze his assets two months ago. There's an ongoing investigation into a Ponzi scheme. He wasn't in charge, but he's named in the filing."

Bree frowned. "Let's see if we can get that warrant today."

"I'll prepare the affidavit as soon as we're done here," Todd said.

Matt made a note. "Who's next?"

"Heather Oscar, the ex-wife." Todd spoke quickly. "Her record is clean, except for a few tickets issued in the year after she divorced Oscar, which seems to corroborate her claims of harassment. Again, no purchases of the paracord on her credit card statements."

Bree's brow furrowed. "The killer would probably have used cash."

"Heather has motive," Matt said. "He lied to her for years."

"In her mind, he completely betrayed her," Bree added.

Matt remembered her passion and loss, and he could imagine her pressing the gun to Oscar's head. "And she also had no alibi."

Todd shrugged. "I suspect most people are home on a Sunday night. I am if I'm not covering a shift. Stores tend to close early. Bars are mostly empty. Folks are getting ready for the upcoming work or school week."

Bree nodded. "Who's up next?"

Todd flipped the page. "Kenny McPherson. Like the others, he has no alibi. He hasn't been out of prison long enough to have much financial history, but he is employed, and his landlady clearly supported him."

Matt checked his notes. "He also has plenty of motive. He has a record of drug use, resisting arrest, assaulting an officer, *and* fighting in prison."

Bree waggled a hand. "But how much of that history was caused or fabricated *by Oscar?*"

Matt wondered if he'd ever worked a case where so many people had a good reason to want the victim dead. "Kenny ran from us."

"Can't blame him if his story is true." Bree drummed her fingers on the table.

"But can we believe Kenny?" Todd cocked his head.

Bree's fingers stilled. "Jim Rogers's story matched."

"But Jim didn't actually *see* Oscar plant the drugs," Matt said. "And Dylan isn't talking."

"Which brings us to Brian Dylan." Bree sat back. "I don't know what to make of him. He was belligerent and uncooperative. He seemed to hate me on sight, even though I'd never met him before."

"He hates you by association." Todd frowned. "He was Oscar's buddy, and you went after Oscar."

"If he was that close to Oscar, then is he a valid suspect for the murders?" Bree asked. "Does he have motive?"

"They were—pardon the cliché—thick as thieves," Todd said. "Maybe Oscar was going to get Dylan into trouble."

"How?" Matt couldn't see it.

Bree shook her head. "I can't think of anything Dylan would gain by killing Oscar. If they committed crimes together, then how could Oscar threaten him without putting himself at risk?"

Todd shook his head. "Maybe they were planning something new and Oscar was going to double-cross him to keep all the profits."

"Maybe Oscar's death is related to that survivalist group Dylan joined, the Hudson Footmen." Matt didn't think Dylan needed a rational reason to fear Oscar. Clearly, the guy was more than one brick short of a wall.

Bree shook her head. "That's pure conjecture with no proof. Dylan is hardly an innocent, but we have no evidence that suggests that he killed Oscar and Camilla."

Matt wasn't ready to move Dylan to the bottom of the suspect list. "He's unstable and armed. He thinks the queen is a friggin' cannibal. He had a whole inventory of paracord in his garage."

Bree agreed with a nod. "But we have no way to establish probable cause for Dylan. His personal beliefs, no matter how weird, aren't enough to make him a suspect."

But they were definitely disturbing.

"What about the phone calls on Oscar's cell to and from burners?" Matt asked. "Could they have been Dylan?"

"It's possible. We know he's into using tech without being tracked," Bree said. "But we can't prove anything unless we find actual burner phones at Dylan's house, and we don't have enough evidence to obtain a search warrant. For now, we focus on the warrant for Bernard Crighton's place."

Todd stood. "I'm on it."

"Make sure his vehicle is included in the warrant." Matt rose. He wasn't through with Dylan yet, but the case against Bernard was gathering momentum.

Sometimes the truth was only a few lies away.

Chapter Sixteen

By four o'clock, Bree stood at Bernard Crighton's front door. Would they find the gun that killed Oscar and his mother? Her heart thumped and excitement rushed through her veins, forcing her to admit how much she enjoyed solving crimes and hunting killers. She might have joined law enforcement to help people, but the thrill of the chase was addictive, almost like a drug.

Bernard opened the door. His gaze went over Bree's shoulder to where Todd and Matt waited with two deputies on the front walkway. Bernard's face went dark. "What's the meaning of this?"

Bree handed him the warrant. "We have a warrant to search the premises."

"You can't do this!" Bright pink spots colored his lean cheeks as he waved the folded papers in the air. "I have rights."

"Yes, sir. That's why we have the warrant." Bree pointed to it and brushed past him. "I'll need you to wait outside with Deputy Juarez."

Bree assigned Todd and Deputy Collins to the first floor of the house. She gestured for Matt to follow her to the second floor. "Let's start with the spare bedrooms."

The first one had clearly been recently redecorated with young grandchildren in mind. The twin beds looked new, as did the toys lined up on a shelf. The closet held clothes for small children. Bree opened a second door into a room decorated for an older male child. These furnishings appeared dated, but the room had been recently dusted and vacuumed. Several school awards in the name of Robby Crighton were dated more than twenty years before. The room was shrine-like.

She made a note to ask about Robby and called for Matt. "Where are you?"

"Walking into Bernard's bedroom," he answered.

She followed him into the primary bedroom. He was headed into the en suite bathroom.

Bree started with the nightstands. Books were piled everywhere. Notepads contained scribbles pertaining to the syllabi of his classes. She opened a journal. Bernard was writing a book on some medieval figure Bree had never heard of. She searched his drawers, lifted the mattress, and checked the cushions of the leather wing chair in the corner. The pockets of his clothes in the closet contained nothing but crumpled dry cleaning receipts, coins, and paper clips.

She examined a row of framed photos on the dresser. Most were snapshots of Bernard with two girls Bree assumed were his daughters. She paused at the oldest picture, taken on the deck of a sailboat. Above their heads, a tall mast wrapped in a bright blue sail framed the shot. A much younger Bernard wrapped his arm around a blonde woman. In front of them, the two girls and a little boy grinned. The whole family was tanned and smiling. In the background, sunlight glittered on a lake. The woman was probably Bernard's deceased wife. Who was the boy? Robby? She used her phone to snap a picture of the photo.

From the bathroom, Matt whistled. "Bingo."

Bree carried the photo to the doorway. Matt stood over an open hamper. His gloved finger hooked a pair of worn khaki pants by the belt loop. Dark red spots spattered the hem, and one knee was soaked through, as if he'd knelt in blood. She recalled the smeared blood at the crime scene.

"Blood?" she asked.

"That's what it looks like to me. What did you find?"

Bree lifted the photograph. "I don't know yet. Maybe nothing." But something about the photo nagged at her.

They finished searching the primary bedroom.

"I'll bag and tag the clothes and the hamper," Matt said.

Bree went downstairs. She found Todd and Deputy Collins in the study. Collins was on her hands and knees checking volumes in the bookcase. Behind the desk, Todd closed a drawer.

"Progress?" Bree asked them.

"Tagged the laptop." Todd motioned toward an old, bulky computer on the desk. "Haven't really found anything interesting. No gun."

Bree eyed the cluttered bookshelves. "How much longer will you need?"

"A few more hours." Todd gestured around the room. "The house might not be big, but he's lived here a long time. The closets and cabinets are stuffed to capacity."

"Keep me updated. We're going to ask Bernard to come down to the station for questioning." Bree went outside.

Bernard paced his front yard. As Bree approached him, a compact SUV roared to the curb, and a woman in her midthirties stepped out and stormed up the walk. A well-fitted charcoal-gray pantsuit subtly enhanced her curvy body. One of the daughters? Must be the lawyer-daughter. A schoolteacher with three kids didn't have the time to put herself together this well.

She eyed Bree's badge with anger and suspicion. "What is going on?"

"I'm Sheriff Taggert." Bree tapped her badge. "This is Investigator Flynn." She waited for the woman to introduce herself, but she merely stared at them. "What is your name, ma'am?"

"Stephanie Crighton." She tucked a strand of her sleek ash-blonde bob behind one ear. A tasteful gold stud gleamed in her lobe.

"Bernard Crighton's daughter?" Bree asked.

"Yes." Stephanie had the same dramatic cheekbones as her father. She waved a wild hand over the house and sheriff's department vehicles. "What is the meaning of this?"

"You'll have to ask your father," Bree said.

"Dad?" Stephanie called over her shoulder. "Tell the sheriff I'm your attorney and will be representing you in this matter."

"She's my lawyer." Bernard's chin lifted in defiance.

Bree sighed. "I'm investigating the murders of Camilla Brown and Eugene Oscar."

"And my father is a suspect?" Stephanie seemed incredulous.

"He's a person of interest," Bree clarified.

"That's ridiculous." Stephanie practically bit off the words.

Bree glanced around. A few neighbors stood on porches. "We're attracting an audience. Let's continue this conversation at the sheriff's station." She gestured toward Deputy Juarez. "My deputy will bring your father to the station."

"Absolutely not," Stephanie barked. "Is he under arrest?"

"Not yet," Bree said.

"Then I'll drive him to the station." Stephanie jabbed a finger at Bree. "You'll be lucky if I don't file a harassment suit."

"I'm not trying to harass anyone." Bree shook her head. "I'm trying to solve your aunt's murder."

Stephanie narrowed her eyes. "And I'm protecting my family."

Bree stepped back. "Then I'll meet you at the station in twenty minutes." She issued a few last instructions to her deputies, then left Todd in charge of completing the search and asked Matt to return to the station with her to assist with the interview.

A half hour later, she and Matt faced Bernard and Stephanie over the interview table. Bernard held a Styrofoam cup of coffee. Stephanie drank from a water bottle.

Bree read Bernard his Miranda rights, and he signed the acknowledgment without comment.

Bree pulled out her copy of the old family photo taken on the sailboat. "Who is this woman?"

"My wife." Bernard's face tightened with grief. "She died when the kids were teenagers."

Bree felt a pang of pity as she tapped the boy's image. "And who is this?"

Bernard's eyes closed for a second. When he answered, his voice was barely audible. "My son."

"Robby?" Bree kept her tone gentle. She felt bad for ripping open an old wound. But she also had a double murder to solve, and Bernard had lied to her.

He nodded.

"When I asked you how many children you had, you said two daughters."

His eyes opened. Anger flashed. "You asked how many children I *have*." He emphasized the tense. "My son is gone. I no longer *have* him—"

Stephanie interrupted. "Is it necessary to torment my father like this? Our family has endured tragedy. It's taken us a long time to heal."

"I'm sorry for your loss." Bree understood grief as well as anyone. "What happened to your son?"

"He died by suicide." Bernard paused, squeezing his eyes shut for just a second before reopening them. Misery shone from his gaze. "Shortly after we lost his mother to cancer. He was thirteen."

"I'm sorry." Bree sat back. She was no stranger to tragedy, and his sorrow resonated down to her soul.

"He went to bed one night, and I found him in the morning. I knew he'd been bullied. He stuttered. He'd had speech therapy, but his mother's death aggravated it. I should have known he was that desperate." Bernard's voice dropped to a whisper, as if he were talking to himself. "I should have known."

The devastation on his face hit Bree hard. A wave of grief swept over her. She pictured Luke and Kayla at their mother's funeral. Sorrow strangled her until she couldn't form words. How could her grief still be this fresh after eight months?

Never in her career had she been rendered speechless during an interview.

Until today.

Stephanie flattened a hand on the table. "Are you done now that you've brought up a very painful subject?"

Bree's brain scrambled to recover its train of thought. She felt Matt's gaze on her. Sweat broke out under her arms.

With a quick glance at her, Matt leaned forward and picked up the questioning thread. "Not quite. In our first interview, you said you hadn't seen Camilla or Oscar since you went to the farm for her birthday a month ago. But Oscar was at your house just a few days before the murders occurred." Matt didn't explain how they knew.

Bernard didn't ask. He simply admitted his error with a weak shrug. "I forgot."

Bree didn't buy that for one second. "You also stated the farm was worthless. Yet we know a developer recently made a lucrative offer for the property." Bree was bluffing—she didn't know if the offer had been good or not.

Bernard blinked away from her gaze. He stared at the wall to his left. "My son-in-law got himself mixed up in a Ponzi scheme. He's lost everything, and unfortunately, he's dragged my daughter down with him. My grandchildren are going to lose their home. Leonard will be lucky if he doesn't go to prison. I ran through everything I had to keep them afloat and hire a decent attorney, but I don't have anything left." He swallowed, his eyes returning to Bree's. "I asked my sister for money. She said no."

"Did she have any money?" Bree had seen Camilla's bank statements and already knew the answer was no.

Bernard folded his hands on the table in front of him. "Not in cash. But she could have mortgaged the farm or accepted the offer from the developer. I've already mortgaged my home and drained my savings."

"Do you think it was fair to ask your sister to give up her home?" Bree asked.

"It's for the children! Their father could go to prison. They'll lose their home." Bernard thumped a fist on the table. "Camilla complained about not having grandchildren for years. All I ever heard was how much she loved children. I thought she actually did."

"You called her a few days before she died," Bree said.

Stephanie interrupted. "You don't have to answer, Dad."

"No, it's OK." He squeezed her hand. "Yes. She turned me down last month, but I thought maybe she might have changed her mind after she'd had time to think about it." His mouth flattened into a grim line. "She hadn't." He released his daughter's hand and shoved his through his silver hair. "Eugene came to see me the next day. He told me to stop badgering his mother and go beg somewhere else." His gaze flittered away and the lines around his mouth tightened. He was holding something back.

"Eugene paid your son-in-law a significant sum of money last year," Bree said.

Bernard's nod was curt. "I warned Eugene. He wouldn't listen, and Leonard sucked him in."

"You knew Leonard was running a Ponzi scheme?" Bree asked.

Bernard shook his head hard. "Of course not. And Leonard wasn't running it. He was suckered too. But Leonard was always pursuing some questionable-sounding scheme. My sister just wouldn't understand."

"I'll bet you were angry," Matt said.

"Dad, don't say any more," Stephanie warned.

But Bernard's eyes flashed, bright with fury. "You bet I was angry. My sister was a selfish woman."

Bree caught Matt's eye and nodded. Matt left the room and returned with a printed photo. "We found these pants in your hamper." He set the photo on the table and pointed to the dark stains on the pant leg. The lab had already performed a rapid test and confirmed the stain was human blood. "This is blood. Human blood."

Bernard stared at the photo, then looked up at Matt. Panic widened his eyes as his gaze darted to Bree's. "It's mine."

Bree scanned him. "You don't appear to have any significant cuts or scrapes."

"When I mowed my lawn the other day, the grass pollen set off my allergies. I had a nosebleed. If I had just committed murder, I wouldn't have tossed my pants into the hamper. I would have burned them or buried them somewhere. But those are my yard work and painting pants. I don't care about stains."

The pants *were* beat-up.

"We're sending the pants for DNA analysis," Bree said. "So, we'll know if you're lying about that too."

"I'm not lying, not about that." Desperation sharpened Bernard's tone. "I can't believe you think I killed my sister and nephew." He sat back, his face stricken.

"You lied about seeing Oscar. You lied about calling Camilla. You lied about the value of the farm, *and* you lied about needing money," Bree pointed out. "Why did you lie about those things?"

Bernard stared back at her. His mouth opened. "I—"

"Don't answer that, Dad," Stephanie interrupted him.

Bernard's mouth snapped shut.

"Because they made you look guilty?" Matt suggested.

Bernard's jaw sawed back and forth, as if he were grinding his molars.

Stephanie put her hand on her father's forearm, as if to physically restrain him. "Are you going to arrest him?"

Bree met her gaze. "Not yet."

Stephanie stood. "In that case, my father won't be answering any more questions."

Even if Bree requested a rush, the DNA test would take a few days. Until then, Stephanie was right. Bree had no physical evidence. Making a case using circumstantial evidence wasn't impossible, but it was damned difficult.

Frustrated, she watched Bernard and his daughter leave the station. She went to the conference room. Todd sat at the table, files and papers strewn across the laminate surface. His laptop was open in front of him.

Matt followed her in, and Bree summed up the interview for Todd before turning to Matt. "What did you think?"

"He had an answer for everything," Matt said.

Bree nodded. "Except for why he lied."

"Because the truth makes him look bad," Matt suggested.

"He isn't very tech savvy. He didn't realize we could easily find the truth," Todd added.

"Maybe," Bree said. "Let's get the original case report on the son's suicide. I want to understand the family history."

"What's next?" Todd asked.

Good question.

Bree needed to clear her head and absorb the information they'd uncovered. "I'm going home. Speculation about motive is getting us nowhere. We need evidence. Let's hope forensics has something concrete for us tomorrow." She grabbed her laptop and stuffed it into her briefcase.

"I'll order the report. I can also ask Jim Rogers if he knows anything about the Hudson Footmen," Matt said. "During Jim's interview, I felt like he was holding back."

Bree felt like she should be going with Matt. She hated to take an evening off, but she needed to see her family. Her relationship with Luke felt uncomfortably fragile this week, and the suicide of the Crighton boy weighed heavily on her. Luke had to be more important than work, no matter how much she wanted—needed—to catch a killer.

Parenting had as many ups and downs as a big coaster. Seeing the family meant she wasn't working. She knew delegation was part of her job, but that didn't mean she liked it. Respect to all the women balancing work and family life. "Be careful. Don't go alone. If you think Rogers or anyone else will talk more freely without me being present, take Todd or another deputy along, even if they just observe from their vehicle."

"Let me know if you want my company," Todd said.

"Will do." Matt gathered his notes. "I'm going to make some more calls about Dylan. I got some weird vibes at his place. He's up to something."

Todd tapped on his keyboard. "I just got a report from forensics. The flower petals are from a *Buddleia davidii*, or butterfly bush. It's not a native shrub but isn't hard to grow. I don't remember seeing any flowers of this color and size at Bernard's house, but now that I know what the bush looks like, I'll double-check in the morning. I'll also run past Kenny McPherson's and Heather Oscar's places and see if I spot one."

"Be discreet," Bree suggested.

"I'll drive my personal vehicle," Todd agreed. "No one will notice me."

Bree left the station and drove home. But talking to Luke at dinner proved as fruitless as working on the case. He mumbled one-word answers and sullenly stared at his plate as he shoveled spaghetti and meatballs into his mouth. His irritation clearly hadn't affected his appetite.

Bree salvaged the evening by playing a board game with Kayla, then sent her upstairs for a shower. She promised to drive her to school the next day. When Kayla settled in to finish her reading homework, Bree stopped by Luke's room.

She paused in the doorway and knocked on the frame. "What are you working on?"

"Pre-cal." He sat at his desk, hunched over his notebook and pencil. "Almost done?"

"Uh-huh." He looked up, his eyes stubborn.

"OK. I'll leave you to it." She turned away from the silent treatment, wondering how long he would stay mad at her. Conflicts were a normal part of parenting, but his rebuffs hurt more than she'd expected.

Restless, her mind returned to the case. She headed to her office to process paperwork, type interviews, and review evidence reports. The investigation was less satisfying than her interactions with Luke. No matter how many times she replayed Bernard's lies, Bree wasn't completely convinced he was guilty.

Chapter Seventeen

Matt used a lacrosse stick to fling a tennis ball as far across his backyard as he could. Greta streaked after it. She made a sweeping turn. Barely slowing, she snatched the ball off the grass and raced back. Dropping it at Matt's feet, she backed away and barked at him.

At eight o'clock, the evening was going dark. He'd spent an hour calling his contacts in the SFPD asking about Brian Dylan. But none of the SFPD officers admitted to knowing him well.

Cady walked across the grass and stopped next to him. "She is so demanding."

"She never gets tired," Matt said with pride as he hurled the ball again.

"You and Brody are going to miss her when she's gone."

Lying at Matt's feet, Brody all but rolled his eyes.

Matt laughed. "I might, but I think Brody will be happy to return to his regularly scheduled naps."

Cady shoved her hands into her pockets. "So I gave the caterer the final guest total."

"I can't believe we sold every ticket to a black-tie night of board games." Matt sent the tennis ball sailing again, but he sensed reservation in his sister's tone.

"We need to talk about that." Cady dug a sneakered toe into the damp grass. "Two local sponsors canceled today."

"What?" Matt turned to face her.

Cady's mouth pursed. "The youth group at the church was going to hold a bake sale. We rented a table for them. But their leader pulled out, citing that garbage story about nude pics of Bree and pornography. He said he can't have the kids mixed up with 'that sort of immorality.'"

Matt swore. "What part of 'fake pictures' don't people understand?"

"I pointed out that the photos were fabricated. He didn't believe me." Cady lifted a hand. "I don't think we have to be worried yet, but if this story gains any more momentum . . ."

"We could lose more money." Matt raked a hand through his hair. The whole fundraiser was at stake. "It's nearly impossible to prove a negative."

"I know," Cady said. "But Bree has to get out ahead of this. She needs to fight it. Her reputation is on the line."

Matt agreed. "Not sure how she's supposed to do that. She gave a press conference. She explained what happened."

"I don't know, but I'd hate to see all the hard work that went into this fundraiser go to waste."

Greta spit the ball onto Matt's shoes. K-9s were typically funded with private donations. Small local budgets couldn't afford the costs. If Bree's department couldn't raise the money, what would he do with Greta? She was a working dog. She needed a job, and it would be a shame to waste her potential. Could he donate her to a different department? He might not see her again.

Which shouldn't matter, right?

His business model hadn't allowed for getting attached to the dogs.

The road to hell and all that.

He said, "The sheriff's department really needs a K-9."

Investigations had been hamstrung on several occasions waiting for a K-9 to arrive from another department.

"I know it."

"Shit."

"Yeah. Shit," Cady agreed. "Talk to Bree, OK? Let her know what's going on."

"I will." But that was a conversation Matt didn't want to have tonight. Bree had enough on her plate. And really, what could she ever do about rumors?

Cady said goodbye and headed for her minivan. Matt took the dogs to the house. Brody stretched out on his orthopedic dog bed. Greta drank a whole bowl of water and lay beside him on the tile, finally tuckered out.

Disturbed by the conversation with his sister, Matt opened his laptop and did a Google search with Bree's name. The number of links and images that search returned shocked him. The story had gained speed like an avalanche.

But what could they do about it?

His phone buzzed, and he answered, "Flynn."

"Hey, Matt. This is Detective Brody McNamara with the Scarlet Falls PD. You helped me with a drug case about five years back when you were working the K-9 unit for the sheriff's department."

Matt laughed. "How could I forget? You and my dog have the same name."

"I'm honored. He's an awesome dog. The way he tracked down that drug dealer was epic."

"He's the best," Matt agreed.

"How is Brody?"

"Enjoying his retirement." Matt glanced at his dog, snoozing hard in his bed, which took up an entire corner of the kitchen.

"And you're working for the new sheriff?"

"Now and then," Matt said. "As a civilian consultant."

McNamara hesitated. "Rumor says you've been asking about Brian Dylan."

Matt straightened. "I have. What can you tell me?"

"Is your inquiry related to that double homicide you're working?"

"He is a person of interest." Matt enunciated the words in a way to let McNamara know that Dylan was indeed a murder suspect.

"This is off the record and unofficial. I don't have any definitive proof, just speculation."

"OK."

"We did an internal investigation after his *incident*"—McNamara paused—"and linked Dylan to the Hudson Footmen, a survivalist group."

"We know that."

"I shouldn't be surprised," McNamara said. "But did you know the Hudson Footmen were evolving into a paramilitary group? They've been loosely linked to online chatter about a planned cyberattack on a hospital. The FBI shut it down before it happened, but it wouldn't surprise me if the Footmen get added to the FBI's list of domestic terror groups. Also, they recently set up an elaborate social media recruitment and funding campaign. Our sources say Dylan is spearheading the recruitment effort."

Matt was surprised. "Seriously?"

"Yes," McNamara said. "They need members and money. They've developed a significant dark web presence. Dylan's involvement in the organization has escalated since he lost his job, and he has some expertise with technology and software."

Matt thought of all the satellites on Dylan's roof. "Is Dylan at a decision-making level yet?"

"We don't know. The Footmen aren't doing anything illegal that we've discovered. They are a legitimate organization. Dylan's involvement was more secondary information, but when I heard you were asking about Dylan, I thought you should know."

"What about Eugene Oscar?" Matt asked. "Have you ever heard his name associated with the Footmen?"

"No. But I would be suspect of any close associates of Brian Dylan."

Matt ended the call and stared into space for a few minutes. Brian Dylan was involved with a paramilitary group. Oscar had been close friends with him. Could the survivalist group be involved in Oscar's death?

Matt picked up his phone and called Todd. "I want to track down Jim Rogers tonight. You in?"

"Yep. I'm not far from your place. I'll pick you up in ten minutes."

"OK." Matt grabbed his keys and wallet from the counter and stuffed them into his pockets.

Brody whined.

"You want to come with?" Matt asked.

Brody went to the door and stood under the hook that held his leash.

"OK." Matt kenneled Greta and he and Brody went outside.

Todd pulled up in his personal vehicle, a compact SUV. He stepped out. Brody trotted over to greet him. "Good to see you, Brody." Todd scratched his neck.

"Do you mind if he comes with us?" Matt asked. "He's bored, and Greta is driving him a little nuts."

"Of course he can come." Todd opened the back door. The dog jumped in and settled on the back seat, his nose pressed to the window.

Todd drove out to Rogers's house, but no one answered their knock. They returned to the SUV.

Matt drummed his fingers on the armrest. "Where now?"

"Let me make a couple of calls." Todd slid his cell from his pocket. He called some friends. A few minutes later, he returned the phone to his pocket. "Someone saw him at the gun range on Route 7."

Todd drove out to the range and parked in the lot. Though it wasn't the range where Matt typically practiced, he'd been here before. A concrete-block building housed the office and indoor range. Trees grew close on either side. An outdoor stall and an area for skeet shooting sat well behind the building. The rear of the property was lit up like a football stadium. The brightness in the distance made the surrounding woods seem darker.

The parking lot was semifull. Matt and Todd stepped out of the SUV. Matt opened the back door and lifted Brody down. The big dog might be useful. Brody was loved by all, even people who didn't like Matt.

The outdoor range was far enough away that the sound of gunfire was muted by distance. Matt spotted Jim Rogers sitting on a split-rail fence in front of the building. His puppy sat at his feet, chewing on a hard rubber dog toy.

Matt and Todd approached him. The puppy abandoned its toy to yip at Brody.

"Leave it," Rogers commanded. When the puppy turned toward him, he praised her. "Good girl." Rogers commanded her to sit, then reached over to greet Brody. "How are you, big boy?"

The puppy jumped up and nipped at the hair around Brody's neck. With a stoic turn of his head, Brody pointedly ignored the pup. He looked back at Matt as if to say, *You want to get a handle on this?*

Rogers shorted the leash.

"Hey, Jim, you OK?" Todd asked.

Rogers was pale and pouring sweat, despite the coolness of the evening. He shrugged and leaned down to scoop the puppy into his arms. Settling her in the crook of his elbow, he stroked her back. "Since I can't shoot, I brought Goldie here to get her used to the sound of gunfire. I thought maybe listening to it at a distance would help me get conditioned to it too." He snorted. "So far, I'm SOL there." The puppy chewed on his sleeve. "Maybe she'll have to be my emotional support dog instead of a retriever."

"Nothing wrong with that." Todd reached forward and ruffled the puppy's ears. "I miss having a dog, but I don't have time to train a puppy." Like Bree, Todd worked long hours.

Matt said, "Cady has a few older, fully housebroken rescues that would be happy to hold your couch in place while you went to work."

Todd looked thoughtful. "Maybe."

"You want me to ask Cady?" Matt asked.

"No." Todd flushed. "I'll call her."

"Why are you here?" Rogers looked at Matt, then Todd. "This isn't your club."

"We're looking for you," Matt answered. Two men walked out of the building. He waited until they moved out of earshot before continuing in a low voice. "I wanted to ask you some follow-up questions about Brian Dylan."

Rogers stiffened. "I already told you everything."

Matt began. "What do you know about the Hudson Footmen—"

Glancing around, Rogers interrupted with a chop of his hand. More sweat darkened the armpits of his gray T-shirt. "It's not smart to mention that name out here."

Matt lowered his voice. "Are members here?"

"I don't know, but I wouldn't want to find out." Rogers continued to scan the parking area.

Matt saw no one except for the two men getting into a truck on the other side of the lot. They weren't close enough to overhear, but he lowered his voice anyway. "Is Dylan in the club?"

"I don't know," Rogers nearly whispered.

"He believes some wild shit," Todd said.

"He does," Rogers agreed.

"What about Oscar?" Matt asked. "Did he follow any of those conspiracy theories?"

Rogers snorted. "Nah. Oscar didn't believe in anything but Oscar." He paused. "But I think even he was starting to get concerned about the increasing wackiness of Dylan's theories."

"Did this create conflict between them?"

"I really have no idea." Rogers lifted a shoulder.

Matt remembered the female shadow in Dylan's window. "Does Dylan have a girlfriend?"

"Dunno," Rogers said.

Brody stood, the fur on the back of his neck rose, and he growled softly in the direction of the darkness. Matt saw no one but trusted his dog. Something—or someone—was out there. The puppy followed Brody's focus. A baby growl rumbled in her throat.

Rogers frowned at his puppy and Brody. He slid off the fence. "I need to go home." He started toward the parking lot. "Don't follow me. I don't have any more information for you." He patted Brody on the head before carrying his puppy away.

Matt and Todd returned to the vehicle.

"He was fine until I mentioned the Footmen." Matt glanced over the seat. Brody sat on the back seat, but his attention was still on the woods.

"Just the mention of the group made him nervous," Todd agreed. "Brody OK?"

"Yeah."

"Maybe he smelled a coyote or something."

"Or something," Matt said. Had someone else been nearby, maybe listening?

"Rogers knows more than he's saying." Todd started the engine. "But we can't prove it. What now?"

"I'm going to do more research on the Hudson Footmen."

Todd dropped him and Brody off. Inside, Matt let Greta loose. Brody settled in his bed in the kitchen. Matt gave Greta an elk antler to chew while he worked.

He turned on his computer, then started up a browser using a VPN, or virtual private network. Given the Footmen's apparent reputation, he wouldn't want them to be able to track his IP address. In a common social media app, he opened a profile under a fake name. Using this profile, he found and followed some crazy-ass antigovernment sites.

Then he searched the Hudson Footmen's page and posts and found their private group. The group's discussion feed was private, but the administrators were listed at the top of the page. He hovered over the names.

Joe Hunt and Bri Bri Dee.

A nickname for Brian Dylan?

The name Joe Hunt sounded kind of fake too.

Matt screenshotted their pages and copied the links to his notes.

Bri Bri Dee's page was also private, and there was no photo available. Matt returned to the Hudson Footmen's group page. He'd send the screenshots and links to Rory. No doubt the forensics lab would have the resources to get more information.

He clicked "Join." While his admission was under review, he went to YouTube. The Hudson Footmen had their own channel. Most of their videos were posted by Joe Hunt and Bri Bri Dee, both of whom had their own individual accounts as well. Matt clicked on the first video and watched a totally weird video of a man in a white coat "demonstrating" that a recent hurricane never happened, that the government had fabricated the event in order to manipulate currency. Matt felt his eyes rolling at the ludicrousness. This "scientist" used radar maps and what he claimed was historical weather data. Matt stopped the video and double-checked the numbers with actual historical data from an international weather site. None of the numbers matched.

All bullshit.

But to some, probably very convincing bullshit.

The next video depicted a well-known politician admitting that the space shuttle *Challenger* explosion had been faked in a TV studio. The man's mouth looked distorted. The movement of his lips did not quite match the cadence of his speech. Also, he didn't blink throughout the one-minute clip. The video was a deepfake. Matt reached for the mouse to click the "Stop" button. He'd seen enough. Before he could click, the screen shifted to scrolling text that proclaimed, YOUR GOVERNMENT IS DECEIVING YOU. A website address appeared next. Do

YOU WANT TO BE PREPARED? JOIN US. SAVE YOURSELF AND YOUR LOVED ONES. ANARCHY IS COMING.

Now it all made sense. They were recruitment videos.

Matt copied the website address: jointhefootmen.com.

The website was for the Hudson Footmen. The site's rhetoric took care to fall shy of inciting violence. They focused on being the antidote to anarchy.

Matt went back to YouTube and watched a few more videos. The content was disturbing as hell, but that wasn't what held his attention. There was something familiar about the production, the style, the general feel of the videos. They weren't Hollywood slick but instead had a homemade quality to them reminiscent of *The Blair Witch Project*. The amateur look gave them an authentic quality. Matt was no expert, but he sensed this false genuineness wasn't accidental.

Then he realized what felt so familiar.

The Hudson Footmen's recruitment videos felt just like the deep-fake porn video of Bree.

If Bri Bri Dee was Brian Dylan, had Dylan made the deepfake video of Bree?

CHAPTER EIGHTEEN

Todd drove home, parked in his driveway, and shut off the engine of his SUV. Sitting in the darkness, he pulled out his cell phone. It was after ten. Too late to call Cady?

Since Matt had suggested adopting a dog, Todd had been unable to get Cady out of his head. Who was he kidding? He'd been thinking about her nonstop for months, which was why he'd volunteered to help with the fundraiser. She'd offered to row while he swam—which was a great idea—but how much could he talk to her while he was in the river?

He *was* lonely, and an older dog would be a good fit for him. But he simply wanted to spend time with Cady. If he adopted one of her dogs, she'd need to come over and assess his house. She'd want to introduce him to multiple dogs. Hell, maybe by the time he actually picked a dog and adopted it, he and Cady would have established some kind of relationship that had nothing to do with the upcoming fundraiser or his triathlon training.

He sent her a text. HEY, WHAT DO U THINK ABOUT ME ADOPTING A DOG?

She responded immediately, and a tiny spark of joy flashed in him. I LOVE IT! I HAVE IDEAS.

He typed back, TALK TOMORROW?

She answered with a smiley face emoji that matched his mood perfectly.

Shoving his phone into his pocket, he stepped out of his car. Though it was late, and he'd had a long-ass day, the text exchange with Cady had energized him better than a thermos of coffee. In his driveway, he stopped and stared at his house.

Sitting in the middle of a one-acre wooded lot, it looked empty, almost like no one lived there. Then again, he didn't really *live* there. He used the house for eating, sleeping, and doing laundry. He'd never invited guys over for a beer. He watched football alone. He'd never cooked a decent dinner.

Never had an overnight guest.

And that thought brought Cady to mind again.

It was time for a change.

As usual, he'd forgotten to leave a light on. He glanced over his shoulder at the neighbors' house across the road. Lights glowed in the windows. Some kind of gold flowers brightened the front beds. Spotlights shone on a few ornamental trees and shrubs. The landscaping wasn't fancy but made the place look like a home, as if the people who lived there cared about more than meeting the bare minimum.

In comparison, his own property was barren—almost forlorn—which he supposed reflected his own state of being.

He'd moved into the tiny bungalow after his divorce six—no, wait—almost seven years ago. He'd progressed from a personal pity party to plain apathy. The split might have been mostly amicable, but it had still left him depressed and uninterested in his personal life. He worked late most nights and had never cared much about appearances. The outdoor space was neat enough to keep the neighbors from complaining. He mowed the lawn and pulled the weeds, but he hadn't put any effort into curb appeal.

He walked around to the side yard and stopped at the picket fence gate. Branches overhead blocked out the moonlight. The rear yard backed to woods, and he'd left it mostly natural. The fence that encircled the cleared portion was four feet high. So as long as the dog he adopted wasn't too agile, it would work just fine. Cady would surely approve.

But the thought of her coming over and giving the place a preadoption once-over made him want to spruce up the yard. He needed lights or landscaping—both, he decided. The inside could use some work too. The walls were still up-for-sale white. He hadn't hung a single picture or piece of art, and his furniture leaned toward essentials only. He couldn't fix everything at once, but he could begin making his house look like a home. He started a mental list for the home improvement store: paint, flowers, mulch.

A twig snapped behind him. He spun toward the sound.

The first blow cracked against the side of his head. The pain exploded through his skull and sent him to one knee. Light flashed across his field of vision, like shooting stars. At first, he thought he'd walked into a low tree branch. Then he sensed more than saw the figures moving around him. With the pain ricocheting in his head like a pinball, it took a breath for him to realize he was being attacked.

He reached for the sidearm on his hip. As soon as his weapon cleared its holster, a second blow struck his elbow, hitting the nerve. White-hot agony raced from his fingertips to his shoulder, and he dropped the gun. A man loomed over him, blotting out the moonlight. He wore camo. Something swung from his hand. Some kind of stick or baton? A brimmed hat shielded his eyes, and a dark bandana covered his face.

The group shifted around Todd. He tried to count them, but his vision went blurry as blood ran into his eyes.

Four? No, five.

His hand went to his waist again, but he was out of uniform. Without his duty belt, he had no Taser, no pepper spray, no anything. Levering to his feet, he spun in a circle, a futile attempt to face all his attackers. A body passed close to him, and he lashed out with a hook punch. His fist caught a soft belly, and the man grunted.

Another blow from the baton struck him low across his back. The pain nearly folded his legs, but he knew once he went down, that was where he would stay.

And the fight would become a beating.

He remained upright by sheer willpower. Staggering, he braced himself and kicked out. His boot caught a knee. Something cracked. The recipient screamed, his knees buckled, and he fell to his ass. *One down.* Satisfaction drove Todd to lash out again. He stomped on a foot, then drove his left elbow under a jaw. The sound of teeth snapping together revitalized him.

A punch sailed toward his face. He dodged it, but a second fist came out of nowhere, hitting him in the eye. Adrenaline blocked some of the pain, but his vision doubled for a few seconds.

He was a decent fighter, but not against five opponents who'd gotten the jump on him. There was no way for him to win. He remembered Oscar's bruised face, and the bullet holes in his knees, shoulder, and forehead. Had his last moments gone like this? Were these the men who'd killed him? Would they torture Todd like they had Oscar?

Something moved on his left. He ducked, and the baton swished over his head, close enough to his face that he could feel the disturbance of air on his skin.

Men circled him.

Todd knew they would probably kill him. He pushed away the regret and fear. He would die tonight. His only choice was whether he would go easy or hard. Hard, he decided.

Fuck them.

He would inflict some damage on his way out. Anger burned away some of his pain. He'd wasted the last seven years. Now, he'd finally found someone he wanted to be with, and these fuckers were going to kill him. Cady's face crossed his mind.

I'm sorry.

He hadn't even asked her on a date. *Stupid.*

A punch to the kidneys rocked him. He stumbled a few steps away, then caught his balance and whirled. Using the momentum of the spin, he whipped the heel of his hand across a face, then raked his nails across the man's eyes. He felt a liquid pop.

"Fuck. My eye." The man grabbed his face with both hands and staggered away.

That's two.

Todd's hand came away wet. He wiped it on his shirt, making sure blood soaked into the fabric and skin and tissue drove deeper under his own nails.

DNA, motherfucker, DNA.

If Bree and Matt had to investigate his death tomorrow, he'd make sure they found some evidence on his body. He reached out again and snagged a wrist and latched on to a watch band. The buckle gave and came away in his hand.

Something cracked against the backs of his knees. Todd's legs crumpled. He crashed to the ground, the watch sailing out of his grip. As he fell, he caught sight of the baton. *That'll do it,* he thought. The grass did not feel soft as his head bounced off it. The baton headed toward his face, and he wrapped his arms around his head. It struck his shoulder. The new pain barely registered on his already-battered body.

A kick to the gut bent him in half. Still covering his head with his arms, he rolled to his side and curled into a fetal position to protect his organs. Boots rained down on him, and he wished he could simultaneously protect his spine. Pain slammed through his back, his shoulders, his legs.

Someone searched his pockets, removed his phone, and crushed it under their boot. In his peripheral vision, he saw one of them pick up his gun and shove it into their pocket.

"Don't you wish you'd stayed out of business that ain't yours?" a male voice asked. "When you disturb a nest of rattlesnakes, eventually, you get bit."

Todd blinked, looking for the source of the voice. It sounded familiar, but the rush of blood in his ears made it impossible to identify his attacker. His eye was swelling shut and blood dripped down his face, obscuring his vision. Blinking, Todd tried to clear his eyes. The night sky came into focus for a few seconds. Then he saw a boot headed for his face. He turned his face toward the ground and closed his arms more tightly over his skull. But he couldn't protect his whole head and face. The heel of the boot glanced off his temple and everything went fuzzy.

Hands picked him up. Pain rocketed through Todd's entire body as they carried him away. He vaguely heard twigs snapping. A few minutes later, they dropped him. He hit the ground with a white-hot bolt of agony.

"Don't drop him!"

"He's fucking heavy. I lost my grip. Anyways, I think he broke my hand."

"Get him in the truck."

Hands under his shoulders lifted his torso. His boots dragged a few feet in the dirt. He wanted to run, but his body refused to work. He couldn't move. Couldn't do anything but dangle helplessly. Someone grabbed his feet. They swung him back and forth.

"One, two, three."

They tossed him. He hit metal. The bed of a pickup truck? Men climbed in after him. Someone threw a tarp over him. An engine turned over, and the vehicle lurched forward. They weren't leaving him behind. They were going to dump him somewhere. Would his body be found?

He had one last conscious thought before blackness mercifully took.

You won't survive the night.

CHAPTER NINETEEN

After dropping off Kayla at the grade school, Bree arrived at the station a few minutes after eight. She grabbed coffee, settled at her desk, and began checking her email. No dick pics, but her second email called her a slut and a degenerate porn star. She felt a little sick as she opened six more just like it. Bree closed the seventh citizen complaint and checked her voice mail.

Nick West from WSNY News had left her a message asking for an update on the murder case. Bree returned his call: she had no updates at the current time, but she appreciated him sticking to the case.

She had an email from Morgan Dane with an available appointment later that morning. Bree clicked the embedded "Confirmation" button.

Marge poked her head through the doorway. "Have you finished your coffee?"

"Why? What's going on?"

Marge came in and shut the door behind her. "Reporters have been calling all morning. Paris Vickers with the *Daily Grind* called three times."

Bree scowled. "What does she want?"

"She asked for an interview or a comment, but it sounded as if all she really wanted was to be able to say she contacted our office and didn't receive a reply. Apparently, there's a petition going around social media calling for your resignation."

Bree rubbed her forehead. "For what?"

"Indecency." Marge shook her head.

"But the pictures and videos are fake." Bree didn't know why she was shocked. The *Daily Grind* wasn't a bastion of journalistic integrity—it was a tabloid rag.

"I know it's all fake, but you have to deal with it."

"How am I supposed to deal with it? It's all over the internet."

"You'll probably need to sue the hell out of them, very publicly, and to make repeated indignant statements about the media being irresponsible."

Bree didn't have the time or desire to put on a show. She wasn't an actor. Anger and anxiety churned in Bree's gut. "I have a murder to solve."

"You won't solve any murders if you're kicked out of office," Marge said.

Damn it.

"Maybe this is the wrong job for me." It wouldn't be the first—or fortieth—time Bree had doubted her new career.

Marge crossed her arms. "Don't tell me you're going to let them win?"

"I am out of my element, Marge. I'm a cop. I have no taste for the politics required of being sheriff."

"You're a good sheriff, and you're better with politics than you think. You come across as genuine."

"I don't want to be good at it," Bree grumbled. "Is Todd in yet?"

Marge shook her head. "I haven't seen him."

"He was running an errand this morning." Bree considered how long it would take him to drive past suspects' houses. An hour or two? "Let me know when he comes in."

"Of course."

Her desk phone rang. Marge reached across the desk and answered it. "Sheriff Taggert's office." Her frown deepened. "One moment, please." She punched the "Hold" button and lowered the phone. "It's that county supervisor, Madeline Jager."

Bree extended a hand for the phone.

Marge held it out of reach. "Be careful. Madeline Jager would eat her own young for good PR."

Bree sighed.

"Deep breath," Marge instructed.

Bree did as she was told. Marge had worked in local government longer than anyone else. She knew everyone, and experience had given her the extraordinary ability to read and judge people. Bree exhaled, and Marge handed over the phone.

Bree pressed the button to release the hold. "Ms. Jager, what can I do for you?"

"Citizens are calling for your resignation, Sheriff."

"Why?" Bree asked.

"You know why."

"Explain it to me." Bree held back the *like I'm five*. She thought it was likely implied.

"Moral decency is a prerequisite for public office." Jager's voice rang with superiority.

"Is it?" Bree asked.

Ms. Jager sputtered. "Well, it should be. You're supposed to be a role model, particularly for young girls. How do parents explain your appearance in pornography to their children?"

"Why are parents allowing their children to view pornography?"

"That's not the point," Jager snapped.

Bree fought her temper. Usually, she had very good self-control, but the situation was taxing her patience. She carefully neutralized her voice. "Then what is the point?"

"The point is that your image was utilized on pornography," Jager said, her voice ringing with a condescension she had no right to feel. "It's indecent!"

"How does anyone control how publicly available images are utilized? We know the videos and photos are fake."

"Do we?" Ms. Jager said, her voice dripping with sarcasm.

An ache formed behind Bree's eyes, but she refused to take the bait. She kept her voice level. "Yes. We do."

Jager huffed. "What am I supposed to tell the citizens?"

"How about the truth?" Bree suggested. "The computer forensics techs can easily tell that the images have been manipulated. My face was superimposed over a pornographic video. Deepfakes are an increasingly common problem, particularly for female public figures. How would you feel if this happened to you?"

"Is that a threat?"

"No, of course it's not a threat." Bree massaged her temple. "Just a fact. You are a public figure. You are also a woman. Therefore, you are vulnerable to this type of harassment."

"You can't threaten me, Sheriff."

Oh, my God. Where's the ibuprofen?

Bree wanted to scream, but she couldn't allow this woman to get the best of her. Jager seemed determined to push Bree into saying something she would regret. Bree wouldn't give her the satisfaction. "What do you want, Ms. Jager?"

Jager hesitated. "The board of supervisors thinks you should consider taking a leave of absence."

Bree had not expected that suggestion. "Why?"

"To deal with this pornography mess."

"Why would I do that? I have more resources to deal with the issue as sheriff than I would as a private citizen. I will not be cowed into leaving office. Caving to bullies only empowers them."

"Well, you have to do *something*." Jager's voice rose.

"I promise I'm exploring all options. Now, unless you have a specific suggestion for me, I really need to get back to solving this double homicide."

Jager skipped the social niceties. "You'll be hearing from me again regarding this matter. This will not be our last conversation. If you won't do something about this situation, then I will." The connection went dead.

"Now, *that* sounded like a threat." Bree returned the phone to its cradle. She looked up at Marge. "I didn't lose my temper."

"No, you didn't, and you deserve a medal. That woman is insufferable." Marge tapped her lip. "Have you talked to Morgan Dane?"

"I have an appointment with her this morning." Bree wasn't sure how she felt about that. It felt wrong for the sheriff to need an attorney.

"She'll help."

Bree shot Marge a look. "Aren't defense attorneys on the opposite side of the law as sheriffs?" Bree had met the attorney before. Their dealings had been short, but she'd seemed smart.

Marge's nod was thoughtful. "Ms. Dane is highly respected, she's not much for theatrics, and she won't put up with any nonsense from the *Daily Grind*."

"Well, I need someone to help with this deepfake mess." Bree had never felt so utterly useless. What kind of sheriff couldn't stop herself from being victimized?

Marge returned to her desk.

Matt knocked on Bree's office doorframe. He gave her a quizzical and concerned frown. "Is everything OK?"

Bree motioned him inside the office. "I just had a call from County Supervisor Madeline Jager." She summarized their appalling conversation.

Matt slid into a chair. "Nice to know victim blaming is alive and well."

Bree leaned on her elbows. "I don't want to be a victim." She could deny it until she was blue, but she *was* a victim, and that fact churned in her gut. She'd spent the first eight years of her life as a helpless casualty of domestic violence. Part of the reason she'd become a cop was to keep from ever becoming a victim again. But someone had changed all that with some photo- and video-editing software.

"Name a victim who wanted to be one," he said.

Bree lifted both palms in surrender. "Good point." She deflated. "How do I prove I didn't do something when evidence already exists, but no one cares about that evidence? People believe what they want to believe. A juicy story about a sex tape is more thrilling than the boring reality of digital photo editing." She lightly slapped both palms on her desk. She needed to move on with her morning. "I'm meeting with Morgan Dane later. Until then, let's get back to finding a killer."

"Do we have a plan for today?" Matt asked.

"I need to check in with forensics." Bree opened her email. "They should at least have preliminary reports for the crime scene and Bernard Crighton's house by now."

Before she could type the email, her cell vibrated. She glanced at the screen. The call was from the high school.

Luke!

Bree's heart lurched as she answered. "This is Sheriff Taggert."

"This is Principal Newton." The principal sounded stern, but then she always did. "I need you to come to the high school."

Fear squeezed Bree's heart. "Is Luke all right?"

"Yes." The principal hesitated. "He got into a fight."

"Luke?" Bree couldn't imagine it.

"Yes, Luke." The principal's voice hardened. "He punched another student."

Luke started it? That was even harder to believe.

"Was anyone seriously hurt?" Bree asked.

"No. But I need you to come and pick him up. He's being suspended for three days. We have a zero-tolerance policy on fighting."

Bree bristled. She thought no-tolerance policies were bullshit. Adults accused of crimes were allowed to explain themselves. Kids deserved the same courtesy. Plus, zero-tolerance policies encouraged bullying. Good kids followed rules. Troublemakers did not. But she held her tongue—by biting her lip hard enough to taste blood. Some discussions were better handled in person. "I'll be there in ten minutes."

The principal ended the call without a response.

"Luke got into a fight." She relayed the call to Matt.

Matt's brows dropped. "Luke?"

"Right?" Bree's mind searched for an explanation. "Luke isn't a hothead. I can't believe he'd get into a fight."

"He's levelheaded," Matt agreed. "If he punched another student, there must have been a reason."

"Would you check in with forensics?"

"Sure," he said. "Good luck. Keep me posted."

"Will do." Bree grabbed her keys and headed for the door. She stopped at Marge's desk on her way out of the station. "I have to run over to the school. I'll be back as soon as I'm able."

Marge nodded. "Is everything OK?"

"I don't know." Bree could only hope.

CHAPTER TWENTY

Matt settled in the conference room with a laptop, a stack of photos, and Rory in forensics on speakerphone.

"I'm emailing you the preliminary forensics reports both from the crime scene and from Bernard Crighton's residence," Rory said. "Unfortunately, nothing stands out at the crime scene that we haven't already discussed. Recovered fingerprints belonged to the victims. We found plenty of interesting trace evidence: goat hair, cat fur, chicken feathers, animal feces . . . but the crime scene is a goat farm, so . . ."

The computer dinged. Matt opened the email and downloaded the reports. As he scanned the list of evidence, he compared the items with crime scene photos.

Rory continued. "The search of Bernard's house was more interesting. We found goat and cat fur on his doormat. Also, traces of chicken feces and feathers on a pair of shoes out in the garage."

Bernard had already admitted to being at the farm recently, so Matt wasn't surprised. "No blood other than what we found on the pants?" he asked.

"No, and per the sheriff's request, we asked for a rush on that DNA test. The lab hopes to have those results in another day or two." Rory paused. Keys tapped over the connection. "But the lab tested the clothing in Bernard's hamper for gunshot residue. They didn't find any."

"Bernard stated that if he'd killed his sister and nephew, he would have disposed of his clothing. Maybe he did just that." But if that were true, Matt had no explanation for the bloodstained pants, other than the blood was actually Bernard's.

"Oh, wait." Rory hesitated. "Our tech found two dried flower petals in Bernard's garage that match the three found at the crime scene."

Matt flipped through the photos of the farm's exterior. "But we didn't find a butterfly bush on either property."

"No. Nor did we find any petals on Bernard Crighton's shoes or in his vehicle."

"He could have picked them up anywhere." Matt stroked his beard. They had no idea when the flower petals had been dropped at the crime scene. But Oscar had visited Bernard's house just a few days before the murders. He could have tracked the flower petals to both locations. "Did the techs check all of Oscar's shoes at the crime scene?"

"We did," Rory said. "We didn't find any on his shoes or in his vehicle."

"Anything else?" Matt asked.

"Those are the highlights. I'll let you know when the DNA analysis comes in."

"Thanks, Rory." Matt ended the call. He shuffled more photos and paused on pictures of Oscar's body in situ.

The flower petals could be irrelevant. Oscar had been at both the crime scene and Bernard's house. Thinking of the flowers, he picked up his phone and texted Todd, who was checking suspects' houses for butterfly bushes. ANY LUCK?

A new email popped into Matt's inbox. It was from the Scarlet Falls PD. He opened it and downloaded the original report from Bernard's son's suicide. The boy had hanged himself from the clothing rod in his closet. He'd used his own belt. No one had been in the house that day except Bernard and his three children. The son had been a short, skinny boy. Interviews of his closest friends confirmed he'd stuttered badly and had been bullied and depressed since his mother died. Neither the responding officers nor the medical examiner had found any sign of foul play. The death had been ruled a suicide without much fuss.

As much as Matt didn't want to empathize with a suspect, his heart broke for Bernard. How could he live in the same house where his son had killed himself? Matt remembered the boy's room, dusted and kept almost as a shrine for decades.

Then again, how could he leave his only connection with the boy he'd lost?

Matt pulled out a copy of the image of Bernard's happy young family on the sailboat. He stared at the smiling mother, the innocent boy. Just a few years after this photo was taken, both the mother and son were dead. Now Bernard had also lost his sister and nephew. Matt thought of Bree and the repeated instances of tragedy and violence in her family. Were some people magnets for bad luck? Maybe Bernard was just a victim of senseless loss.

Unless the DNA report of the blood on Bernard's pants came up as a match for his sister or Oscar, they had no physical evidence linking Bernard to the murders. He had told lies about his whereabouts and contacts with the victims, and he had motive. Matt set the sailing photo aside. Motive wasn't evidence.

He checked his phone, but Todd hadn't answered his text. Matt sent another. Then he called Todd and left a voice message. "Where are you? Call me back."

Marge opened the door. Her face was locked in an angry frown. "Check out the live feed for the *Daily Grind*. Paris Vickers is doing a hit piece on the sheriff."

Matt opened a browser, went to the site's social media page, and clicked on the live video. He maximized the window and sat back to watch. Marge walked around the conference room table and watched over his shoulder. A banner scrolled across the bottom of the screen: NEW SHERIFF DEPARTMENT SCANDAL UNVEILED?

Paris batted her tarantula-leg eyelashes at the camera. "Recent nude images of the new sheriff of Randolph County have appeared on the internet this week. Is Sheriff Taggert a former porn star? What else could she be hiding? The *Daily Grind* wants to know."

One of the fake nude images of Bree popped onto the screen. Strategically placed black boxes barely blocked out the woman's private parts. Paris went into detail describing the photographs and the video. The screen blinked to another image, and Matt's heart stopped cold.

Pictures of him and Bree at a local restaurant played on the screen in a slideshow. They'd dated in public several times. Matt had been pleased no one had noticed or seemed to care.

But he'd been wrong. Someone cared.

Just as Bree had feared, taking their relationship into the public eye had left her open to criticism. The montage stopped with a photo of Bree leaving his house in the predawn twilight.

Fuck.

Behind him, Marge coughed.

Paris's face split in a predatory grin. "And why is Sheriff Taggert having dinner with Criminal Investigator Matthew Flynn? More importantly, why is she leaving his house at five o'clock in the morning? Is the relationship between the sheriff and her employee less than professional?" Paris's eyes gleamed with excitement. She was enjoying every second of her fifteen minutes. "And, on top of the sexual scandals plaguing the sheriff's department, we have an insider tip that the sheriff has a conflict of interest within a current murder investigation."

The scene shifted to Bernard Crighton and his lawyer-daughter, Stephanie, on a modern studio set. Their names appeared in white text below them.

Paris sat on a matching stool angled toward her guests. She wore sky-high heels and a skirt bordering on too short. Her ankles were crossed and tucked to one side, her knees pressed tightly together. "On

Tuesday evening, Camilla Brown and her son, Eugene Oscar, were found shot to death on the family farm."

She introduced Bernard and Stephanie. "First of all, my deepest condolences on your loss."

"Thank you, Paris," Stephanie said. "Our family is grieving, which is why our situation is so heinous."

Paris tilted her head. "Is it true that the sheriff is treating your father as the prime suspect?"

"That's how it seems." Stephanie took her father's hand and squeezed it. "I can't even say how much this week has hurt."

Bernard added, "I can't believe anyone would think I killed my own sister and nephew."

Paris leaned forward, folding her hands on her knees. "Mr. Crighton, please tell us why you think it isn't right that Sheriff Taggert is investigating the murders of your sister and nephew."

"Because my nephew, Eugene, used to work as a deputy for the sheriff's department. Before Sheriff Taggert took over, he had a spotless record with two decades of service. Sheriff Taggert herself forced my nephew out of the sheriff's department just two months ago, and people are saying there was more to my nephew's retirement than was made public." Bernard swallowed. "I believe my nephew had a conflict with the sheriff. I believe he was trying to highlight corruption in the department." He looked directly into the camera. "I also believe this is why he was killed."

Paris's eyes glittered, and she pounced. "Are you saying you believe that the sheriff killed your nephew to silence him?"

Regret thinned Bernard's lips as he clearly realized he shouldn't slander the sheriff. Then his chin lifted with defiance, as if he didn't care. "I—"

Stephanie interrupted him with a quick, hard stare. Then she turned to Paris, and her features softened. "Of course we can't make any specific accusations, but people are saying the timing is very suspicious."

Paris turned to face the camera. Her lips curved in a sated smile, as if the juicy details Bernard had revealed energized her. "You heard it here from the *Daily Grind* first. Sheriff Bree Taggert is in charge of the murder investigation of one of her former deputies, with whom she had a recent disagreement." The camera moved into a close-up of Paris. "And guess who discovered the bodies?" She waited for a dramatic pause. "You guessed it. Sheriff Bree Taggert."

Matt reached for his phone as Paris Vickers called for Bree's resignation.

Chapter Twenty-One

Bree left the station through the rear door and hurried to her SUV. The tires squealed as she pulled out of the parking lot. She eased off the gas pedal. This was *not* a lights-and-siren emergency.

But it felt like it.

She called Dana to let her know about Luke.

"No." Dana sounded shocked.

"Yes." Bree breathed.

"It'll be OK." Dana's voice came through the Bluetooth speakers.

"I know." But nerves kept her fingers tight on the steering wheel as she drove to the high school. "Parenting is harder than I expected. Some days, the worry feels like it's eating a hole right through me. I wonder if it gets any better after they grow up."

"I doubt it."

Bree snorted. "Thanks for the reassurance."

Dana said, "You worry because you love them. That's never going to change. You just have to learn to live with it."

"You're probably right." But the thing that ate away at Bree was her fear that she was screwing up, that she would make major mistakes raising the kids, that she wasn't good enough.

"You can't control everything."

"And that is the problem."

"You're doing a great job with them," Dana said as if she could read Bree's mind.

"I wish I could be sure of that. Some days I feel like someone pushed us all off a boat, and I don't know how to swim, let alone save them. I'm floundering along trying not to let any of us drown." And potentially failing. Pressure built in Bree's chest until it felt as if it would burst. "What would I do without your help?"

"You need to chill," Dana said. "I've seen you face murderers with less stress. Luke isn't perfect. Stop expecting him to be. It's not fair to either one of you."

"You're right." Bree parked the SUV at the curb in front of the school. "I'm here. I'll call you when we're done."

A tension headache throbbed at the base of Bree's skull. She reached for the door handle.

Dana said, "Deep breath."

Bree filled and emptied her lungs.

"Now go find out what happened, and be Aunt Bree, not Sheriff Taggert."

"Thanks." Bree ended the call and climbed out of the vehicle.

Something didn't feel right about the situation. All kids made mistakes. She didn't expect Luke to be perfect. But he just wasn't a fighter. He wasn't the kind of kid who came out swinging. He harbored some residual anger from his mother's death, but he internalized emotion. He dealt with his grief by exhausting himself with work. In that way, Luke was a lot like Bree.

Could she have been wrong? Had she missed a sign that he'd backslid?

She went into the office. Luke and three other boys sat in the outer lobby. A counter separated this reception area from the administrative personnel and offices. Behind the counter, several women worked on computers. An older woman with her hair in a tight bun manned a phone and kept one experienced eye on the four sulking boys.

Luke sat in a plastic chair against one wall. He held an ice pack to his mouth and glared at three boys on the other side of the room. Among the other boys, Bree counted two blackening eyes and a split lip. Outnumbered three to one, Luke had given as good as he'd gotten.

She shouldn't be proud of that, but whatever. Parenting was weird.

The tallest boy sat in the middle of the trio, flanked by two dark-haired teens. A long bang of blond hair fell over his forehead. As Bree entered the room, his mouth twisted into a smug—smackable—sneer. Something in his posture made him appear to be the leader. Bree had been a cop long enough to know instinctively that this one was the problem.

She approached Luke and crouched in front of him. He kept his gaze on the other boys. The hate and hot fury in his eyes startled her. She lifted the cold pack away from his face. His lip was swollen, and a bruise was darkening his jaw below his mouth. She replaced the ice and spoke in a low voice. "Are you OK?"

He gave her a jerky nod. But he didn't look at her, and the discomfort in Bree's chest cranked tighter.

"Let's go out in the hall," she said. "I'd like to hear what happened from you first."

His gaze shifted to meet hers, and he shook his head once. The muscles of his face were hard as stone, his mouth strained, as if he were working hard to keep quiet and didn't trust himself to speak.

The familiar helpless, flailing feeling flooded Bree. Her instincts told her he needed to know she had faith in him—no matter what. But what could she do if he wouldn't talk to her? She gave his forearm a quick squeeze. His mouth twitched. Then he shifted his eyes over her shoulder again and resumed glaring at his opponents.

Bree stood and crossed the floor to the counter. She gave her name to the woman with the bun on the other side. The woman eyed her uniform. "I know who you are." She picked up the phone and pressed a number. "Sheriff Taggert is here."

A few seconds later, a door opened, and the principal emerged from an office. A sturdy woman in her late fifties, she wore a navy-blue pantsuit and radiated an air of no nonsense. Bree had interacted with her only a few times. Most of their discussions about Luke's emotional health and schooling had been with the guidance counselor.

She hated to leave Luke there alone, facing his opponents. But she had no options.

Bree rounded the counter.

Principal Newton held out a hand. "Sheriff Taggert. Thank you for coming."

They shook hands, and the principal gestured to her doorway. "Let's talk in my office."

Bree entered the office. With cinder block walls and no windows, the space reminded Bree just a little of the county jail.

Principal Newton closed the door, rounded her desk, and sat down. She tossed her glasses on the blotter and rubbed her forehead.

Bree sat in a chair facing her and waited.

The principal dropped her hand to her lap and sighed. "I don't even know what to tell you. None of the boys will talk."

"Do you have the fight on surveillance video?" Bree asked.

The principal shook her head. "We don't have a hundred percent coverage of the school. We have the entrances covered, along with most of the hallways and the cafeteria. The fight happened in the locker room. We obviously can't have cameras in there." She leaned forward and rested her forearms on the desk. "The gym teacher who broke up the fight said he saw Luke throw the first punch at Bobby. Bobby came back swinging, then his two friends joined in. From there, the situation deteriorated into general melee, with usual encouragement from the crowd."

"But the teacher has no idea what started the altercation?"

"No." The principal lifted both hands in the air. "I tried grilling them each individually, but none of them will say what started the fight. Not that it matters from a punishment perspective. I have no leeway when it comes to dispensing punishment for fighting. Regardless of the cause of the fight, all four boys will be suspended for three days."

Exasperation heated Bree's belly. She wanted to defend Luke, but how could she? She had no idea what had happened. "Zero-tolerance policies aren't the answer."

The principal nodded. "It's a district decision. My hands are tied." But deep, disapproving lines bracketed the principal's mouth. "It's no secret that I've been lobbying to change the guidelines. But until that happens, I have no option. You should contact the school board. I expect your arguments will garner more respect than the average parent."

Frustration welled in Bree. "Suspension seems like the least appropriate punishment. Some kids will view it as a vacation. Others will feel like outcasts. Either way, you haven't changed behavior, and taking them out of the classroom makes them fall behind in their studies, which is the opposite of the goal of education."

The principal flattened her palms on her desk. "I can't change the penalty, but I would very much like to know what made Luke lash out. He's a junior, and *he's* never been in my office before." Her tone suggested the other boys might have.

Bree nodded. "So would I."

The principal frowned. "I also have to tell you that an additional infraction could jeopardize Luke's eligibility for the baseball team. I don't want to see that happen."

Baseball was one of Luke's passions. Right now, he played fall ball with a regional travel league. But in the spring, he'd try out for the school team. He would be devastated if he couldn't play. He was hoping for a scholarship.

The principal wasn't at fault, but Bree couldn't bring herself to thank her. "Please keep me informed."

"I'd ask the same of you."

With a nod, Bree left the office. In the lobby, a man in a suit stood at the counter glowering at everyone, including the tall blond boy. From his irritated expression, she assumed he was the boy's father. The man's brows shot up as he took in Bree's uniform. He pointed at the blond boy. "Did you get yourself arrested?"

"No, sir," the boy mumbled.

"You're going to be sorry you dragged me out of work." His tone was harsh.

Bree walked by but offered no explanation. She couldn't muster much pity for the blond kid. Luke might not be ponying up the details, but she knew him. Whatever had happened had been caused by the other kid. *Let them sweat.*

Luke stood as she approached. He gave her a questioning look.

She gave him a quick headshake. "Let's get out of here."

Luke grabbed the backpack at his feet. Then he hurried out of the building, smacking the bar on the exit door with both hands. Right behind him, Bree headed for the SUV.

The morning sun heated the top of her head. Luke's shoulders slumped as he dragged his feet on the concrete walkway.

Bree turned him to face her. "So, you want to tell me what happened?"

"No."

"The principal says you threw the first punch."

"Yeah." Luke bit off the word.

"Why?"

Silence.

Frustration fizzed inside Bree like Alka-Seltzer. "I can't help if I don't know the problem."

"You can't help anyway." His tone was hopeless.

"Luke, talk to me," she all but pleaded.

He shook his head, then paused at the curb. "What about my car?" he asked. Bree had given him the old Honda Accord she'd brought with her from Philadelphia.

"Go get it," she said. "Go directly home. I'll meet you there."

Without speaking, Luke dug out the key from his pocket and headed for the students' lot behind the school.

Bree listened to radio chatter and chewed two antacids during the short drive home. Her cell phone buzzed, but she ignored it. For once, her focus had to be Luke.

Ten minutes later, Bree turned into their driveway and parked in front of the house. Luke parked next to her. He bolted from the car and headed for the barn. She followed him. The horses were in the pasture. At the sight of Bree and Luke, the three animals headed toward the fence. Riot broke into a trot, put his head over the fence, and nudged Luke's pocket.

Luke rested his head on his horse's neck.

Bree gave him a few minutes. When he still didn't speak, she said in a soft voice, "You're suspended for three days."

His eyes misted as he fought tears. "It's not fair."

"Why isn't it fair?"

"Because they're assholes."

Bree resisted chastising him for his language. Swearing was the least of her worries at the moment. "I know you. You don't start fights."

He flushed. A single tear escaped. He swiped a jerky hand across his cheek. "They were showing pictures around school."

Bree knew instantly what pictures he meant, and she felt sick.

Luke's face turned bright red. "And a video."

Fuck. Fuck. Fuck.

She breathed. She wanted to break something. "They're fake."

"I know," he snapped. "There weren't any tattoos in the pictures or video." His tone turned from angry to resigned. "I pointed that out. Bobby laughed, said it didn't matter. He was sharing the video with everyone." He gritted his teeth. "He called you a whore, and I punched him."

"Oh, Luke." Bree's heart ached. He'd defended her. She loved this kid beyond belief. She felt every ounce of his pain. "Bobby is the blond?"

He nodded. His hands curled into fists. "I just couldn't think. I got mad, and I reacted. I know I shouldn't have let him bait me."

"You're right," Bree said. "Bobby is a jerk."

He lifted his eyes to hers and snorted, breaking a small amount of the tension.

The hell with the school and the suspension.

"I appreciate you standing up for me, but you need to control your temper. I don't approve of fighting."

He looked away and stared at the ground. His eyes watered as if more tears threatened to break free.

Bree continued. "Violence isn't the answer. It's exactly the reaction Bobby wanted from you." She squeezed his arm. "If you step out of line again, they won't let you play baseball."

His gaze shot back to hers. He opened his mouth, then closed it as he struggled for control.

It broke Bree's heart. "Please don't let him bait you into another fight. I wouldn't be able to forgive myself if I was the reason you couldn't play ball or get a scholarship, if I let my job interfere with your future. That would be more devastating to me than any embarrassing fake video. Does that make sense?"

He swallowed but said nothing.

"If someone physically attacks you, I would never tell you to stand down. You can always defend yourself if it's necessary. But this is different." She searched for the right words. "You can't punch every jerk you run across. There are too many of them. You wouldn't have time for much else."

His mouth quirked. "I guess."

"Bobby and his friends are in trouble often?" Bree asked.

He nodded. "He thinks a suspension is a vacation."

"Then they don't have as much to lose from getting into a fight."

Something dawned in Luke's eyes.

Bree continued. "You get good grades. You're a star on the baseball team." She paused. "When some people get jealous, they try to bring other people down instead of raising themselves up. And you have to realize that there are people who just aren't as capable as you are of the kinds of success you've achieved. Not everyone is smart. Not everyone is athletic. Not every kid in school has an adult who gives a damn about them."

Staring across the field, Luke snorted. "I guess I'm lucky?" His words brimmed with sarcasm. He'd lost his mother to violence, and his father—currently in prison for fraud—was worse than useless.

"In some ways, yes." Bree paused, searching for the right words, afraid she'd get it wrong. "I've lived through a great deal of tragedy."

Luke glanced at her.

Bree rarely spoke of her childhood with the kids. "But I consider myself lucky. I have you and Kayla, Uncle Adam, Dana, Matt. At first, I resisted appreciating all I've been given. I tend to look at the worst-case scenario. But I'm trying to do better. I'm learning to enjoy family and friends, to treasure each day, to look forward instead of back. I can't change the past, and I can't control everything, but I can damn well affect my future."

"But what if everyone believes those pictures are real?" Luke finally met her gaze.

"I can only do what I can do," Bree admitted.

"Will you lose your job?"

"It's possible, but it's only a job." There. She'd said it out loud. "I will survive without it."

"It doesn't seem right that you could lose it for no reason."

"No, it doesn't. The world isn't fair, but you know that. I can't control what other people think, say, or do. But I can control my own actions."

He scratched Riot's withers. The horse bobbed his head and lifted his upper lip in approval. Like Bree and Adam, Luke's soul was older than his chronological age. Tragedy and loss had aged him. Bree wasn't often grateful for the horrors of her childhood, but today she appreciated her ability to empathize with Luke. How many people could understand what it was like to lose your mother to murder?

"So you have three days of riding Riot."

"You're not going to ground me or anything?"

"Nope. Promise me you won't do it again, no matter what jerks like Bobby say or do?"

"OK." Luke sounded reluctant, but his voice rang with sincerity. He'd keep his word.

"I understand why Bobby wouldn't tell the principal why you punched him. He'd get into additional trouble for possessing and sharing pornography at school. But why didn't you tell her?"

His face flushed. He blinked but said nothing.

"Let me guess. You didn't want the principal to see the images. I've seen the pictures and the video, Luke. I know they're bad, but remember, it isn't me."

He admitted, "I know they're fake, but . . ." His cheeks reddened.

"It's still embarrassing," Bree finished. "I get it. But I'm going to tell her. She's worried about you. Plus, she should know what Bobby was up to. Harassment is illegal, and I'm sure distributing pornography at school is against the rules."

"OK, I guess." Luke looked away. Looking a little relieved, he rubbed his horse's neck. "Is it OK if I go for a ride?"

"Yeah. That's a great idea."

He went to the barn for a lead rope. Bree headed for the house. In the kitchen, Ladybug greeted her like a furry cannonball. Scratching the dog, Bree watched Luke bridle Riot, swing up onto his back like a TV cowboy, and ride across the meadow bareback. He'd been riding horses practically since he'd been born. He looked like a centaur. Without asking, she knew where he was going—the hilltop in the distance where they'd spread his mother's ashes. It was the same place Bree went when she needed to feel Erin's presence.

Bree called her brother, Adam, and gave him a quick summary of Luke's suspension. "Do you have some time over the next few days to spend with Luke?"

"I'm headed to New York. The gallery manager wants to meet in person to talk about my latest painting."

"Is that good?"

"I don't know." Adam's laugh sounded nervous. "It's different from my other work. Maybe he hates it."

"I think it's the best piece you've ever done," Bree said.

"Thanks. I guess we'll see," Adam said in a resigned voice. "How about I take Luke with me?"

Bree hesitated. Adam used to be very removed from everyone—including her and the kids. Since their sister died, Bree had asked him to be more involved in the kids' lives, and Adam had delivered. She needed to trust him. Plus, a guys' trip with Adam could soothe the sting of not being able to go camping with his friends. "I think he might like that."

"Great," Adam said in a more cheerful tone. "I'll call him."

"Thank you, Adam."

"You don't have to thank me. We're family."

"Yes, we are." Bree ended the call, feeling more hopeful. No matter what happened with her job, she had her family, Dana, and Matt. She would be OK.

Dana stood in the middle of the kitchen, her hands on her hips. "Well?"

Bree filled her in.

"Rotten little fuckers," Dana said. "Deepfake and revenge porn are new ways to abuse women, to take away their power."

"This could literally happen to any woman."

"You need to get your power back."

"Suggestions for doing that?" Bree asked.

"I'd do another press conference. Reveal what's happening. Name names."

"Can't." Bree shook her head. "It's part of an active murder investigation. I've already been accused of orchestrating Oscar's death to conceal corruption. Imagine if I went public with the knowledge that Oscar died shortly after uploading those deepfake images. Plus, we don't know where the videos came from yet. Oscar didn't make them. He just shared them. Matt has some suspicions but no evidence to back them up."

"Then find out who made them." Dana mashed her lips flat. "Think of how many other women will be targeted. Do you want them to be too embarrassed to stop it? Should they just suffer in silence because their abuser found a new way to hurt them?"

"No," Bree admitted with reluctance. "I know you're right, but I can't go public with the suspects and motives in an active investigation."

"I know you can't, but you need to crush some nuts and shut it down."

Bree's phone vibrated and she glanced at it. "It's Matt. I have to get back to work. I've been ignoring him for the last thirty minutes."

"You go. I'll take care of Luke." Dana turned toward the refrigerator. "I'll make some of his favorite foods tonight: chicken parm and lemon bars."

"Thank you for the one thousandth time. I don't know how I would manage to give these kids a decent home without you. You provide the stability they need."

Dana's eyes went misty. "Yeah, well, the appreciation goes both ways. I was so busy kicking asses, I didn't take the time to have kids." Dana had been married and quickly divorced twice. "Thanks for sharing yours."

"For someone who never had kids, you're a hell of a mom." Bree grabbed her phone and headed for the door. On the way to her SUV, she called Matt. "I'm sorry. I needed to focus on Luke. Now I'm headed to Morgan Dane's office. What's up?"

"Have you seen the news?"

Bree's stomach sank. "No. Why?"

"Paris Vickers is calling for your resignation."

CHAPTER
TWENTY-TWO

Still digesting the Crightons' accusations, Bree parked in front of a duplex near the business district of Scarlet Falls. The first-floor unit housed the offices of Morgan Dane, Attorney at Law, and Sharp Investigations. Bree had been here once before, to interview Lincoln Sharp during a previous case.

Bree entered the building, and Morgan Dane greeted her in the foyer of what once had been an apartment. Tall and slim, the lawyer wore a pale blue silk blouse and a single strand of pearls. Her long dark hair hung to her shoulders in elegant waves. The way she enhanced her femininity in a tasteful way reminded Bree of Stephanie Crighton. Did they teach dressing for success in law school? Or was it a learn-by-doing activity? Either way, standing next to Morgan, Bree felt awkward in her bulky body armor under her uniform, thick duty belt, and practical shoes. However, Bree did have a handgun, collapsible baton, and handcuffs handy.

"How are you?" Bree held out a hand. She had met Morgan during a previous case and had been impressed.

"Better than you." Morgan shook it. "Come on back to my office. I hope you don't mind, I roped my husband, Lance Kruger, into our meeting. From what I know of your case, we'll need him." She turned and walked down a hallway.

"All right, but I didn't give you any details on my case." Bree followed.

"You didn't need to." Morgan glanced back. "Technically, I'll hire the investigation firm, so they operate under our attorney-client privilege." She led the way into a medium-size office. A huge whiteboard covered one wall. A tall, beefy blond man drank from a mug.

Morgan introduced them. "Sheriff Taggert, this is Lance Kruger."

They shook hands.

"Coffee?" Lance asked.

"No, thanks." Bree wanted to keep this appointment as brief as possible.

Morgan went behind her desk. Lance perched on the corner. They were a ridiculously good-looking couple, like models for a wedding cake topper.

Bree sat in a guest chair and spilled her guts about the email threats she'd been receiving, then described the deepfake video and images the county forensics department had traced to Oscar's computer.

"I can issue the takedown orders." Morgan folded her hands on her blotter. "We have a cybersecurity expert on staff who is excellent at internet sleuthing. She'll be able to track down shares of the video."

Lance lifted his mug. "In the interest of full disclosure, the expert is my mother."

Morgan's eyes sharpened. "Even she won't be able to find every copy. Once something hits the internet, it's out there for good, and these seem to be going viral, but we'll make it costly for any major site to knowingly share the deepfakes. We'll sue them all. I'll make sure to include the *Daily Grind* and name Paris Vickers." She frowned. "We saw the press conference."

"I'm not litigious," Bree protested. The thought of suing dozens of news agencies made her queasy.

Morgan nodded. "I understand, but in this case, you need to be. You are protecting your reputation, possibly your career. The lawsuits need to make a very loud and very public statement."

Bree must have looked doubtful.

"The images and story are titillating." Morgan swiveled her chair. "A female sheriff appearing in pornography? That's fantasy fodder. The less reputable news agencies will continue to share the video and pictures as long as they generate interest and activity. By suing anyone who publishes them, we cause them to incur legal expenses. We have to make sharing the images cost more than the clicks they generate are worth."

"That's depressing," Bree said.

Morgan sat back. "That's reality."

Bree knew she was right. "OK."

"So, we're doing this?" Lance asked.

"Yes." Bree nodded. There was no point hiring and paying for the best attorney in the area if you weren't going to take her advice.

Lance rose. "I'm going to call my mom and get her started with tracing the deepfakes." He excused himself and left the office.

Assuming the meeting was over, Bree shifted forward, preparing to stand.

"I'd like to talk about another matter." Morgan drummed her fingers on the desktop.

"Okaaaay." Bree settled herself back in the chair. She sensed she wasn't going to like where the conversation was headed.

"The video isn't my only concern." Morgan leaned forward again. "Regarding the other piece from Paris Vickers and the *Daily Grind*, the interview with Bernard Crighton and his daughter, the lawyer—"

"I'm not resigning," Bree interrupted.

"No. Of course not," Morgan said. "But you *do* have a conflict of interest with the Eugene Oscar murder investigation."

Bree blew out a hard breath.

Morgan continued. "Eugene Oscar worked for the sheriff's department. You and he had a conflict. Regardless of the labeling of his exit from the department as retirement, it's known among enough people that you forced him out."

"There's a paper trail of misconduct," Bree protested.

Morgan shook her head. "Which is irrelevant to the discussion."

Bree's instinct was to argue, but she was paying for the lawyer's advice. So Bree shut her mouth and listened.

Morgan tapped a forefinger on the desk. "To make matters worse, if Oscar is the one who uploaded the deepfakes, then you have a personal motive as well as a professional one."

"We didn't know about the deepfakes until after he was dead. The computer forensics tech discovered them on Oscar's computer."

"I understand. But that is impossible for you to prove, and it's terrible optics. If it's leaked to the media—and there are always leaks—you'll be eviscerated on social media."

The word *optics* made Bree grind her molars. "I just want to do my job."

"I come from a family in law enforcement, so I do understand your perspective," Morgan commiserated. "Love it or hate it, social media is our new reality. We must make decisions with it in mind."

Bree exhaled. Did she really have to step away from the investigation? Worse, call the State Police Bureau of Criminal Investigations and hand over her case?

Morgan softened her voice. "Think of it from the family's perspective. You had a major disagreement with Oscar barely two months ago."

"I only wanted him out of my department."

"You tried to have him charged." Morgan held up a hand. "I know. Officially, he retired, but everyone knows."

"He rendered our evidence inadmissible, but we weren't able to prove he'd done so intentionally." Bree had been able to prove only incompetence.

"And he got away with it," Morgan pointed out. "Doesn't that make you mad?"

"It's annoying, sure, but he's out of my hair now . . ." Bree stopped herself. From an objective perspective, she had plenty of motivation to kill Oscar.

Morgan continued: "Now he's dead, and you're in charge of his murder investigation."

Damn it. Morgan was right. Deep down, Bree had known she was too close. She just hadn't wanted to admit it.

Morgan tilted her head. "Also, there's the risk that Bernard Crighton and his daughter will push their agenda until the case is taken from you. It's far better for you to be the one instigating the turnover rather than having the investigation ripped out from under you."

She made an excellent point.

"You're right." Bree emptied her lungs in a hard *whoosh.* "As much as it kills me to do so, I'll recuse myself from the investigation. I'll call BCI today and ask them to take over."

Morgan nodded her approval. "Put out a press release."

Bree exhaled. "I will."

"I'd like to read the statement before you make it," Morgan added.

Bree raised a brow.

Morgan's lips curved. "I'm very good with PR."

"I do not enjoy dealing with the media," Bree admitted.

"Well, then, all the more reason to run the press release past me." Morgan's smile broadened.

"All right." Bree sighed, but she felt marginally better about the situation. Morgan Dane exuded both confidence and common sense. The situation still sucked, but Bree would get through it. She'd had worse. This wasn't the first case she'd had to give to another investigator. She'd live. "Is there anything else I need to do? What about the photo of me and Matt Flynn?"

"Are you involved in a relationship with him?" Morgan asked.

"Yes."

"Do you intend to continue that relationship?"

"Yes," Bree answered.

"Then we will be assertive about your right to date whomever you choose."

Saying it out loud, with no reservations, made her realize that she'd made a choice. Not long ago, she had lived for her work, with no one to share her life but her cranky tomcat. Now she had a life worth living. She'd sacrificed and fought for happiness. She would not give it up. "If it boils down to a choice, then I choose him over the job."

"Let's hope it doesn't come down to that." Morgan pursed her lips. "Before this business with the deepfakes, you had an excellent reputation. People really like you. You generally have great PR. Let's focus on the other legal issues for now. Then we'll figure out how we can spin your relationship with Matt into something positive that the community will embrace."

Spin, another word that gave Bree heartburn. "What do I say if I'm asked?"

"The truth. Matt isn't employed by the county. You're dating. End of story. You have a direct, no-bullshit gaze. Use it."

Bree nodded. "Anything else?"

"I can't think of anything at the moment, but I'll call you if I do. Please don't hesitate to call my cell if you need me." Morgan wrote a number on a business card and handed it to Bree. "I'll keep you informed on the progress with the deepfakes."

Bree rose and held out a hand. "Thank you."

"You are very welcome."

They shook hands over the desk.

Bree didn't ask for a cost estimate. What was the point? She needed them.

She left the office and slid into her vehicle. On the way back to the station, Bree made the call to BCI. As she discussed the case and made arrangements for the files to be picked up that afternoon, she felt less confident about the case surrender. It wasn't in her nature to give up.

The murder investigation was now out of her control. All she could do was hope her decision didn't come back to bite her on the ass.

CHAPTER
TWENTY-THREE

Matt paced as he waited for Bree in the conference room. He'd pressured her to stop hiding their relationship. Being accused of impropriety was exactly the reason she'd wanted to be discreet. But he hadn't wanted to sneak around. He wanted more from a relationship. Companionship, friendship, loyalty, sex.

He wanted it all.

Had he been selfish?

Was this his fault?

Bree was the first person he'd met in his life with whom he felt the kind of connection that could lead to a lifetime commitment. He'd never even considered it before. But *she* made him want more.

She walked into the conference room, closed the door, and sank into a chair. Propping her elbows on her knees, she dropped her head into her hands. "We're giving up the case."

Matt rested a hand on her back. "Seriously?"

"Seriously." She lifted her head and summarized her meeting with Morgan Dane.

"Ask yourself a few hard questions." Matt rubbed between her shoulder blades. "Why is Bernard going on the attack? Why didn't he help you find his sister's killer? And most of all—why did he tell so many lies?"

Bree scrubbed her hands down her face. "He's hiding something."

"Yep, and you were getting close to the truth. The easiest way to keep you from exposing his secret is to force you out of office or off the case."

"And it worked." Her back straightened. "I caved." She glanced at the reports and photos spread out over the table. "Marge is going to inventory, copy, and box everything up. I want a record of everything they take. Major cover-our-butts action. Are all your reports finished?"

Matt nodded. "I'll shred my personal notes."

Cops' personal notes could be subpoenaed by defense attorneys and were generally destroyed after an arrest was made and the case handed over to the prosecutor's office.

"Good," Bree said. "BCI is sending someone for the files later today. They don't want to waste any time."

"The situation is out of your control," Matt said. "But Bernard won't be able to pull the same stunt with BCI. I know some of the detectives over there. They're good. They won't give him a pass because he's indignant and his daughter is a decent lawyer."

"I hope not."

"It's the right thing to do, even if giving up the case is the last thing I want you to do."

"Yeah, I know. But it still stinks."

"It certainly does," Matt said. "But look on the bright side. No more late nights, right? More time with the family. How did it go at the school? Is Luke OK?"

"Some kid at school was sharing the deepfake video. Luke punched him, right in the face."

Matt smiled. "Good kid."

Bree snorted. "You would say that. He's been suspended."

"In this case, that's a badge of honor. He stood up for you."

"He did." She seemed to shake off her mood.

"If I saw someone sharing that video, I'd punch them too."

"I've no doubt of that." Her eyes softened for a few seconds, then she frowned. "I haven't heard from Todd this morning. Have you?"

"No. He didn't answer his phone."

Worry lines bracketed Bree's eyes. "I'll send a deputy out to his house to check on him."

Someone knocked. Matt pulled his hand off Bree's back as the door opened, hating that necessity. *Damn it.* This was exactly what he hadn't wanted: a relationship that felt as wrong as it did right.

One that needed to be hidden.

Marge slipped into the room, closing the door behind her and leaning on it. "Madeline Jager is in the lobby. She called three times while you were gone. Now, she's ragey. Want me to send her away?"

Bree stood and flattened a hand on the table. "No. I'll talk to her. If I avoid her, she'll smell weakness."

"OK." Marge sounded doubtful as she turned and opened the door.

"Sheriff Taggert! You can't avoid me!" Madeline shouted from outside the door.

"Christ on a cracker," Marge muttered under her breath. "She must have snuck past the desk."

Matt braced himself. It felt cowardly, but he'd been hoping to slink away before Bree confronted Jager. Angry politicians made *him* ragey. Their emotions always seemed insincere and manufactured for a specific response.

Calculated.

Jager brushed past Marge, who cocked an irritated brow.

"It's all right, Marge," Bree said.

Marge bowed out, and Matt was a little jealous.

Standing in the doorway, the county supervisor was *too* everything. Like a Hollywood star with unrealistic expectations of fighting her age, her hair was too red, her face too plastic, her heels too high. Right now, her anger was just as over the top. "I've been trying to reach you for hours. The sheriff is supposed to be available during business hours."

"It's been a busy morning," Bree said.

Jager propped one hand on a hip and glared. "Well, I need to speak with you."

"OK." Bree gestured toward a chair.

At Bree's immediate agreement, the defiance seemed to leave Jager, like air leaking from a raft. She closed the door and crossed to the table.

"Did we have an appointment?" Bree asked.

Jager pulled out a chair. "No, but—"

"Of course I'll always try to be available to the county supervisors, but we've been working a double-murder investigation." Bree motioned, Vanna White–like, to the crime scene photos spread out on the table.

Thinking Bree would want to keep the images under wraps, Matt started gathering the photos. Bree stopped him with a look and an almost imperceptible shake of her head.

Matt rose. "I'll give you some privacy."

"You're part of this," Jager snapped.

Matt bit back a retort, but it wasn't easy. Instead, he said, "I'm Matt Flynn." He held out a hand. "Have we met?"

She glanced at his hand as if it were covered in manure. "I know who you are."

"OK, then." Matt lowered his hand and sat back down with a shrug.

Bree waited for the county supervisor to sit before taking her own seat. She faced her across the table.

Jager leaned on her forearms. Her gaze dropped to the table and the crime scene photos. Her eyes widened, and she recoiled. Matt noted she was staring at a particularly bloody photo of Oscar's dead body, still tied to the chair. Bree's crow's-feet deepened slightly, and Matt realized she'd wanted the photos to put Jager off guard.

Disconcerted, Jager blinked a few times, then visibly regrouped. "Sheriff, corruption won't be tolerated."

"What corruption?" Bree asked.

"All of it." Jager waved a loose hand between Bree and Matt. Bree lifted an eyebrow and waited. Matt sat back, crossed his arms, and watched. On one hand, he felt bad for insisting on taking their relationship into the public arena and bringing this kind of scrutiny to Bree's door. He'd made her job harder, her world messier. On the other hand, Bree could handle herself. In that respect, he sensed the next exchange would be popcorn-worthy.

"You're going to need to be more specific." Bree folded her hands on the table and held Jager's gaze with an unflinching stare.

"We'll start with the pornography." Jager huffed.

Matt couldn't hold back. "Which is fake."

Jager shot him a dirty look. "And *your* relationship"—she wagged a finger between him and Bree—"is completely inappropriate."

Bree tilted her head. "How so?"

"What do you mean, how so?" Jager stammered. "Is it true that you're sleeping with Investigator Flynn?"

"The nature of our relationship is none of your business," Bree said.

"I'll take that as a yes." Jager thumped on the table with one fist. "He works for you. He's literally sleeping with his boss."

Matt raised a hand and wiggled his fingers. "And I'm right here."

Jager spared him a brief irritated glance, then returned her focus to Bree.

"Actually, Mr. Flynn is an independent civilian consultant," Bree corrected. "He is not an employee of the county."

"Tomato, tom-ah-to. The county pays him. It's the same thing." Jager shook her red bangs off her face.

"Except, legally, it's not." Bree's tone projected zero tolerance for bullshit. She gave Jager her stern face. "Matt and I are dating. There's nothing illegal about it."

"It might not be illegal, but it's definitely unethical to channel county money to your boyfriend." Jager adjusted an earring. Personal grooming was a sign of stress. She wasn't as confident about her accusations as she was pretending to be. Jager was a lot of bluster. Unfortunately, in politics, bluster was very effective.

"Matt is a former deputy." Bree nodded toward him. "He was a seasoned investigator long before I came to Randolph County. There is no one who doubts his expertise. We only call him in when we have a case too complex for me to handle solo. I have too many other responsibilities to be able to dedicate my time one hundred percent to any one investigation. Since there's no room in the budget for a dedicated detective, by using Matt on a case-by-case basis, we save the county a significant amount of money."

"That is not how the board sees it." The muscles of Jager's face shifted as if she were trying to say something but couldn't decide on the right words. "You have a conflict of interest with your current investigation."

"Do I?" Bree asked.

"You knew the victim." Jager's frustration all but seeped from her pores.

"This is a small town." Bree lifted a shoulder. "Everyone knows everyone."

"He used to work for you." Jager pushed: "You forced him out."

"That *is* true," Bree acknowledged. "Which puts me in the unique position of having background knowledge of one of the victims."

"I heard he was the one who published the pornographic pictures of you," Jager said, her tone smug.

Bree shouldn't have been surprised. Leaks happened. "We didn't know that until the day after the bodies were discovered."

"Prove it." Jager pushed away from the table.

Bree's face tightened, showing the first chink in her defense. "How do I prove I didn't know something? It's not possible."

"Well, then . . ." Jager trailed off, as if she'd made her point. "Mr. Crighton and his attorney have alleged that you are targeting him as the prime suspect for his sister's murder to distract from your own potential guilt."

"In that regard, now that certain facts have come to light about Eugene Oscar's life, I've decided we're too close to the investigation. I've already called on BCI to take the case. I don't know which detective will be assigned, but I'm sure you can find out. Someone from the Albany office is en route to pick up the files."

Jager opened her mouth to respond, but no words came out. She hadn't expected that.

The door opened. Marge stood in the opening. "Sheriff, I need to see you. Now."

"We're in a meeting," Jager protested.

"Excuse me." Ignoring the supervisor, Bree hurried around the table and out the door. It closed with a solid thump.

Matt stared at Jager, letting the uncomfortable silence hover for two long minutes. She glared back at him for a few seconds. Then one of them broke eye contact, and it wasn't Matt. Jager checked her phone. Then Bree pushed the door open and motioned for him. "We have to go."

Jager leaped to her feet. "You can't blow me off."

Bree ignored her. Matt met her gaze. She was wearing her cop face. Only someone who knew her well would read the worry in her eyes. He rose and headed for the door, leaving the county supervisor sputtering, "I've never been treated so rudely."

Bree craned her head to peer around him. "Ms. Jager, I apologize for cutting our discussion short. You can schedule another meeting with my administrator." She pivoted on her heel. Matt followed her out of the station.

"There's a fire at the vacant farm next to my place. The responding deputy says there's a message for me. Fire department has been called." She rushed across the blacktop and jumped into her SUV.

Matt slid into the passenger seat and buckled his belt. Flipping on the light bar and siren, Bree stomped on the gas pedal and sped out of the parking lot.

"I'd better call Dana." Bree used her hands-free setting. After Dana answered, Bree said, "There's a fire next door."

Dana paused, then said, "I'm looking out the window. I see a thin plume of smoke. Nothing crazy."

"Is Luke back from his ride?" Bree asked.

"I don't know. I'll check the barn. Hold on." After a brief pause, Dana said, "He's not back. I'm going out to look for him. I'll keep you posted."

"Same." Bree ended the call. Her fingers tightened on the steering wheel until the knuckles went white. The tires squealed as the vehicle took a turn fast.

Matt grabbed the armrest as the SUV leaned through a curve in the road. Bree cut several minutes off the short drive by pushing the SUV to its limits. As they neared the farm, they could see black smoke rising into the air. Bree slowed, then turned into the driveway. A patrol vehicle was already parked on the grass. Bree pulled up next to it.

Fifty feet in front of the vehicles, a bonfire burned on the front lawn. Matt stared through the windshield. "Why would someone set a bonfire?"

"If it were winter, I'd say to keep warm, but it's seventy-five degrees today."

"Some people just like to destroy things. Others just like fire." Matt scanned the property. The barn was huge and falling down. Beyond it, empty fields rolled into the distance. There was a huge garage as well, and a silo. "What kind of farm was this?"

"They grew corn and wheat, kept chickens, raised the occasional steer or pig for meat. I only met them a handful of times before they went bankrupt."

Matt noted the knee-high weeds around the foundation and heavy graffiti on the barn and house. "How long has the place been empty?"

"A few months," Bree said.

Matt focused on the house and froze. It was a two-story white building, a stereotypical farmhouse, complete with a wrap-around porch. A tree had fallen onto the porch roof. The words FUCK SHERIFF TAGGERT had been painted across the front of the house. "I guess that's the personal message."

Bree sighed. "Looks like it."

Matt squinted at the windows of the house. Then he turned toward the barn, looking for potential snipers. "Feels like a trap."

"Yep." Bree grabbed the radio mic and reported her arrival on scene to dispatch before stepping out of the vehicle.

Matt got out and closed the passenger door. Warm wind sent dead leaves tumbling across the cracked grass.

Juarez walked over. He was one of the newer deputies in her small department. He'd finished his field training and was out on solo patrol, but he had only about a month of real experience. He still sported an academy buzz that made him look like one of the cast of *21 Jump Street*.

"What's the situation?" Bree asked.

"Fire department is on the way." Juarez pointed to the message for Bree. "I thought you'd want to see it." The red-and-white lights from the roof of his patrol car swirled on his face, highlighting the tension in his features.

Bree scrutinized the area. Matt did the same. The bonfire appeared to have been built from broken boards taken from the partially collapsed front porch. Sections had been ripped out of the steps. Vines covered the foundation. Reachable windows had been boarded up, but several sheets of plywood had been pried off and tossed aside.

There were a dozen locations someone could watch them from without them knowing. A creepy sensation crawled up his spine.

"Have you checked the property?" Bree asked.

"No, ma'am." Juarez flushed. "I wanted to wait for backup."

"Smart." Bree nodded her approval. "This situation has the potential to be an ambush."

Juarez's tanned throat shifted as he swallowed. Another sheriff's vehicle drove up, and a deputy stepped out.

Matt shrugged into his vest and retrieved Bree's rifle from the back of the vehicle. He couldn't shoot a handgun to his satisfaction with his off hand, but his aim with a long gun was still excellent. "House, barn, or garage first?"

"We'll take them left to right: barn, house, garage." She started toward the barn. Juarez followed at her heels. Matt brought up the rear. They jogged across the grass toward the barn. The double doors were open, and they could see into the big, empty space. Except for two small pens, the space appeared to have been used to store large equipment.

Juarez went up a ladder and checked the loft. "Clear."

"House is next." Bree turned. She sent her deputies to the back door. She and Matt approached the front. They skirted the missing boards and climbed the steps.

Matt noted multiple potential points of entry for trespassers. The front door hung open. The plywood covering a low window had been pried off, the panes smashed. He peered through the broken glass. Enough sunlight streamed through the window and door that they wouldn't need flashlights. There was no furniture inside. Overturned milk crates formed a semicircle facing the wood fireplace. The floor was covered with cigarette butts and trash. Someone had used the house as a shelter or party spot. The homeless were always looking for somewhere to sleep. Kids were always looking for a place to drink, smoke weed, and have sex. Abandoned buildings were great places for drug dealers to conduct business and for addicts to crash.

They flanked the front door. Through the doorway, he could see down a narrow hall into the kitchen.

A can rattled. A rat squeaked and darted across the floor of the living room, its thin pink tail disappearing down the corridor. Under his body-armor vest, sweat dripped down Matt's spine. The hairs on the back of his neck prickled.

Bree went through the door first. Matt shifted the rifle to his shoulder and followed her. She always led from the front, never the rear. Matt slipped into the room after her. Empty rooms were easy to clear, and they rapidly moved from the living room to the hallway that led to the back of the house. Matt and Bree had cleared enough buildings to work as a team with little communication.

Juarez and the other deputy were at the kitchen door. They entered the kitchen from the back as Bree and Matt emerged from the hallway.

"Clear." Matt shifted the AR-15 to the stairwell. With Bree at his heels, he went to the bottom of the stairs. Peering through the spindles, he put his rifle to his shoulder again. Wary of a potential ambush— stairwells were called *fatal funnels* for a reason—they wasted no time clearing the steps, then proceeding to the three bedrooms and two baths on the second floor.

They filed downstairs and headed out the back door toward the extra-large garage. With three bays plus a set of huge rolling doors, the structure had likely been used to store combines and other heavy farm equipment.

The door to the garage sagged on its hinges. Matt put his shoulder to the frame. When Bree and her deputies were in place, he opened the door and went through into a small office with a restroom. "Clear."

The water must have been turned off, because the toilet and sink were both in pieces. The office opened into a hallway that led to two storage rooms and finally opened into the huge vehicle storage space. Across an expanse of concrete, two more doors were closed.

Keeping low, Matt filed through the final opening and pressed his shoulder to Bree's.

Wind blew through a missing window. Trash and dead leaves tumbled across the concrete. A rope creaked. Matt's heart jolted.

In the back of the area, a human figure hung from the neck. Matt's thoughts went to his unanswered texts from Todd.

No. Please, no.

CHAPTER TWENTY-FOUR

Pulse slamming, Bree leveled her weapon at the hanging figure.

Next to her, Juarez jumped and yelled, "Freeze!"

Bree registered instantly that the figure wasn't touching the ground. Hung by the neck, whoever it was had to be dead. With a twinge of dread, she thought of Todd. Relief surged through her when she realized the body wasn't big enough to be his.

Matt exhaled hard. "It's not him."

"I know." She shifted her attention to the rest of the space.

Juarez's ragged breathing sawed in and out of his lungs.

Bree moved through the opening and swept her weapon around the space. She glanced at her deputies. The older one had experience, but Juarez's eyes were wide with adrenaline. She didn't need to check in with Matt. She knew he was solid.

For a brief second, she considered sending Juarez to the rear. But he needed the experience and confidence that finishing this task would give him. How would he gain experience if they didn't let him? If she pulled him back, the only thing he'd gain from this call was the knowledge that she didn't trust him. If she didn't trust him with her life, she couldn't expect the rest of her deputies to work with him. Lastly, there was only one way to find out how a new officer responded in a stressful situation. So, she kept him moving.

Fear wasn't the issue. Intelligent people were afraid in dangerous situations. But could he control his fear? He needed to function despite the fear. That was the key. Ordinary people ran away from danger. Cops ran toward it.

With a gesture, she sent him to the other side of the garage, toward the closed door. He nodded, his face pale in the sun pouring through a broken window near the ceiling. Matt and the older deputy veered left, covering the back of the garage.

Bree took point. The door, off its hinges, lay on its back like a wounded soldier. She examined the visible slice of room, then met Juarez's gaze.

He nodded and mouthed, "Clear."

She gestured and slid through the doorway into another spacious room. A pegboard was attached to the wall. Wear marks on it suggested it had been used to store tools. The air smelled faintly of oil, and scratches on the walls showed where a long piece of furniture had once stood. A workbench maybe. Farm equipment needed maintenance and repair. They had to do it somewhere.

The room had no additional exits. A dirty mattress lay in the corner. Someone had been sleeping here. A broken office chair sat in the opposite corner. Missing three of its wheels, it listed drunkenly to one side. Juarez pulled his flashlight and shone it on the mattress. His light illuminated a sleeping bag. Bree covered Juarez while he walked closer and kicked the sleeping bag away with a toe. Empty.

Juarez's lungs expelled air like a bellows. Bree stood still for a few seconds until it no longer sounded as if her deputy was going to hyperventilate and until her own breathing approached normal. She slid her gun into its holster. "Good job. Let's get back to that body."

Juarez nodded. He looked a little sick from the adrenaline rush, but his eyes held both relief and satisfaction.

They turned and filed out of the room. With knowledge that no threats remained in the building, Bree returned to the hanging body and the details she hadn't noticed while she'd been focused on clearing the building. For one, the garage carried the faint smell of garbage but no decomposition. Even a relatively fresh body put off an odor. Urine and feces released at the moment of death.

She pulled out her flashlight and switched it on. Even before the light fell on the figure, her brain was registering that something was off about the shape. The limbs were oddly bent, almost cartoonish. Relief welled, followed by curiosity. Not a body.

What is it?

She moved closer. "Mannequin?"

Matt's rifle hung by his side, pointing at the floor. "I don't think so."

They walked closer. Bree shone the beam on the shape's face. It was flat with garish features printed on it. The mouth was disturbingly puckered, an actual hole, lined with bright red lips permanently fixed in an O.

The older deputy gasped.

"Shit." Juarez flinched. "Sorry," he said, as if embarrassed he'd been frightened.

"Don't be," Matt said. "That thing is scary."

Bree studied it. "Is it some kind of weird doll?"

Matt cleared his throat. "Sort of."

In the corner of her eye, she caught bright red spots on Juarez's face. She turned back to the doll. It almost looked like a balloon . . . A wave of gross washed over her as she realized what it was. "For the love of Pete . . . It's a blow-up sex doll."

She glanced at Matt, expecting him to be shaking his head, but there was no sign of humor on his face. His mouth was locked in a grim frown as he stared at the doll. She turned back and played her light down the rest of its body.

As one would expect, the doll was naked. Her beam fell on its huge breasts, where a badge had been drawn on with black Sharpie. Someone had written SHERIFF TAGGERT in block print. Three red spots had been drawn onto the chest. The paint had been allowed to drip.

Like bullet wounds.

A sense of dread settled over Bree, and the relief she'd felt a minute earlier dissipated like smoke in the wind as she examined the rest of the doll. A police baton protruded from between its legs. A handcuff dangled from one balloon-like hand, and the rope around its neck had been fashioned into a noose.

Bree stepped back. She had no words.

"Clearly, this is a threat." Matt's tone was controlled, but the undercurrent was angry.

"Ma'am?" Juarez had moved a few feet away and pulled out his own flashlight. He faced the opposite direction, sweeping his light over the rest of the space. The six-bay space was mostly empty except for takeout containers, bottles, and other trash. On the walls, faded graffiti had been written over with fresh, bright red paint.

The new profanity covered the walls with messages. Bree read KILL THE WHORE, FUCK TAGGERT, and SLUT TAGGERT WILL PAY. All around the words, the "artist" had painted crude yet clear images of a large-breasted female being raped in multiple positions. In case she didn't grasp the fact that the females being raped were supposed to be her, the artist had labeled them with a sheriff's badge and her name.

She felt a little sick as she took in a depiction of a violent gang rape. The female was on her hands and knees, being assaulted by three males simultaneously. The male kneeling behind her held a rope tied around her neck. Bloody tears leaked from her eyes.

There was no reason for her to be embarrassed. She hadn't done anything. Yet she was filled with shame. The scene was graphic and disturbing and humiliating in a way that wasn't logical.

Matt muttered something under his breath. "Sick."

Get a grip.

She glanced at Matt. His features were locked in his stony cop face, as were the other deputy's. Bree turned to Juarez, who clearly hadn't mastered the flat cop stare. His cheeks were still beet red.

Bree had been a patrol officer, then a homicide detective in Philadelphia before she'd moved back to her hometown of Grey's Hollow. She'd seen things this young rookie likely couldn't yet imagine. He was a local, not a jaded city cop. He hadn't witnessed the terrible crimes Bree had. He'd gone to Catholic school. He was, for lack of a better term, a nice young man.

And with that thought, Bree felt a thousand years old.

But then, her hardened exterior had as much to do with her personal past as her career. At the age of eight, when her father had shot their mother and then killed himself, Bree had ceased being a child. She'd lived true horror in grade school.

Juarez cleared his throat. "What should I do with it?"

Bree mustered her no-nonsense attitude. "The usual. Take photos, bag it, and type up your report. You can try and get prints." She looked around. "Did the property owner make the call?"

"No, ma'am." Juarez vibrated with anger. "It was a mobile number." He pulled a notepad from his pocket. "The name was Mr. Skunt."

"Skunt." Matt raised a suspicious brow.

Blushing more, Juarez reached for his radio mic. "I'll confirm with dispatch."

Bree stopped him. "Use your cell."

Even as she said it, she realized trying to keep the details from the rest of the department and other local law enforcement was futile.

But Juarez pulled his cell phone from his pocket and made the call. A few minutes later, he ended the call with a frown. "The caller was male. He gave the name of Mr. Louis Skunt."

Repeating the name silently to herself, Bree sighed.

Matt said it out loud. "Loose Cunt."

"Yeah." Juarez's tone went flat. "Dispatch didn't get it, and neither did I."

Bree said nothing. Her older deputy shook his head.

Matt pointed to the wall, then to Bree. "This is a direct threat to you."

She read the messages on the wall again. Her gaze fell to the drawn-on badge with her name written on it. Fear coiled in her belly. This was way too close to her home and her family, and the threat was extremely personal. "Yes, it is."

Juarez propped a hand on his duty belt. "I should have realized the caller wasn't legitimate right off."

"Don't beat yourself up." Bree circled a hand in the air. "No one would have expected this."

"This is no prank." Matt shook his head. "The call might have used a fake name, but this threat is very real."

Bree admitted it with one quick nod. "But it isn't the first threat or nasty message I've received. Hell, it isn't even the first one I've gotten this week." But this one was different.

Juarez blinked in surprise at her.

"I get nasty phone messages and emails all the time." She gestured toward the walls. "Many are sexually explicit or violent," she admitted. "This is, however, the most elaborate and disturbing threat."

"Someone went to a good deal of effort here." Matt leveled her with a look that said he wasn't happy.

Bree pulled out her cell phone and took photos of the doll and messages. The flash went off with each photo, highlighting the ugliness. When she'd finished, she turned away and walked out of the building.

The deputies and Matt followed her outside. After the dimness of the building, the sunlight seemed harsh, and she shaded her eyes. She caught a whiff of smoke. The fire was running out of fuel and burning itself out, but sirens wailed.

Bree stared across the field at her own house in the distance. "Why did they pick this place?"

"It's vacant. Close proximity to your house means it was a good bet that you'd come personally. Plus it's threatening to have this"—Matt gestured toward the garage—"near your home. Also, your place is wired tight and covered with security cameras, which makes it a riskier target."

"And Dana is there—armed," Bree added, grateful for her highly suspicious and very capable best friend.

"This was as close as they could get to you and yours."

Too close.

Two engines turned into the driveway and parked. Firemen unrolled hoses and put out the small fire in a few minutes.

Bree's phone buzzed. She read a text from Dana. LUKE IS BACK. ALL FINE HERE.

She answered, THX. Then she added, TAKE EXTRA CARE THERE.

Dana replied, WILL DO.

Bree went to her vehicle and opened the door. She turned to Juarez. "Follow up with the property owner. You can try to trace the mobile number, but it'll probably be a burner."

"Yes, ma'am." Juarez's jaw sawed back and forth, as if he was grinding his teeth. "I'll dust for prints too." He lowered his voice. "I don't want to speak out of turn here, ma'am. But please be careful."

"Thank you for your concern. I do appreciate it."

Juarez grabbed a fingerprinting kit from his vehicle and headed back toward the garage. The older deputy followed. Trusting her deputies to process the scene, Bree climbed into her SUV.

Matt slid into the passenger seat. "Like Juarez said, someone has it out for you. Please be careful."

"I will." Bree waved a hand at the building. "There's a lot of hate out there these days."

"And lately, a good portion of it is directed at you."

She swallowed and took two deep breaths. She couldn't let fear paralyze her. She needed to catch this bastard, and for that she'd need a cool head.

With a glance back at the graffiti on the house, she vowed that she would stop him before he made good on his threats.

CHAPTER TWENTY-FIVE

In the passenger seat of the SUV, Matt tried to cool the rage burning through him. He was a supporter of law and order, but the threats to Bree made him want to exact some vigilante justice.

Bree stopped at a light and glanced at her phone screen. "Collins is at Todd's place. His personal vehicle is parked at his house. He's not answering the door."

Dread lumped like cold oatmeal in Matt's gut.

Bree gunned the engine.

Fifteen minutes later, they parked in front of the small bungalow. Matt scanned the large lot. Woods provided privacy—but also isolation.

They stepped out of the vehicle.

Deputy Collins stood next to her patrol car. "I walked around the house. All the doors are locked. I looked in the windows but couldn't see anyone." She gestured toward Todd's SUV. "The hood is cold."

So the SUV hadn't been driven recently. Matt and Bree went to the front door. Bree knocked and pressed the bell. The ring echoed inside the house.

The front door was solid steel. They went around back and climbed the steps of a wooden deck. The rear door had nine panes of glass set into the top half. Matt cupped his hand over his eyes and peered inside. Dark and empty. The house felt vacant, and he knew before setting foot inside that Todd wasn't here.

The locks were dead bolts—not easy to pick. Bree pulled out a collapsible baton and used the handle to break a pane of glass. She reached through the hole and unlocked the door, then led the way inside straight into the kitchen.

"I'll check the bedrooms." Matt headed for a short hallway. No Todd in the main bedroom or attached bath. No keys or wallet on the dresser. The second bedroom was also empty. Matt checked the closets. No Todd. There were times when he hated being right.

Collins ducked into a half bath.

They met back in the living room. By the front door, a bowl sat on a small table. Matt peered inside. "Did either of you see his keys or wallet?"

Bree shook her head.

"No," said Collins. "Yet his vehicle is here."

"I don't like this." Matt scanned the surfaces of the furniture.

"Me either," Bree agreed.

Through a window, Matt spotted a shed in the backyard. "Did you look in there?" he asked Collins.

"No," she said.

Matt went out the back door. He crossed the yard and opened the wooden door. Nothing but lawn tools and equipment. Bree was walking around the house. Matt followed her.

She stopped in the side yard, staring at the ground.

"What?" he asked.

She held up a hand in a stop gesture. "Don't move."

Matt froze. Something silver flashed in a small pile of dead leaves. "His keys."

Bree squatted and leaned closer to the ground. She pointed to a few spots on the grass. Dark red blotches the size of quarters. "And blood."

Matt's sense of discomfort shifted into a blaring alarm.

Straightening, she surveyed the ground. "We need to search the area." From ten feet behind them, Collins said, "I'll call for additional units."

"Watch where you step," Bree called. "Blood is hard to see out here."

Matt pulled out his phone. "Cady is probably at my place. I'll have her bring Brody over. He'll find Todd faster than fifty deputies."

"Collins, bring evidence markers back with you!" Bree shouted to her deputy.

With her gaze on the ground, Collins rushed toward her vehicle.

Matt dialed his sister's number.

She answered on the second ring. "Yes?"

"Todd's gone missing. Would you bring Brody to his house?" Matt gave her the address.

"Oh, n-no!" Cady stammered. "Of course. I'll be there ASAP. Do you know what happened?"

"No. Not at all." Ending the call, Matt spied another spot of blood about five feet away. "The grass is crushed here too."

Collins returned with another deputy in tow. She handed Bree a small stack of yellow evidence markers.

Bree set one next to the original splotches of blood and the second group Matt had found. Crouching, she examined the nearby ground.

Matt glanced at the neighbors' houses. He turned back to Todd's house and scanned the facade. "I don't see any surveillance cameras on Todd's house, and we're too far away to trigger the motion sensor on his doorbell camera, but let's check with the neighbors."

"On it." The other deputy strode toward the house across the street.

Matt went back into Todd's house and grabbed a dirty T-shirt from the laundry hamper.

Bree continued to search the grass for more blood. By the time Cady arrived with Brody, she'd found a spot on the driveway ten feet away.

Cady let Brody out of her minivan. "I brought his working harness too." She handed it to Matt.

He crouched in front of his dog and fastened the harness. Brody snapped to attention. Matt let him have a long sniff of the T-shirt, then gave him the command to find.

The dog ignored the blood spots. He raised his nose, seeking a scent on the air. Then he surged ahead, walking in a spiral. Expanding the circles, he headed toward a thick patch of underbrush. His head dropped, and he took a deep sniff of the foliage.

With complete faith in his dog, Matt let him do his thing. Brody needed little guidance.

Looking back at Matt, he sat and barked.

"He found something." Matt moved forward and crouched. "Does anybody have a flashlight?"

Bree rushed forward. She shone a light on the underbrush. Something glimmered. "There! Collins!" she shouted. "I need an evidence marker. Bring the camera."

Collins hurried to her patrol car, then back to the brush. She snapped a picture, placed the yellow triangle on the ground, then snapped another before stepping back.

Bree pulled on a pair of gloves and reached into the thicket. When she sat back on her heels, a silver watch dangled from her finger. "Does anyone know if this is Todd's?"

Matt leaned in for a better look. "I don't think so. Todd's watch is black."

Bree pulled an evidence bag from her pocket and dropped the watch into it. She glanced at Collins. "Keep looking here. See if there's anything else."

Collins pulled a flashlight from her duty belt and shone it into the brush.

Brody, satisfied they'd found the evidence he'd sniffed out, stood and pulled on the leash. Matt followed, the tension in the leash radiating through his bones.

"Where's he going?" Collins asked.

"No idea, but he's never wrong." Matt let Brody work. "You'll learn to trust your dog."

Brody surged ahead, leaning into the harness. Every dozen feet or so, he paused, smelled the air, and adjusted his trajectory. He was keen on whatever smell was in his nose.

"There's a path through the underbrush." Bree pointed to a trail of broken twigs and crushed grass.

They walked through the woods between Todd's house and the neighbor's, until they reached the road. Brody stopped and growled. Matt spotted a smear of blood on the weeds at the edge of the blacktop. From the underbrush to the street, two long lines were scraped into the dirt.

"Drag marks," Bree said.

Matt nodded, his sense of urgency building.

Nose down, Brody shuffled to the pavement. He raised his head and sniffed in several directions, then sat and whined.

"Good boy." Disappointed, Matt rubbed his ears. "The trail ends here."

"They took him away by vehicle." Bree stood in the road and looked hard in each direction.

Matt pointed to the shoulder of the road, where the earth was soft. "We have tire tracks." Which would be useful only when they had a vehicle for comparison.

Bree reached for her phone. "I'm calling forensics to get those cast. They can give Todd's front yard and the woods a second look."

They returned to Todd's driveway.

Cady, who had been leaning on her minivan, shifted forward. "Did you find him?"

Matt shook his head.

Cady nodded toward the evidence markers on the grass. "That's blood, isn't it?"

Matt didn't want to worry her. He knew she liked Todd, and suspected Todd liked her back. If her asshole of an ex-husband hadn't made Cady man-and-relationship-shy, something would probably have developed between them by now. Cady might be his little sister, but she wasn't a child. As much as he hated to deliver the bad news, she deserved the truth. "Probably."

She nodded and put a knuckle to her mouth.

Bree joined him in the driveway. They stood together in front of Todd's vehicle.

"We went to the gun range last night, talked to Jim Rogers." Matt thought back over the conversation. "Maybe someone saw us and didn't like it."

Bree surveyed the front yard and surrounding forest. "Or didn't like something else he was working on. We have been stirring things up."

"That's the job, right?" Matt imagined Todd pulling into his driveway. "Todd gets out of his vehicle and heads up the driveway."

"Someone comes out of the woods and jumps him."

Matt eyed the trampled grass next to the driveway. "More than one person."

"He would have fought back."

Matt nodded. "Todd's no slouch in a fight. He would have left marks on anyone who jumped him."

"Forensics will collect blood samples. Maybe some of it is from his attackers." Bree held up the evidence bag. "One of them lost a watch."

Matt held out his hand, and she dropped the evidence bag into it. He turned the watch over and examined the back. "There's an engraved inscription." He tilted it for better light. "AD EOW 6/16/1983."

They looked at each other.

"EOW," Matt repeated.

"End of watch." Bree's mouth turned down at the corners. "A memorial for a fallen officer."

And Matt knew. "AD is Arthur Dylan."

"Let me guess." Bree's brows dropped in fierce intensity. "That was Brian Dylan's father."

Matt handed her the evidence bag, whipped out his cell phone, and called Marge.

"Did you find Todd?" she asked immediately on answering.

"Not yet. Do you know the date Deputy Arthur Dylan was killed in the line of duty? It was in the '80s."

"Hold on. It's engraved on the plaque in the hallway." Her breaths quickened as she rushed through the station. She wheezed. "June 16, 1983."

"Thanks."

"Matt, find him," Marge pleaded.

"We intend to." Matt lowered the phone and turned to Bree. "You heard?"

"I did." Bree was already headed toward her vehicle. "Dylan grabbed Todd, but why?"

As they approached the driveway, Cady stepped forward. Her face was pale, making her freckles stand out. "Well?"

Matt slipped his phone back into his pocket. "We think he was taken away in a vehicle."

"Oh, no!" Cady hugged her own waist.

"We're going to find him," Matt said with more conviction than he felt. Would they find him alive or dead? But damn, his sister did not need any more stress in her life.

The line between Cady's brows deepened. "Do you want me to take Brody home?"

Matt glanced back at his dog. "No. I might need him." Dylan's property was extensive. But if Todd was there, Brody would find him.

"I have a portable bowl and some kibble." She ran to her minivan and took a tote bag from the back seat. Returning, she thrust it at him. "I'll leave them with you in case you need it."

"You saved me a trip home." The day was bound to be long. Matt didn't mind missing meals but wouldn't allow his dog to go hungry. "Thanks." He kissed his sister's cheek. "I'll keep you posted."

Nodding, she turned and went back to her van, her steps dragging.

A deputy came running from across the street. "Bingo. The neighbor has a camera on his vehicles. There have been break-ins lately. Last night, starting at 10:06, a pickup truck loaded with men drove past Chief Deputy Harvey's house three times."

"Tell me you could see the license plate," Bree said.

The deputy's eyes gleamed. "Got it. The vehicle belongs to Shane Bartholomew. He lives in Grey's Hollow."

"Pick him up. Bring him to the station," Bree instructed.

"What do I tell him?" the deputy asked.

Bree paused. "Tell him we need his help in solving a crime. Don't treat him like he's a suspect. Treat him like he's important."

"Yes, ma'am." He returned to his vehicle and drove off.

Bree headed for her own SUV. Brody trotted at Matt's side as he broke into a jog to catch up with Bree.

"We need a search warrant for Dylan's place." He opened the back door, and the dog jumped in.

She glanced at the watch in the evidence bag in her hand. "This is the only piece of evidence we have. It's not enough to prove a crime even happened, let alone establish probable cause for a warrant. All we know is that Todd is out of reach. There are a couple of blood spots on the driveway, and we found a watch we *think* belongs to Brian Dylan in the woods. We *believe* Todd was jumped and abducted, but we don't have any actual evidence that happened. He could have cut his hand and gone to a doctor for stitches. He could have lost his phone."

"We need someone to confirm that Dylan wore that watch."

Bree nodded. "Let's hope this Shane Bartholomew is that person."

CHAPTER TWENTY-SIX

Bree stood in the monitoring room and stared at the screen showing interview room one and sized up Shane Bartholomew. Her deputy had found him at home, sleeping. His truck had been parked in his driveway. Spots of blood had been visible in plain sight in the truck bed, and an electronic search warrant had been obtained. A forensics tech was currently going through the pickup for additional evidence. Any lab tests on trace evidence would take too long, but the tire tracks on the road near Todd's house matched Shane's pickup. The vehicle caught on surveillance video definitely belonged to him.

They had no evidence Shane had done anything wrong, but they needed him to spill his guts.

Next to her, Matt sat at the table staring at the monitor, a laptop open in front of him. While they gathered enough evidence for the warrant to search Dylan's property, Bree sent a deputy to sit on the road and watch his driveway. Unfortunately, the deputy wouldn't be able to see the house, but he'd know if anyone entered or exited the property.

On the screen, Shane sat at the table, chewing a thumbnail. He was an average-looking twenty-one-year-old. About five nine, lean build. There was nothing remarkable about him. He was no Brad Pitt, but he wasn't Quasimodo either. A jittery foot exhibited his nerves, and hunched shoulders conveyed his lack of confidence.

Matt looked up from his laptop. "Shane is currently unemployed. He used to work in the electronics department at Great Buy. He was recently fired after harassing the female employees."

"What did he do?"

"He masturbated onto their lockers."

"There's an image I didn't want in my head," Bree said. "How does he know Dylan?"

"Like Dylan, he's interested in all sorts of conspiracy theories and belongs to many of the same social media groups, including the Hudson Footmen."

"So that's how he knows Dylan."

"Probably, but Shane is also a self-proclaimed incel."

Bree had read articles about incels, short for *involuntary celibates*, a self-described group of men who couldn't find women willing to have sex with them. These incels were angry and hostile toward women. They felt as if they were entitled to the sex they were being denied. A movement that had begun as a support group for dateless men evolved into a hate forum.

Matt said, "How do you want to work him?"

Part of a successful interrogation was reading the subject and determining which interviewer would get the best results. In this case, Bree sensed that Shane wouldn't speak in the presence of a powerful female. She was the very thing he blamed for all his woes. Matt, on the other hand, was everything that Shane wanted to be.

Matt could be his hero.

"As much as I'd like a crack at him, Shane hates and mistrusts women. You're an alpha male to his very apparent beta. He'll be much more likely to open up to you." She glanced at him. Physically, Matt was about as alpha as a man could get. He looked like he could snap

Shane like a crayon. "We don't have time to make mistakes. We need to crack this little jerk."

"All we have on him is a video of his truck driving by Todd's house. We have no evidence that Shane did anything wrong."

"He doesn't know that. But I wouldn't focus on what he did anyway. Concentrate your questions on Dylan. As you said, we have no real evidence against Shane. But we know he was near the scene, so it's reasonable to question him about what he might have seen."

"OK." Matt stood and cracked his neck. She watched him assume an arrogant persona like a Halloween costume as he went out the door.

Bree slid into the chair facing the monitor and turned up the volume. Matt swaggered into the interview room. He stood, looming over the table—and Shane—for a split second. Once his dominance was established, Matt introduced himself to Shane and extended a hand. "Thank you for cooperating."

Shane nodded, enthusiasm warring with his anxiety. "The deputy said you needed help solving a crime."

"Yes." Instead of taking the chair across from Shane, Matt rounded the table and perched on the corner of the table. Not only did he maintain physical command, but he encroached on Shane's personal space. Matt pushed right through a socially acceptable boundary as if he were entitled to do so. He didn't ask permission. He didn't apologize. He took up space as if that were his right and established himself as alpha.

Shane didn't protest. He accepted Matt's superiority like an eager puppy.

"What's up?" Shane's voice begged for approval. "How can I help?"

"Well, here's the thing." Matt shook his head. "I hate to even ask. It feels wrong, but I need some info on a pal of yours. He's in deep trouble."

Shane sat up straighter. "Who?"

Matt's mouth tightened, as if what he was about to do were distasteful. "Brian Dylan."

Shane's shoulders shifted backward an inch as caution crept into his interest.

Matt held up a hand, and his voice oozed with understanding. "I know. He's your buddy. I have buddies too, and I wouldn't want to give them up for anything."

Shane nodded hard.

"But here's the thing. Dylan has been going off lately. Some of the shit he's done . . ." Matt paused, again conveying his discomfort with the topic. "I'm sure you've seen it too."

Shane bobbed his head. "He's been weird. That's for sure."

"I want to talk to him before he goes completely off the rails." Matt hesitated for emphasis. "Before he does something that he can't come back from."

Shane frowned. His head inclined just a touch, agreeing with Matt without speaking.

"Any idea what's up with him?" Matt asked. "I'm worried. Me and Dylan worked together for years."

"You were tight?" Shane's chin lifted.

"Oh, yeah," Matt lied without hesitation.

"He never mentioned you."

Matt shrugged. "Haven't seen him lately. I was out of action for a while. Got shot." He lifted his hand and pointed to the puckered scar in his palm, then raised the hem of his shirt and turned his upper body to show where the bullet had hit him in the back. With his heavily muscled and scarred torso, no one looked more badass than a bare-chested Matt.

Shane's eyes bugged. "Shit." His voice vibrated with awe.

"It happens." Matt shrugged off the injuries. "Part of the job."

Bree shifted in her chair. As impatient as she was for Matt to get to the meat of the interview, she respected his ability to gauge the suspect and not rush the process. They wouldn't get another opportunity. Once Shane realized he was in trouble, he'd stop talking.

"Back to Dylan." Matt dropped the hem of his shirt as if his wounds weren't important. "What's up with him?"

Shane shook his head. "He's been weird ever since he hooked up with that bitch."

Matt nodded knowingly.

"She fucking ruined everything." Shane sulked, scraping the toe of his sneaker on the floor. "Hardly seen Dylan since she's been in the picture."

"I hear ya. Bros before hoes, am I right, my man?" Matt extended a closed fist.

With a vigorous nod, Shane bumped it. "Yeah. I mean, I don't hate all women. Just those stuck-up bitches."

"Right," Matt agreed. "What's this bitch's name?"

"I don't know. We weren't introduced." Resentment edged into Shane's tone.

"What'd she look like?"

"I didn't see her face. She was wearing a hat, and I only saw her from a distance."

"Can you tell me anything about her?"

Shane's brow dropped as he concentrated. "Older lady, but in good shape for her age. She's got a nice set of tits on her."

Matt grinned. "That explains Dylan's lapses in judgment."

Shane chuckled. "I guess it does."

"But seriously, I'm worried about him." Matt flattened his lips and exhaled through his nose. "I heard a rumor that he got himself into some trouble last night."

Shane stiffened.

Matt leveled a stern gaze at Shane. "Do you know anything about that?"

Uncomfortable, Shane scooted his butt in his chair.

"Dude . . ." Matt lifted both hands in a *really?* gesture. "I thought you were going to help me help Dylan." He started to turn away. "I guess I was wrong."

Bree recognized the movement for what it was: dismissal—disapproval—of Shane.

Shane, still seeking validation, leaned forward, as if trying to maintain the connection to Matt. "No. Wait." He licked his lips. "I was with him last night."

Matt settled back down, reestablishing the connection, but his shoulders were tilted back, maintaining a slight distance, as if Shane would have to work to regain his approval.

A few beads of sweat broke out on Shane's forehead. "Dylan called me last night. He asked me to help him teach a guy a lesson."

"So you said yes," Matt said in a *like anyone would* tone.

"Yeah." Dylan glanced away for a second. In the center of his chest, his shirt darkened with sweat. "Me and a few other guys."

Matt waited.

"We met at Dylan's place, then drove over to this other dude's," Shane said vaguely.

"Do you remember the address?" Matt asked.

Shane tugged at the collar of his shirt. Sweat rings had formed under his arms and across his chest. He looked like he'd run a 5K through the tropics. He gave the name of Todd's road.

"Did you know the guy you were supposed to school?"

Shane shook his head. "Dylan called him Harvey."

"Who else was there?" Matt asked.

Shane dried his palms on his thighs and rattled off a few names.

Bree wrote them down. Fury simmered hot in her veins. Five. It had taken five men to take down Todd. How was Matt keeping his cool?

"What happened?" he asked in a casual voice.

"We roughed him up a little." Shane evaded Matt's gaze and shifted his body position again.

"That's it? You just smacked him around a few times and left?" Matt's tone made it clear he didn't believe that for a second.

Shane slid his ass across the seat. "Well, that was the plan, but the dude fought back fierce. Did some damage to Johnny's knee, and Fox's eye was a fucking mess."

Matt let the silence drag out until Shane had to fill it.

"We were gonna just leave the dude there, but Dylan changed his mind. He was pissed the guy fought so hard. So he made us carry him to the truck and toss him in the back."

"Your truck?"

Shane stared at his feet.

"We have your truck on video," Matt said.

"Yeah. My truck," Shane admitted.

"Then where did you go?" Matt pressed.

"Back to Dylan's house."

"Was Dylan's new bitch there?" Matt asked.

Shane nodded. "Dylan went into the house, and we could all hear her yelling at him. She kept calling him stupid." His face twisted in raw hatred, and the ugliness of it took Bree by surprise.

To give Matt credit, he didn't respond at all.

Shane continued. "I don't care how hot she is, no piece of pussy is worth putting up with that behavior. Bitches need to know their place." His eyes narrowed into hostile slits. "Dylan put a stop to it, though. I heard the slap from the driveway." Pleasure glimmered in his face.

Bree's stomach turned.

Matt didn't seem to notice. "Did any other guys stay?"

"Nah. We all went home. Dylan said he could handle things from there."

On the monitor, Matt simply nodded. "Do you know what happened to the guy?"

"Dylan said he was going to dump him in the woods. Make him find his way back." Shane tried to grin, like it was funny, but he couldn't pull it off.

"Do you think the guy could still walk?" Matt's question had a new edge.

Shane stared at the wall for a few seconds. Finally, his shoulder jerked. "I dunno."

Matt's throat shifted as if he was swallowing his anger. He smoothed his tone. "What did Dylan do with him?"

"I went home." Shane's face creased, and his eyes shuttered, as if he had just realized he was in deep, deep trouble. "I want a lawyer."

"Yeah. You're going to need one. The man you beat and helped abduct is the chief deputy of the Randolph County Sheriff's Department, and we found blood in the back of your pickup. How much do you want to bet that blood belongs to Chief Deputy Harvey?"

Shane's mouth gaped and closed again. His face drained of color.

"That's right. You assaulted and kidnapped a police officer." Matt stood. "You'd better pray he's still alive." Matt left him sweating.

Bree called for a deputy to handcuff Shane and arrest him on assault and kidnapping charges. She relayed the three names he'd given Matt to another deputy to have the other men arrested as well.

She met Matt in the hall. "That was one of the best interrogations I've ever seen."

"I need a shower after that." Matt fell into step beside her.

She headed for her office. "Distasteful or not, you put out just the right vibe. We got more than enough for a search warrant for Dylan's house."

"I'm not sure if Shane's confession will be admissible against him, though. I was afraid if I stopped to Mirandize him, he'd shut up."

In her doorway, Bree stopped, spun, and faced Matt. Anger flushed heat through her veins. Her chief deputy had been beaten and abducted. Had he been targeted because he'd been doing his job or because of his association with Bree? Was Bree partly responsible? Maybe if she'd conducted the investigation differently . . . She shook off the guilt. It would not help her find Todd. "You did the right thing. Shane isn't important. He isn't even a small fish. He's vegetation. We need to find Todd, and you just got us everything we need to go after him. I'll fill out the affidavit electronically, then call the judge." She hurried to her desk.

They had to follow procedure. They had to obey the letter of the law. But Dylan would not. If he had kidnapped Todd, what would he do to him?

Was Todd still alive?

CHAPTER TWENTY-SEVEN

Sunset was approaching as Bree parked behind a patrol vehicle on the side of the road near Brian Dylan's property. She tamped down her fury at Shane Bartholomew's interview. She would make it her personal goal to send Dylan to prison for as long as possible.

In the passenger seat, Matt was silent, but the hand resting on his thigh was clenched into a white-knuckled fist.

She glanced at him. "Be right back."

He nodded. In the back seat, Brody pressed his nose to the one-inch gap in the window.

Bree got out of the SUV and approached the patrol car.

Her deputy lowered the window and greeted her. "Ma'am."

She leaned in. "No activity?"

"None." He frowned. "I suspect they cleared out before I got here."

If Shane had been honest, Todd was abducted the night before. Dylan had had plenty of time to bug out.

And dispose of Todd.

She returned to her own vehicle. Brody whined, his plaintive tone voicing frustration and impatience. She reached over the seat and gave him a pat. "I know. We feel the same."

The sky glowed blood red over the trees. Additional patrol vehicles lined up behind her. A forensics tech was en route. The judge would review her affidavit ASAP. Bree didn't doubt he would approve the warrant. She'd more than established probable cause, and he was already aware that circumstances were exigent and her deputy's life was on the line. The judge had signed the warrant to search Shane Bartholomew's truck earlier. Bree wanted a team in place, ready to move in, the second the warrant came through.

Matt had been quiet since the interview with Shane. They both knew the chances were good that, unless Dylan wanted a hostage, Todd was dead.

Hostages complicated escapes. If Bree were in Dylan's situation, she wouldn't risk it. She'd cut ties and disappear.

Her phone buzzed. The number that appeared on Bree's screen belonged to the state police. She answered. "Sheriff Taggert."

"This is Phillip Ash. I'm an investigator with BCI. I'm reviewing the Oscar and Brown case file. I'd like to ask you some questions about the murders."

Bree turned her attention to the phone. "Go ahead."

Ash cleared his throat. "No. I don't want to do this over the phone. I'd like you to come down to the BCI office in Albany."

Bree paused. The Albany BCI office was a solid hour's drive from Grey's Hollow. Normally, she would have obliged, but not today. "When do you want to schedule this meeting?"

"Immediately," Ash said. "Tonight."

"Tonight isn't possible. I'm in the middle of an important operation."

"If you won't cooperate, I'll have to subpoena you," Ash said in a lofty tone.

Bree shared a *what the hell?* look with Matt. She'd dealt with BCI in the past with no issues. They'd always been professional and supportive.

"When did I say I wouldn't cooperate?" Bree asked. "I handed you the case, remember? Just because I can't rush to Albany on a moment's notice? You know I'm a working sheriff, right? I'm on the job at this very moment, about to serve a warrant. You haven't even had time to review the entire murder book."

He didn't respond.

Bree had no time or patience for this bullshit. "Am I a suspect?"

He went quiet for a few seconds, then spoke in a highly reserved tone. "We just have some questions."

Yep. She was a suspect.

Ash continued. "We've had a few calls from the media about the case already. People are talking. We want to get a jump on any rumors."

Bree breathed. Rumors didn't concern her. Her chief deputy was missing. "I'm about to serve a search warrant. I expect the ensuing property search will take up the rest of my night."

"Tomorrow then." Ash's voice went tight with irritation, like a man who was accustomed to being obeyed. "First thing."

Matt gestured with a throat-cutting motion and mouthed, "Call Morgan. Do not agree to this interview without her."

Bree agreed, and she was in no mood to placate the investigator. "I'll need to consult my attorney and see when she's available."

"Who's your attorney?" Ash asked in a clipped, impatient voice.

"Morgan Dane."

She thought she heard a muttered curse and smiled. Morgan had quite the reputation. Annoyed, Bree rubbed it in, just a little. "Do you know her? I believe she once worked at the prosecutor's office in Albany."

"I know her," Ash grumbled. "But I'm surprised you've already engaged a defense attorney. Not great optics, in my opinion."

Optics. There was that word again. Bree rolled her eyes. *I didn't ask your opinion.*

She bit back the snarky response. He could bitch and moan all he wanted. She had every right to bring a lawyer with her. If he'd played nice and just asked her about the case, cop to cop, she would have talked freely about the investigation. But he'd decided to be political and play hardball.

You reap what you sow, pal.

On one hand, bringing Morgan might make her look guilty. Bree couldn't change that. On the other, going into a formal BCI interview without representation, knowing she was a suspect, would be foolish. Bree would not be stupid. Ash was covering his ass with the press and the brass. Bree would not be the sacrifice that got him a promotion.

Fuck it.

Bree's brain hurt from trying to sort out the political ramification of every sentence before she spoke. She had to find Todd. She'd deal with Ash and BCI tomorrow. As long as she found her chief deputy alive, she didn't even care if they arrested her. But she hoped Morgan was as good as her reputation, because Ash had a burr up his butt regarding her.

"I'll contact Ms. Dane and get back to you," she said.

"When?" Ash snapped.

Bree worked to keep her voice even. "After I hear back from her."

"I expect a phone call tomorrow."

"You'll get a callback within a reasonable length of time. Ms. Dane is a busy woman. Good night, Ash." Bree ended the connection before he could respond.

"What a dick," Matt muttered. "Seriously, he's jonesing for you."

"Why?" Bree wanted to throw her phone out the window. Instead, she sent Morgan a text.

"Sheriff is an elected office. You can't be fired. Maybe he thinks you could be the leg up he needs to further his own career."

"The governor appointed me. He can also remove me."

"He'd need a damned good reason. Gossip wouldn't cut it."

"True."

"You've been popular so far. But these deepfakes jeopardize your reputation. Until now, you've been shielded by the voters' will, but if they turn on you . . ."

"I'm through and no longer an asset. Maybe Ash thinks he can take the credit for bringing me down." She sighed.

"Exactly."

Bree mulled that over. "I don't care. Not tonight." Her phone vibrated. She read the screen. "There's our warrant. Let's go."

There was no way to sneak up on Dylan in their vehicles, not the way he'd set up his property. Bree motioned for her deputies to follow her in their vehicles. They parked in front of a bend in the long driveway, the last spot their vehicles wouldn't be visible from the house.

Matt and Bree stepped out of the SUV. Matt opened the rear door. Impatient, Brody tried to jump down, but Matt stopped him with a command, then lifted him out of the vehicle.

Despite the coolness of the evening, sweat dripped down Bree's back under her body armor. "He probably has cameras or an alarm of some sort. With all the surveillance on his house, I can't imagine he would have left out the approach."

"Not much we can do about that." Matt checked the Velcro on his vest and shortened Brody's leash. The dog stood beside him, tensed and poised to work.

Bree regripped her rifle, adjusted her earpiece, and initiated a communications check with Matt and the four deputies she'd brought. When each team member had responded, Bree was satisfied. She motioned them forward.

Given the exigent circumstances, she had emphasized in the affidavit that she feared for Todd's life. She had requested—and had been granted—a no-knock warrant, with the judge's warning that she had better be right or he'd never sign another one for her.

Bree led the way, jogging down the long driveway. Gravel crunched underfoot, and she moved to the side of the lane. They slowed as they rounded the bend. The house came into view. Though the sun hadn't fully set, the thick canopy prematurely darkened the clearing. They crept forward, using the deep shadows as cover.

Matt motioned toward himself and the detached garage. Bree nodded. He skirted the clearing and approached the building from the side. Rising onto his toes, he shined his flashlight through a high window. Brody sniffed at the foundation but didn't seem interested. The dog could smell and hear what they could not see. She doubted there was anyone inside.

Matt's voice sounded in Bree's ear. "One vehicle. An SUV, not Dylan's truck. Too dark to read the license plate."

"Roger that," she answered. If Dylan's truck wasn't in the garage, then he was probably driving it. He probably wasn't even here. Bree contacted dispatch and requested a BOLO alert on Brian Dylan and his vehicle.

Matt returned to her side. With the deputies behind them, she and Matt jogged toward the house. At the edge of the clearing, Bree signaled to Collins and Juarez to loop around back and watch the rear exit. Her earpiece crackled as Collins softly announced they were in position. Then Bree and Matt hurried across the clearing to the front door. She nodded to Matt. He tried the knob. Locked.

She motioned another deputy forward. He carried the battering ram to the front door, swung it, and made solid contact just above the doorknob. The door was solid steel, and it took several good hits before the frame splintered and the door swung inward.

Thanks to regular training exercises, they entered the house as a team. Bree pivoted left, sweeping her rifle into the corners of the room. Matt and Brody went right, and the deputies followed suit. Brody didn't pull in any particular direction. Bree doubted anyone was home.

The house was multilevel. A split staircase opened off the foyer. They divided into two pairs. Matt and Bree went up a set of steps while her two deputies headed down. The two extra bedrooms were sparsely furnished and simple to search. Bree ducked into the primary bedroom. A double-size bed dominated the space, but the room was mostly empty.

She opened the closet. "Clear."

"Clear." Matt emerged from an attached bathroom. He'd let out the leash to give the dog some freedom. Brody was on guard but still not alerting. Matt frowned at his dog. "No one's here."

"Agreed." Bree had learned to trust Brody. He might not officially be with the department anymore, but the dog hadn't forgotten a thing. And he was uncannily right every time. She spoke into her lapel mic and checked in with the deputies downstairs.

"All clear down here, ma'am," one responded. "No Chief Deputy Harvey."

"Outbuildings are clear," Collins said. "No sign of the chief deputy out here either."

Bree dropped her hand and turned to Matt. "We'll sweep the grounds next, but he probably moved out last night."

Matt waved a hand. "Looks more like barracks than a bedroom. I'm sure he had bug-out bags ready."

Nodding, Bree moved downstairs.

Her two deputies exited a room. Through the doorway, Bree could see a large desk topped with multiple monitors. "Did he leave computer equipment?"

"Just the peripherals." The deputy pointed to the desk. "There's a piece missing, probably the main unit and hard drive."

Nodding, Bree led them out of the house. In full dusk, they switched on flashlights to illuminate the ground. The wind shifted to blow scent from the direction of the river. Brody lifted his nose, let out a thin whine, and danced.

"He smells something," Matt said.

"I've got footprints." Juarez's voice sounded in her ear. "I'm around back."

Bree hurried around the house to the backyard. Once Brody cleared the side of the house, he lunged toward the river. Matt could barely hold him back.

Juarez pointed his flashlight at the ground. The soil under the trees was soft. A set of boot prints led away from the house toward the river. Matt let Brody move forward. The dog needed no footprints. He followed a scent on the air.

Bree followed them, maintaining a parallel path and taking care not to disturb the prints themselves. They led to a cliff.

"Whoa, boy." Matt commanded Brody to sit. The dog obeyed, but his reluctance was clear in his stiff posture. His gaze and full attention were focused on the drop-off.

Bree walked to the edge and shone her light into the abyss below. The drop was about forty feet. Cutting through the darkness, her beam barely reached the rocky riverbank below. Horror paralyzed her for one heartbeat. In the weakened light, she could see the distinct outline of a body.

Chapter
Twenty-Eight

Matt stared over the edge of the cliff. Below, weeds, rocks, and sandy earth composed the riverbank. The body lay facedown, but Matt could see that it was male, dressed in jeans and a T-shirt.

When he'd last seen Todd, the chief deputy had been dressed in jeans and a T-shirt. Matt tamped down his rage and sadness.

At his side, Bree was already moving away from the edge. "Let's get down there."

To the north, the ground leveled off some. Matt spotted a trail that zigzagged down the slope to the river. He pointed and headed for it. "There!"

With Bree on his heels, they ran for the descent. Brody was reluctant to leave the cliff's edge, but once he saw the trail, he all but dragged Matt down it.

In his ear, Bree issued commands to her deputies, instructing them to call an ambulance and fetch a first aid kit. Matt didn't hear the rest of her orders. At first he thought the river was drowning out her voice, but then he realized it was the sound of his own blood rushing in his ears.

But Matt couldn't unsee the man's body. As much as he wanted him to be alive, in his heart he knew it was too late. While they'd been dicking around, following procedure, adhering to the letter of the law, a man had lain here dead.

Maybe he'd even been actively dying.

The deputies dispersed, presumably to follow orders. Matt's focus tunneled to his own footsteps on the rocky path as Brody lunged into his harness. The dog's weight forced Matt to concentrate or fall on his face. By the time they reached the bottom, sweat had soaked his shirt under his vest. Bree raced for the body. Matt held the dog back for fear of contaminating the scene.

The corpse lay in about two inches of water. Bree slowed. She stopped just ahead of Matt. The beam of her flashlight shook. She was doing the job, but she was as panicked as he was.

Todd was a hell of a chief deputy—and a good man.

Matt stopped. He almost didn't want to know. Sickness rose in his throat as Bree approached the body. Her gaze was on the ground. She was likely making sure she didn't step on any evidence. Matt shone his flashlight on the body. Even from ten feet away, he could see the grayish-blue tone of the skin.

Crouching, she pressed two fingers to the neck, then shook her head. "No pulse, and he's cold. Really cold." She reached for his shoulder and turned the body just enough to see the victim's face. She gasped and nearly lost her grip.

Not Todd.

Matt also sucked wind as he took in the very dead face of Jim Rogers. Rogers and Todd were about the same size. Both had short brown hair. Both had been dressed in jeans and T-shirts the last time Matt had seen them. It was no wonder Matt had confused them from the back.

Relief—then guilt—rocked him. He shouldn't be glad that it was Rogers instead of Todd.

Rogers wasn't a horrible person. He'd done some bad things, but he had clearly regretted them. He'd struggled with his change of heart, and his remorse had been evident over the past months.

Bree rocked back on her heels. It seemed to take a few seconds for her to reset. "I didn't expect that."

"Me either." A wave of nausea swept over Matt as his adrenaline rush abruptly ceased. He let it pass through him. No choice really. Couldn't stop it.

Bree got to her feet, visibly steadying herself. She leaned on her thighs and took a few deep breaths before touching her mic. "It isn't Chief Deputy Harvey."

Brody lay down at Matt's feet and rested his head on his paws. Matt crouched and stroked his head. "Good boy."

"Is he OK?" Bree asked.

"He gets depressed when he finds dead people."

Bree stepped away from Rogers. She canceled the ambulance and called the medical examiner.

Matt stood. "Could you see how he died?"

"Looks like he took a bullet to the back."

Their eyes met in the darkness. Matt didn't need light to feel the connection. He wished he could go to her, to share the relief and sadness they were both feeling, to bolster his reserves for the next phase of the search for Todd. Their relief might be premature. Todd could also be dead. But they were on duty. If anyone caught sight of them and took a picture . . .

Her career didn't need another hit. So Matt held back.

But she crossed the ten feet of damp ground and put her arms around him. He returned the hug, tentatively. "Someone might see," he said into her ear.

"I don't care." She leaned her forehead on his chest. They stood there for a full minute, drawing strength from one another. Finally, she lifted her head and stepped back. Her eyes glimmered with moisture. "Thank you."

"I needed it too." Matt touched his own face and was surprised to find it wet. He wiped it on the shoulder of his polo shirt. "Why was Rogers here?"

"He could have been here to help Dylan or to confront him about something." She turned to stare at the body. "Considering he's dead, I would bet on the latter."

"I hope so." Matt couldn't believe Rogers would have backslid that far. His bitterness toward Dylan had felt real.

"Me too. Rogers . . ." Bree shook her head. "I don't know. No point in speculating."

"Nope." The only way they'd discover the truth was to get back to the investigation.

Her spine straightened. "We still need to find Todd."

"Yes. Maybe we can find a clue to his whereabouts in Dylan's house." Matt called Brody to heel. "*Fuss.*"

They headed for the trail to find Collins standing at the base of the slope, her back to them. She'd been blocking the path and giving them privacy, Matt realized, and ensuring no one else saw their embrace.

As they approached, Bree cleared her throat, and Collins turned around. She had a pretty good poker face but couldn't entirely keep the warmth and respect from her eyes. "What now, ma'am?"

No matter what the press reported, no matter what the brass did, Bree's deputies would have her back.

"Now we look for other signs of where Dylan could have gone." Bree whipped out her phone. "I'll have Marge search property and tax records. If Brian Dylan owns any other properties in the area, she'll find them. He must have gone somewhere."

CHAPTER
TWENTY-NINE

An hour later, Bree sat at Dylan's desk in his home office. Scratches and bright patches on the desktop indicated where pieces of equipment had been removed. Dylan had been ready. She closed the pencil drawer, frustration adding power to the slam. "Are you having any luck?"

Across the room, Matt looked up from a filing cabinet he'd been searching. "No. All I've found is a bunch of useless paperwork. Dylan kept everything, including the instruction manual for a fifteen-year-old leaf blower and the receipt for a lawn mower he bought in 2002." He closed the drawer.

"We need to ID the girlfriend." Bree dragged a hand over her face.

Matt scratched his jaw. "Shane could only describe her as a large-breasted older lady. He didn't even say large, just that they were *nice*."

"Which describes a third of the female adult population of New York State."

The clock was ticking. The longer Todd was missing, the less likely it was they'd find him alive.

Her phone vibrated, and she checked the screen. Marge.

She answered. "Did you find anything?"

"No." Marge sounded tired, not just physically, but emotionally drained. "I can't find any property in the area owned by Brian Dylan. I'll keep expanding my search. Just wanted to give you an update."

"Damn." Bree thought about Shane's description of Dylan's lady friend. *Older woman. Nice tits.* An image of Heather Oscar popped into her head. "Try Heather Oscar."

Bree ended the call.

"You think Dylan was sleeping with Heather Oscar?" Matt asked.

"I was thinking of Shane's description of Dylan's woman. I admit I'm reaching, but Heather is attractive and in good shape for her age. Oscar and Dylan were friends for years. Heather and Dylan could have met."

"We should have thought of her."

"No evidence pointed to her. We still don't have any evidence to implicate her. A twenty-one- year-old's description of *nice tits* doesn't cut it." But Bree was getting desperate to find Todd.

"Ma'am?" Collins stuck her head in the doorway. "We found a couple of pictures you might want to look at." She walked into the room. In her gloved hand she clutched some papers. "They're photos printed on regular paper." She dealt them out onto the surface of the desk. In the first image, Dylan held a fish from its gills against a backdrop of a lake and trees. Picture number two was of him holding another fish. In the background, Bree could see a dock, along with water and woods.

Matt leaned over the desk.

"He likes to fish." Bree moved to the third image and tapped a green building in the background. A fourth shot showed Dylan in a boat, holding a fish. The entire backdrop was water. Bree returned to image number three. She looked up at Matt, then Collins. "Do either of you recognize this place?"

Collins shook her head.

Matt squinted at the photo. "No, but you have quite a few deputies who fish."

Bree nodded to Collins. "Show these around to the other deputies. Maybe one of them recognizes this building."

"Yes, ma'am." Collins gathered the papers and walked toward the door.

"Collins?" Bree called.

The deputy glanced over her shoulder. "Ma'am?"

"Good work," Bree said.

Collins flushed, nodded, and left the room. Bree removed the last desk drawer, turned it over, and checked the bottom and back. Then she shone her flashlight into the empty space. Nothing.

"Ma'am?" Collins returned, with Juarez in tow. "Deputy Juarez thinks he knows this building." Collins set down the stack of photos. The one with the green building sat on top.

"It's Grey Lake." Juarez pointed to the image. "I grew up fishing and camping there. This looks like Dockside Fuel and Bait at the north end." He held out his phone and tapped on its screen. "See?"

She squinted. He'd pulled up an online photo of the establishment.

Matt leaned over the desk. "That's it!" He began to pace. "We know Dylan fishes at Grey Lake. That doesn't mean he went there."

"No, but it's all we have to go on," Bree said.

Matt's face reflected her own doubt.

"There's a boat in one of the pictures." Bree sorted through them until she found the right one. "So we don't know where he stays on the lake."

Bree stared at the photos again. She could see a silver rail and a bit of white fiberglass behind him. A sliver of blue in the corner of the image caught her attention. "What's this?"

Matt stared at the photo. "Fabric. A sail?"

Bree recalled the photo of the young family on their sailboat. She opened her phone and scrolled through her photo app. "Here it is." She set her phone next to the printed picture. "The color of the sail is the same."

Dylan was on the Crightons' sailboat.

Energized by the discovery, Bree called Marge. "Look for a property on Grey Lake owned by Bernard Crighton."

"You think one of the Crightons was working with Dylan?" Matt asked. "So, Todd's kidnapping is tied to Oscar's murder?"

"I don't know what to think, but motive is less important than evidence. Also, we're not working the murders anymore, so officially, we aren't considering the two crimes as linked at this time. We are looking for Todd." Bree and Matt shared a look. Having listened to her phone call with BCI, he likely understood she didn't want to call the investigator.

Bree tapped on the picture. "It would be a huge coincidence if Dylan was on a sailboat that just happened to match the one the Crightons owned."

Matt added, "Dylan and Oscar worked together for years. There's no reason Dylan couldn't have met Oscar's relatives at some point."

"Where was this taken?" Bree offered her phone to Juarez. "Do you know?"

Juarez took the phone and squinted at it. "The sails are down, and it looks like the photo was taken while the sailboat was tied up. I can see part of a dock." He expanded the image on the phone with his thumb and forefinger. "I don't see any other boats or slips, so maybe the house had its own dock. That's all I can see."

"That's great." Bree took back her phone. "Thank you, Juarez."

"Yes, ma'am," he said. "We all want to find the chief deputy."

Bree's phone vibrated with a call. "It's Marge." Bree answered. "Did you find anything?"

"I did," Marge said. "There are no properties owned by Bernard Crighton, but I did find one deeded to Stephanie Crighton." She read off an address.

Bree covered the speaker and repeated the house number and street to Matt. "Find this property on a map app."

"It's a waterfront lot on the north end of the lake." Matt looked up. "Not far from Dockside Fuel and Bait."

"How is Stephanie involved?" Matt asked.

Older lady. Nice tits.

Bree turned to Juarez, the youngest person in the room. "Would a thirty-five-year-old woman be considered *older* by a twenty-one-year-old?"

"Yes, ma'am," Juarez said. "No offense."

"None taken." Bree rose. Puzzle pieces began to shift into place in her mind. She met Matt's gaze. "Are you thinking what I'm thinking?"

"Stephanie Crighton is Dylan's new lady friend," Matt said.

Bree nodded. "Collins, Juarez, you're with us. Let's go check it out."

All she could do was pray she was right.

Because she also knew in her heart, if Todd was still alive, it wasn't likely he would survive the night.

Chapter Thirty

A wave of pain roused Todd. The surface underneath him shifted, and nausea rolled over him like a bulldozer. He swallowed and breathed until it passed. When his stomach settled, he cracked an eyelid but couldn't see much except darkness. Fresh air washed across his face, telling him he was outside, but clearly night had fallen. Something dried and sticky, probably blood, blurred his vision. He gave up and closed his eye.

The floor under him lurched. Was it actually moving, or was the motion in his head? He remembered taking a boot to the skull.

The floor shifted again. This time he was relatively sure it was not his imagination but actual movement.

Todd took stock. He was curled on his side. His hands were bound behind his back, and his ankles were tied together. Without moving his body, he wiggled his hands and feet to get the blood moving. More of his body hurt than didn't, but miraculously, he could still move all his fingers and toes.

Hard surfaces all around him told him he was crammed in a confining space. Under him, metal mesh cut into his shoulder. He jolted, and something creaked. A wheel. He was in a cart of some sort.

If he was in a cart, then someone was pulling or pushing it.

Where was he being taken?

The cart lurched and began bouncing in a rhythm. Todd heard *thump, thump, squeak.*

He didn't want to give away his conscious state, but he risked opening his eyes slightly, just enough to peer through his lashes. Actually, he could open only one eye. The other felt like it was swollen closed. The dried blood on his eyelid cracked enough that he could see. The sky above him was black and dotted with stars, and a half moon cast silvery light. He made out the silhouettes of two people in front of the cart. A man pulled the handle.

Dylan?

No wonder the voice of his attacker had sounded familiar.

The second person was partially hidden behind Dylan's shadow. To Todd's surprise, the first voice he heard was a woman's.

"I can't believe you kidnapped a cop." Her voice rang with condemnation.

"He's our insurance," Dylan said.

She stepped out from behind Dylan. Backlit by the moon, her features were indistinct. "He's a liability, you moron."

Todd had to agree. Abducting a cop was a stupid move that would attract more attention than it was worth.

"Don't call me that," Dylan snapped.

"Stop right there!" Her tone went cold and threatening. "If you ever lay a hand on me again, I'll saw off your dick while you sleep." Clearly, she was not going to take any shit from Dylan. Todd would have approved, but a little voice in the back of his aching head told him the woman was the more dangerous of the two.

Dylan said nothing. Probably a wise move on his part.

"Every cop in the state will be looking for him," she said. "We need to get rid of him."

"I guess he is a loose end," Dylan agreed in a reluctant voice. "I just wanted him to stop asking questions about the Footmen."

"Why? *Why* does that matter?" The woman clearly did not give two fucks about the Hudson Footmen.

"You don't get it. The Footmen are doing important things. They don't need the cops sniffing around their business."

"Kidnapping one only increases scrutiny from law enforcement," she pointed out. "Did you think about what you would do with him afterward?"

A few heartbeats of silence confirmed that Dylan had not.

But she obviously had ideas. As horrible as Dylan was, he hadn't killed Todd.

Yet.

But this woman, she knew the score. "You can't be impulsive. You need to plan."

"So what now?" Dylan asked, his tone suggesting he now realized he'd been stupid.

"We dump him."

"Then what?"

"Then we go back to our original plan. *My* original plan," she clarified. "And it doesn't involve any extracurricular activities like kidnapping or harassment. We lay low. We don't do anything to attract any more attention to ourselves. We let the sheriff take the heat for the murders, and we quietly move on."

We dump him.

Todd heard water lapping. His blood chilled as he realized where he was and identified the thumping noise and the reason the cart was bouncing. It was rolling down a dock, the wheels hitting uneven boards.

They were taking him to a boat.

They were going to *dump* him overboard.

The cart stopped moving. Fabric flapped. Something metal rattled. The boat?

Fear pooled cold in Todd's belly. He stiffened, then forced his body to relax. If Dylan knew he was awake, he'd probably knock him out again—or worse. Tied, Todd was helpless, but the thought of being unconscious as well—with them free to do whatever they wanted without him even being aware—brought sickness roiling back.

Todd fought it. He concentrated on controlling his respirations and heart rate. Even and slow. His muscles needed to be limp.

Rough hands hooked under his shoulders, and Dylan tried to drag Todd out of the cart. Todd fought the urge to kick or respond in any way. His face scraped on the metal mesh bottom. Though not as strong, Dylan was about the same size as Todd, but deadweight was a bitch to maneuver.

Dylan breathed hard. "Get his feet."

The woman grabbed Todd's ankles, and they heaved him through the air. He landed on a flat surface. It felt like fiberglass under his face. Pain sang through every inch of Todd's body as he slid into something hard. He'd have bruises on top of bruises.

If he was lucky.

CHAPTER
THIRTY-ONE

Matt opened the rear door of the sheriff's SUV and prepared to lift Brody down to the ground in front of Stephanie Crighton's house. The dog had other ideas and leaped out of the vehicle. Brody's nose was in the air, and the fur on his back stood on end. He sensed something. The hairs on the back of Matt's neck lifted in response.

Bree and her deputies assembled on the side of the road and turned toward the house.

Built of cedar and glass, the lakefront home looked like it belonged to a successful attorney. Landscaping lights shone on trees and brightened ornamental shrubs. Matt pointed to a bush with pink flowers. "Is that what I think it is?"

"Butterfly bush," Bree said.

Inside, the house was dark.

"We don't have a search warrant."

"No, we don't, but I'm not waiting another second." Bree drew her sidearm. "Extremely exigent circumstances."

Life-or-death matters could negate the need for a warrant, and no one could argue that an abduction wasn't an emergency; however, it wasn't a risk-free decision. The sheriff's department could be sued.

Evidence discovered could be challenged by a defense attorney. A warrantless search could affect the outcome of a criminal trial.

In this case, they wanted to find Todd. They'd worry about the details later.

Juarez and Collins hefted AR-15s. They all adjusted their earpieces.

Matt touched his microphone. "Do we have a plan?"

Bree's voice sounded in his ear. "Follow the dog?"

"Sounds good." Matt squatted and presented Todd's T-shirt to Brody. The dog ignored it. An intuitive canine, he knew what to do. He was leaning into his harness before Matt could give him a command.

If Todd was nearby, then Brody would find him.

Matt walked behind the dog. Brody didn't give the house any attention. Putting his nose to the ground, he followed a path around the side of the building. Periodically, he lifted his head and sniffed the air. A two-car, detached garage sat in the shade of a huge oak tree. There were no windows on the overhead doors. Brody sat at the base of one and pawed the concrete.

Bree knew the dog's cues by now. Matt didn't have to say a word. She led the way around the garage to a side door. Collins stepped forward and approached the entrance. Covering her eyes, she peered through a glass pane in the upper half of the door. "Don't see anyone."

Brody maintained his focus on the building. Though the evening was cool, sweat dripped down Matt's back and soaked his shirt at the base of his spine. Bree pulled her baton from her belt and used the butt to break a pane of glass. She reached through and unlocked the door. Leading with their weapons, they went through the doorway. A compact SUV and a large pickup truck shared the space. Collins peered in the truck cab. Juarez circled the SUV.

At the same time, Bree dropped to one knee and checked under the vehicles.

Matt glanced over the side of the truck bed. A tarp was thrown into the corner. It was too flat to conceal a person. There was nowhere else to hide.

The dog tugged on the leash, and Matt followed him. Limping slightly, Brody trotted to the back of the pickup and whined softly.

Matt read the license plate. "Dylan's truck."

Bree gestured to the SUV. "And this is Stephanie Crighton's vehicle."

Standing on his hind legs, Brody sniffed at the tailgate. Matt held him back and waved Juarez toward the truck bed. "Let's see what's under the tarp."

Juarez pulled up the tarp and shone a flashlight into the bed. Then he uttered one word. "Blood."

Matt scanned the grooved metal. There was much more blood than the spots they'd found in Shane Bartholomew's pickup. Dark streaks ran from the middle of the bed to the tailgate, as if a bleeding Todd had been dragged out. Outrage and dismay churned in Matt's gut.

Not enough blood to assume Todd had died.

But there was no proof he was still alive either.

"Are we assuming it's Todd's blood?" Collins asked, her face grim.

Matt glanced down at Brody. The dog was focused and agitated. "Yes. Trust the dog. He has senses you can't even comprehend."

Todd was one of the good guys. He didn't deserve to be beaten and hauled around like a slab of meat.

Or worse.

Brody walked the perimeter of the garage, then he pulled toward the back door. Todd wasn't here any longer. The dog wanted to get back to work. Matt let him lead the way. Bree and her deputies followed as they left the garage.

A gentle breeze stirred branches overhead. The dog paused and sniffed a circle.

"Is he following the scent in the air or on the ground?" Collins asked.

"Either. Both." Matt and Brody enlarged the circle, spiraling outward. "K-9s track scent cones in the air. Scent concentrates at the tip of the cone. The dogs also follow the microscopic skin cells everyone sheds constantly. There isn't much wind, and it just shifted. Give him a minute. He'll reorient himself."

Again, Brody ignored the house. Matt would have bet a million dollars Todd had never been inside it.

The lots were large on this side of the lake. This house was elevated to take advantage of the views. A long, sloping back lawn the size of a football field led down to the water. A dock extended out over the lake. A long sailboat bobbed at the end of the dock. Next to it, a smaller motorboat was tied. Moonlight shimmered on the water's glassy surface.

Brody pulled toward the dock. Matt had no doubt Dylan and Stephanie had headed for the boat. Grey Lake was miles long and deep in places. Bodies had been pulled from its waters in the past. Swimmers who'd drowned . . .

Murder victims.

"Stop!" Bree's quiet command halted the procession. "I see movement on the dock."

Matt squinted into the darkness. The moon cast enough light that he could discern two shapes.

Had their small rescue party been heard?

Brody's front feet danced. Matt put a hand to his head to shush the whine he sensed was coming. The wind died, and the night was too quiet. Sneaking up on the dock wouldn't be easy.

They eased into the shadow of the big oak. In order to get to the dock—and the boats—they would have to cross a hundred yards of open ground. Were the people on the dock watching? Were they armed?

Matt considered simply turning Brody loose. The dog could cover the distance faster than any man, but he could also get shot. And he was favoring his shoulder. Probably hurt it jumping out of the SUV. It wasn't likely he'd be able to jump onto a moving boat.

One of the figures leaped onto the motorboat. The other moved around on the dock.

Shit.

"They're casting off." Matt knew he wouldn't be able to catch the boat before it pulled away. Brody leaned into the leash. Matt held him back. The dog would alert Dylan and Stephanie to the presence of law enforcement. If Todd was still alive, that could put him in jeopardy. They might kill him immediately. Matt glanced at Bree.

"Matt, go!" Bree gestured. "Collins, take the dog. Matt's the fastest one of us here."

He handed the leash to Collins and gave Brody a command. "Take him back to the vehicle. Crack the window." The night was cool. Brody would be fine.

"Give Flynn your AR," Bree commanded Collins.

Collins traded the AR-15 for the leash. Brody obeyed, but he was not happy about being sidelined. As Collins led him away, the dog cast a look back at Matt as if asking, *Are you sure?*

Matt cradled the rifle and sprinted toward the dock.

"Request backup," Bree instructed Collins via the headset. "See if the state can send out a helicopter and call out the marine unit."

Randolph County had their own boat and dive team, but the equipment was kept at a marina at the other end of the lake, miles away.

They were on their own.

CHAPTER
THIRTY-TWO

Bree raced toward the dock. Her legs churned as she pushed for more speed. Matt was in the lead, his long legs eating up the distance. Behind him, she and Juarez raced side by side.

Matt stopped at the edge of the dock as the boat pulled away.

They weren't going to make it.

Matt ducked behind a piling. Bree and Juarez caught up. Breathing hard, Bree leaned on her thighs and sucked wind. She felt like someone had taken an ice pick to her lungs.

"Couldn't catch them," Matt said, barely winded.

Bree scanned the shore. The next-door neighbor also had a dock with a fishing boat outfitted with an outboard motor. She whispered to Juarez, the fisherman, "You know boats?"

He nodded. "Yes, ma'am."

She pointed to the neighbor's boat. "Will that one be able to catch Dylan?"

Juarez squinted at it. "I think so. It's older but has a bigger outboard."

Bree looked at the house next door. All the windows were dark, and it had a vacant air. "Can we commandeer it?"

One thing television actually got right was the ability of police to borrow a vehicle if they were involved in a dangerous situation and have no reasonable alternative. That said, if they crashed it, there'd be hell to pay.

"Let's find out." Juarez turned. Crouching, he ran along the shoreline. Bree and Matt followed close behind him. Juarez was clearly very familiar with watercraft. He jumped into the boat and went to the center console. The vessel was about eighteen feet long, with a single outboard engine. Juarez opened and closed compartments. Something cracked. A minute later, the motor started up.

Bree and Matt untied the lines and jumped aboard. The boat rocked, then settled as they stilled. Juarez manned the wheel, piloting the small boat across the water. Bree could see the running lights of Dylan and Stephanie's boat a hundred yards ahead.

Bree stood next to her deputy. "Did you hot-wire it?"

Feet spread wide, Juarez pointed to a key in the ignition. "Didn't have to. Key was in the glove box. I might have broken into that. My dad always kept a spare key on board in case someone dropped the primary key overboard." He moved the throttle forward and the boat leaped ahead. The bow rose, then dropped as the boat hit plane and leveled off.

Bree used her radio to update dispatch.

They began to close the gap. Clouds drifted across the moon, throwing the lake into darkness. The outboard engine wasn't unusually loud, but the night was exceptionally still and quiet. Even if the moon stayed hidden, surely Dylan and Stephanie would hear the approaching motor above their own.

Barely a hundred feet separated the vessels when Bree saw movement on the deck ahead. One silhouette was at the wheel. The other struggled to lift a long, seemingly heavy object.

Matt pointed. "Look!"

A long, dark shape was lifted to the side of the boat.

Bree knew what that shape was. "Todd." Horror tightened her chest as she realized what was happening.

Matt nodded. "And they're going to throw him overboard."

CHAPTER

THIRTY-THREE

Todd lay on his side in the stern of the boat, exactly where he'd landed when Dylan had dropped him a second ago. Pain ratcheted through his body. He looked through the lashes of his good eye.

"I need help," Dylan said. "He's too bulky."

The boat slowed as the woman left the wheel to help Dylan. They rocked and drifted in the water.

Dylan rolled Todd toward the side of the boat. Agony racked Todd's body. His ribs cracked against something, knocking the wind out of him. His lungs shut down, and he couldn't hold back a gasp. As his chest expanded and convulsed, more pain wrapped around his rib cage and squeezed. The hell with it. It didn't matter if they knew he was conscious anymore. They were going to shoot him in a minute, then toss him overboard.

His body wanted to go into survival mode. It wanted to fight. Unfortunately, with his hands and feet still bound, his options were limited. Still, he thrashed his feet and twisted his body to make their work harder.

"I told you to kill him," the woman yelled.

Dylan paused, then yelled back, "He'll be dead soon enough."

It sounded as if Dylan didn't want to shoot him. Why not? He couldn't be squeamish if he'd shot Oscar and his mom right in their fucking heads. That scene had been a horror show. After the first messy shot, you had to have a strong stomach to pull the trigger again and again.

"No," the woman yelled. "He has to be dead. No loose ends."

"Who made you the boss?"

"You are the stupid one who complicated my plan by kidnapping a deputy. Now you have to fix it."

"Fine." Dylan huffed. "Where's the gun?"

"I have it. Get him closer to the edge. I want to keep the blood off the boat."

Dylan's hands hooked under Todd's shoulders. His breaths grew ragged as he struggled with Todd's weight. "Grab his feet."

Without propulsion, the boat turned with the current.

"Don't we need to weigh him down?" asked the cold-blooded bitch. "Do we have something heavy we can tie to him?"

"No need. He doesn't have any body fat. He'll sink right to the bottom." Dylan was right. Dead bodies sank at first, then floated to the surface after decomposition gases formed. Depending on water temp and location, that could be a few days.

The woman grabbed his ankles. Despite Todd's struggles, they heaved him onto the edge of the boat. The engine, now idling, glugged.

"Hold him still," the woman said. Fabric rustled.

With their engine quiet, Todd heard a second motor approaching. *Another boat!*

Dylan's head snapped around. "Someone's coming. If you're going to shoot him, hurry the fuck up."

The woman was rooting in her pocket, probably for the gun. Todd caught the glint of moonlight on metal as she pulled out a pistol. He shifted his eyeball in the other direction. Nothing but water, dark and terrifying, stretched out in an endless, shifting void. He was an excellent swimmer, but he'd never practiced with his hands and feet tied. He wasn't a fucking SEAL. Was the water a better option than a bullet? She couldn't miss at this range. A gunshot would be quick and clean. Drowning seemed more terrifying. But he couldn't give up. His survival instinct took over.

He had no choice.

He pulled his knees to his chest and kicked out. His bound feet caught the woman in the belly, knocking her backward. The impact also broke Dylan's grip and sent Todd's shoulders over the edge of the boat. He dangled, but Dylan's fist closed on his pant leg.

"Get him!" the woman yelled.

Dylan grunted and swiped at Todd's bicep. Todd twisted away and kicked off Dylan's grip. Todd slid over the side. He free-fell for a split second, then hit the water headfirst. The lake was cold and shocking. He tumbled and lost his bearings in the darkness. He opened his eye and saw moonlight above him. With his arms bound behind his back, it took him a few seconds to right himself. His lungs burned. He kicked toward the light. When his head broke the surface, he spit out a mouthful of water and gasped for air. Unable to tread water, he felt himself sinking. Panic stole his control, and he thrashed. Water invaded his mouth and nose. His throat closed, suffocating him. His vision blurred. He sputtered and coughed. Even though his face was wet, he could feel tears burning his eyes and clogging his nose.

He was going to drown.

Stop!

Floating was hard for him even without being tied, but it wasn't impossible. Fighting for calm, he tilted his head back and inflated his lungs like an inner tube. To save energy, he moved his feet as little as possible, kicking them in small movements like a dolphin's tail only when necessary if the water was over his face when he needed to breathe.

He could keep his mouth and nose above water for a while, but he must remain calm.

Panic would kill him.

As he hung, suspended in the water, his breathing didn't return to normal, but it did begin to slow. His heart rate decreased from full-out sprint to hard run.

A gunshot rang out, startling him. He jolted at a disturbance in the water a few feet away. Water sloshed over his face and into his eyes, and he lost control of his respirations.

As if not drowning while submerged in a dark lake with one's hands and feet bound weren't challenging enough.

She was fucking shooting at him.

The woman was leaning over the side of the boat, obviously scanning the water for him. She waved the gun in one hand. "Get a fucking flashlight!"

Todd used his abs to dolphin kick, trying to put some distance between him and the boat. The greater the distance, the less accurate a handgun was to shoot.

But he had only one option. If he stayed above the surface, she would see him. Then she would shoot him. Then he'd definitely drown.

To save himself, he'd have to do the one thing his body was fighting against.

He had to go under.

Todd exhaled. With the air out of his lungs, his lean body sank. The water closed over his head. An odd calm washed over him as he watched the moonlight fade.

A second shot rang out. The bullet hit the water with a quick splash. Todd slowly kicked away from the sound.

The blackness had seemed terrifying just a moment ago. Now he was hoping it was dark enough so she couldn't see him.

CHAPTER

THIRTY-FOUR

Matt watched the silhouettes struggle, saw the body go into the water, heard the sound of gunshots. He needed to go in after Todd. But he couldn't see him.

"Can you get me closer?" he shouted at Juarez.

With a nod, Juarez eased the throttle forward, and the boat surged faster. The AR-15 strapped to the deputy's back swung. He steered to the right to give the area where the person had gone into the water a wide berth. The boat leaned into the turn. They crossed over the wake of the lead boat. Their bow porpoised, the hull slapping on the water after it topped each wave and crashed down.

Stephanie's boat surged ahead. Were they making a run for it?

Fighting for balance, Matt grabbed the life ring from the back of the seat and staggered to the side.

Next to him, Bree gripped a rail with one hand. Her feet were spread for balance. Matt handed her Collins's AR-15. Bree rested the rifle across her body. Her eyes were on the water. She shouted, "Could you see if it was definitely Todd who went into the water?"

"No. Too dark." Matt's gaze swept the water, looking for a face. But all he could see was darkness and more darkness.

"There!" Bree pointed. A pale face appeared above the surface. Then he went under again.

Matt looped one arm through the life-ring rope and brought one foot up onto the side of the boat. The boat rocked as he pushed off without waiting for it to stop. He dived into the lake.

The water closed over him. Towing the life ring, he stroked toward the spot where he'd seen Todd. When he reached the approximate location, he spun, treading water, looking for Todd.

A head popped up a dozen feet away.

"Todd?" Matt yelled.

The head went under.

By the time Matt swam to him, he'd surfaced again. Hooking the life ring under one arm, Matt grabbed him with the other. It *was* Todd, and he was alive. Relief almost made Matt weak. "Grab the ring."

Shivering, Todd gurgled an answer.

Holy shit.

His arms and legs were bound. He couldn't hold on to the ring.

How was he even still alive?

"It's OK. I've got you." Matt couldn't free Todd's hands and ankles. The best he could do was keep both of their heads above water until Bree and Juarez could swing around and pick them up. Todd was pale and gasping. His face was beat to shit. Probably the rest of him too.

An engine screamed toward them. Matt turned, hoping to see Juarez at the wheel. Panic bolted through him as he realized it was the wrong boat. Stephanie Crighton was headed right toward them. There was no way for Matt to get them out of the boat's path. He couldn't swim fast enough with a fully bound Todd and a life ring in tow.

"We have to go under." Todd spit out some water. "Let me go."

Matt had no choice. If they stayed on the surface, they'd die.

"Deep breath." Matt shoved the ring away and dived down. Exhaling as he swam down, he tried to keep hold of Todd. He would not lose the chief deputy, not after finally getting him back. But Todd wiggled out of his grip, dolphin kicking toward the bottom. Thankfully, neither of them had much body fat. They both sank like bricks.

CHAPTER

THIRTY-FIVE

Todd lost control of his respirations. His heart sprinted wildly. Below the surface, he forced himself to swim down. Down. Down. Until his feet hit the bottom. He kept going until his ass landed in the mud.

Oxygen starved, his lungs were on fire. Dizziness disoriented him.

His instincts screamed to surface. To swim toward the light. Toward air.

He heard the engine whine and felt the disturbance in the water as the boat passed over him. He counted to three, not wanting to get sliced by the propeller.

Then he pushed off the bottom of the lake toward the moonlight. His face broke the surface. He gulped air. He could still hear the whine of an engine. Which way was it going?

"Go down!" Matt's voice shouted.

Without looking to see where his friend was, he leaned his head back, raising his chin, trying to get one last sip of air into his lungs. Exhaling, Todd let himself sink again.

How many times could he do this? Exhaustion and panic were eroding his strength like high tide took down a sandcastle. The boat passed over him again. Todd pushed off the bottom one more time.

His face broke the surface and he inhaled air, along with some water, through his nose and mouth.

"Todd!" Matt yelled from somewhere behind him.

Todd didn't answer. Lake water burned the back of his throat and gagged him. Fuzziness encroached on his vision, and he was light-headed from lack of oxygen. Gasping, he couldn't maintain the deep, steady breaths he needed to keep going.

In a few minutes, he was going to have to float. Otherwise, he'd drown.

Then that crazy bitch would run him over.

Matt grabbed his sleeve. Todd shook him off. If he died, he wouldn't take Matt with him. Unable to keep his head above water any longer, Todd let himself sink.

All the way to the bottom.

CHAPTER THIRTY-SIX

Bree aimed her rifle at Stephanie's boat, but the vessel was moving fast and turning too quickly. Stephanie passed over the place where Bree had last spotted Matt and Todd, then her boat roared away.

Bree turned her attention from shooting the suspect to finding Matt and Todd. She lowered the gun and scanned the lake.

Where are they?

Fear wrung out her insides like a wet rag. They passed close to a navigation buoy. A red light blinked above white mile-marker numbers. Using her radio, Bree reported their location to dispatch. "What's the ETA on the marine unit?"

A few seconds later, the dispatcher said, "Twenty-one minutes."

Too long.

She tapped Juarez's shoulder. "How deep is this water?"

"I don't know." Juarez gestured toward the empty dashboard. "This boat is old-school. It doesn't have any electronics. Not even a depth finder."

The running lights of Stephanie's boat appeared in the darkness. She was circling back to finish the job. That bitch just wouldn't give up.

"She's trying to run them over again!" Bree pointed into the dark. She could just see a pale face in the moonlight.

Todd or Matt?

"We need to get them out of the water," she yelled.

"Hold on, ma'am!" Juarez shouted.

She grabbed for a rail as her deputy brought the boat around in a sharp turn. He straightened their course. As they crossed back over their own wake, the deck pitched under her feet. Then the ride smoothed out again.

Bree turned back. Stephanie's boat was a hundred yards away and closing the distance fast. Bree turned and scanned the water again. "Two o'clock."

Juarez turned toward the person, keeping their boat between him and the approaching vessel. He eased back on the throttle. "She's heading toward us."

"I know." Bree took a position on the bow. She braced a foot on a seat and leveled the AR-15 at the oncoming boat. Aiming at the silhouette behind the wheel, Bree squeezed off two shots. With the deck rolling under her and the movement of her target, she didn't have much hope of hitting Stephanie. But she hoped to put a bullet close enough to the captain to make them veer off course.

The boat kept coming. She squeezed off another shot. Surely, Stephanie would turn.

Or would she play a deadly game of chicken?

Clammy sweat poured down Bree's back, and sickness churned in her belly. If she was wrong, the other boat would ram hers, and they would all die. "Hurry up!"

"I see them in the water." Juarez moved the boat forward. He left the wheel to lean over the side. Bree glanced over. She could see two heads above the water.

Juarez straddled the gunwale and tried to haul Todd out of the water, but with Todd's hands and feet bound, the task was proving very difficult. Todd was essentially deadweight. In the water, Matt tried to help, but he had no leverage.

Bree turned back to the approaching boat again. It wasn't wavering from its course. In about thirty seconds, it would crash into them. She slid her finger into the trigger guard and fired another shot. Stephanie kept coming, headed straight for them.

The boat rocked. Bree glanced behind her to see Matt climbing up the swim ladder next to the outboard. He rushed to Juarez's side, reached over, and grabbed hold of Todd. Together, Matt and Juarez dragged Todd over the side. The boat rocked again at the change in weight. The three men fell to the deck in a sloppy, wet pile.

Bracing herself against the pitch of the deck, Bree shot at the oncoming boat once more. Stephanie was almost on top of them. One of Bree's bullets must have hit something, because the boat finally swerved. It passed close enough that Bree could see Stephanie at the wheel. Next to her, Dylan gripped the dashboard.

As the boat passed, Bree fired a few rounds at the engine.

The deck rocked harder as Stephanie's wake reached them. Bree kept her weapon pointed at Stephanie, but the boat was pitching too violently for her to take aim. She grabbed for a rail but wasn't quick enough. She lost her footing and went down. Her ass hit the deck, and pain sang up her tailbone. She lunged to one knee and leveled the rifle again. No shot.

Juarez lunged across the deck, grabbed the wheel, and gave the engine some gas. He turned the boat so the approaching waves hit the bow at a forty-five-degree angle and the hull was better able to absorb the wake. He yelled back at Bree, "Are we going after them?"

Bree hurried to Todd. He looked rough but his life didn't appear to be in immediate danger. As unprofessional as it felt, she wanted to hug him. After she'd worked with—and trained—him for the last seven months, Todd felt like a little brother. She held back for fear of hurting him. "How badly are you hurt?"

Matt lifted seats and opened little cubbies all over the boat. He came back with a first aid kit and a folding knife. He cut the ropes binding Todd's wrists and ankles. Todd fell back, relief seeming to exhaust him. Shaking, he lay on his side and rubbed his wrists. "Go!" he croaked. "Don't let them get away."

"You're sure?" she asked.

Todd shivered, coughed, and gestured toward the retreating boat.

Matt opened the first aid kit. Sitting on the floor of the boat, he dug in it for Mylar blankets, which he wrapped around Todd's shoulders.

"I'll live." Todd's teeth chattered. "Let's get them."

Bree considered his condition for two seconds. Hypothermic. Beaten. But no gushing blood or obvious broken bones. The chance of internal injuries gave her pause, but the determination in his eyes made her decision. She tapped Juarez on the forearm. "Go after them."

Juarez's face split in a feral grin. "Yes, ma'am."

"Can you catch her?"

"Yes, ma'am." Juarez gunned the engine. The boat leaped forward.

Stephanie had a head start, but the boat they'd commandeered had more horsepower. Juarez wasn't timid about speed once everyone was settled and secure in the boat. They gained steadily.

Bree kept one eye on Todd. Wrapped in two Mylar blankets, he gritted his teeth. The ride was smooth on the flat water. Juarez was following Stephanie's wake, staying in the center of the V. But Todd was freezing. She suspected sheer determination was keeping him upright. He should be headed for the ER.

Damn it. She didn't want to let Dylan and Stephanie get away either.

They drew closer.

In the moonlight, Stephanie looked back. Her boat sounded like it was already at top speed. Dylan was at the back of the boat, watching the deputies gain on them. Stephanie lifted her hand and pointed behind her.

"Gun!" Juarez crouched behind the windshield.

"Get down." Bree ducked, even though they were too far away for an accurate shot with a pistol. Stephanie could get lucky.

A muzzle flash blinked. Dylan toppled over the stern and into the water.

Bree recoiled. Stephanie had shot Dylan. *What the hell?* Bree shook off her shock.

"Hold on!" Juarez tugged the wheel. The boat cut right so he didn't run over the man who'd just pitched into the water.

Bree lost her footing and tumbled ass over feet. Her shoulder crashed into the center console. Todd and Matt slid across the floor.

Bree levered to her feet. "Where's Dylan?"

Juarez eased the throttle back. "In the water. She shot him." He jerked a thumb behind them. "I'll swing around."

Bree wanted to catch Stephanie. Could she leave Dylan to drown? No, she couldn't.

Fuck. Fuck. *Fuck.*

She watched Stephanie's boat race away. Yeah. No doubt about it. Stephanie was lucky.

Juarez steered the boat in a wide arc and slowed.

Bree spotted something pale in the water. "He's at one o'clock."

Dylan was floating facedown. Dead? Bree wanted him alive—to answer questions and to answer for his crimes.

The boat circled. Juarez eased up to him, and Matt hauled him out of the water. Bree knelt next to him and checked his pulse. Nothing. She gave him rescue breaths. Matt started chest compressions.

"Where to, ma'am?" Juarez asked.

"What's close by?" Bree looked up. Dylan needed a hospital.

"There's a park ahead with a beach and dock." He gestured forward, in roughly the same direction Stephanie had gone.

"Go." Bree gave Dylan two more puffs of air. She could hear her deputy on the marine radio, giving their location and calling for an ambulance. Then Juarez gunned the engine, and the boat shot off.

Matt and Bree continued to work in a rhythm. Between breaths, Bree ran her hands over Dylan's body and found a bullet wound high on his shoulder. After a few minutes of CPR, Dylan coughed. His body jerked to life. Bree rolled him onto his side while he expelled water from his lungs and stomach. When he'd finished, she rolled him back and found his pulse. It throbbed weakly against her fingertips. Blood welled from his shoulder wound. Now that they'd brought him back, they needed to stop the bleeding, or they'd lose him again.

Matt opened the first aid kit once more. Ripping open gauze, he stacked it on the shoulder wound and applied pressure. Todd relinquished one of his Mylar blankets. That he would try to save the man who'd almost killed him spoke volumes about her chief deputy.

At Matt's raised eyebrows, Todd shrugged. "Prison will be way worse than death."

Dylan's eyes fluttered open for a few seconds. Fear, shock, and pain widened his pupils before he passed out again. Bree checked his pulse. Still alive.

"Too bad Stephanie got away." Matt sat back on his heels.

"No worries," Juarez yelled from behind the wheel. He pointed.

Bree stood and squinted at Stephanie's boat. Stephanie had been ahead of them, and she'd had a decent lead. How had they caught up to her?

They overtook Stephanie. Her engine sputtered and coughed.

Juarez glanced over his shoulder and grinned. "One of your shots must have hit the engine and damaged it. She's barely doing five or ten miles per hour."

The *thump thump thump* of a helicopter approached. Bree squinted at the night sky. A minute later, the state police chopper passed overhead, spotlights searching the lake. She waved as the light passed over her. The chopper doubled back and hovered above Stephanie's boat for a few seconds. A booming voice from a loudspeaker instructed her to drop her weapon, drive to the beach ahead, and raise her hands.

Even if she got her engine running at full speed, Stephanie couldn't outrun a chopper.

Flashing lights to the right caught Bree's attention. She spotted emergency vehicles. Juarez cut their speed. Collins and Brody were on the beach waiting for them, along with two state police cruisers, two ambulances, and an EMT unit. Bree turned back to Stephanie's boat.

With a glance at Matt applying a pressure bandage to Dylan's shoulder, Bree hefted her rifle and returned to the bow. At the wheel of her own boat, Stephanie still held a handgun.

Juarez turned. "Permission to escort her in?"

Bree pointed the rifle at Stephanie and aimed. A red dot appeared in the center of her chest. Stephanie dropped her handgun and put both hands on the wheel.

Bree kept the sight on her anyway. "Granted."

Ahead, Stephanie pulled up to the public dock. State troopers boarded her boat and took her into custody. Bree lowered her rifle and sat on the side of the boat, her adrenaline suddenly gone. She barely noticed EMTs treating Dylan and Todd.

They were all alive, even Todd. She'd been almost sure they were going to find him dead. Relief made her legs weak.

She could have lost Matt tonight. While he'd been in the water, she hadn't allowed herself to think about the potential for disaster. Even as Stephanie had tried to run Matt and Todd over, Bree had blocked her fear and concentrated on responding. But now that Matt was safe, delayed panic washed over her like cold rain.

He perched next to her. "You OK?"

She glanced at him. "Shouldn't I be asking you that? You were the one who went into the water."

He lifted a damp shoulder. "I'm durable."

She snorted but had no response. They sat side by side, watching the EMTs off-load Dylan by gurney. Todd insisted on walking from the boat under his own steam.

She looked over the side at the water, black and bottomless in the dark. "I can picture a dozen ways tonight could have gone horribly wrong."

"Yep." Matt shifted sideways an inch, until their shoulders pressed together. "But it didn't."

Bree leaned into him.

"Everyone is OK, Bree," Matt said.

"Not sure Dylan is going to make it."

"Everyone who counts," Matt corrected. "If he doesn't, it isn't because of anything we did. He got himself into this mess. He tried to kill Todd. We did everything we could to save him anyway."

She nodded. "There are times this job is incredibly weird."

"You know it."

On the beach, Brody barked. Collins could barely hold him back.

"I need to go see my dog." Matt stood and turned toward the dock.

Bree rose but didn't take a step. She kept her voice low. With all the commotion, no one would overhear. "Have I told you I love you today?"

He turned and smiled over his shoulder. Before he could respond, a state trooper summoned them from the dock. It didn't matter. She knew he loved her. He didn't have to say it with words.

CHAPTER THIRTY-SEVEN

Hours later, Bree walked down the corridor toward Todd's room. She'd managed a brief power nap in the waiting room, and her eyes were gritty. She stopped in the doorway. His face was battered. Most of his visible skin was covered with bruises. He'd been dehydrated and hypothermic and diagnosed with a concussion.

She stood in the doorway for a couple of minutes, marveling that he was alive, thanking his incredible will to survive, and cursing Brian Dylan and Stephanie Crighton. He opened his eyes as she walked in. Eye, really. One was still mostly swollen shut.

"How are you?" she asked.

"I'm OK," he said in a raspy voice. He lifted his left hand. An IV ran into his forearm. "Whatever is in here is definitely helping."

"They're keeping you overnight?" Looking at him, she wondered that they could release him anytime soon. Miraculously, X-rays and scans showed no broken bones or major internal injuries. But nearly every inch of him was bruised.

"Yeah." Todd grimaced. "I'd rather go home."

"Better safe than sorry." Bree gestured to his IV. "Besides, the good drugs are here."

"Good point," he admitted. "It's all superficial." He waved a hand without lifting it off the bed. "I'll be back to work in a week or so."

"You will certainly not come back to work until a doctor clears you," Bree said.

"Oh, no. The stern face." His mouth curved in a loopy smile, then he winced as if the motion hurt.

Bree couldn't hold back a laugh. Her chief deputy was normally very serious. The drugs must be talking. She should go before he said something that embarrassed either one of them. Not that he would remember.

He reached for a plastic cup on his bedside table. After swallowing some water, he rested his head back on the pillow, as if that small movement had exhausted him. "I feel stupid."

"What? Why?"

"I let myself get jumped. I let down my guard."

"That's ridiculous. You were at your own house. No one expects to be ambushed in their own yard."

His shoulder twitched, and he glanced away.

Anger shot through Bree, and she almost wished they hadn't saved Dylan, the bastard. "You listen here. You have no reason to feel stupid. It took five guys to take you down, and you inflicted some damage on them. You kept a cool head under the most dire and terrifying circumstances."

He stared at his cup.

Bree lowered her voice. "I—we are all grateful that you survived. You are one tough nut."

"I guess." Todd blew out a quick breath through his nostrils.

She touched a spot on his forearm that wasn't black and blue. "Get some rest." She vowed he'd get counseling in addition to physical therapy before he returned to work. He would be dealing with the mental and emotional fallout of his ordeal long after his physical injuries had healed.

He closed his eye and drifted off into a drugged slumber.

Footsteps scuffed in the hallway. Bree turned. Cady stood in the doorway, her face pale, her eyes worried. Bree wasn't surprised to see Matt's sister there. She'd felt vibes between her and Todd for some time.

"I need to go." Bree headed for the door. On her way out, she nodded to Cady. "You'll look after him?"

"I will." Cady went inside.

"Then I'll be on my way." Bree left Todd in Cady's very capable hands.

Dylan was still in surgery, so Bree headed to the station, where the state police investigator was taking statements. They'd touched base on the phone earlier, but Bree wasn't in a rush to talk to him. The sun was rising as she parked in the lot. She slipped into her office via the back door.

Marge brought her coffee and two apple cider doughnuts.

"You're the best." Bree bit into a doughnut.

"I know." Marge smiled. "Investigator Ash is in the conference room. He's already talked to the deputies involved with the incident. I gave him coffee and a doughnut. He'll keep until you're ready."

Bree washed the rest of the first doughnut down with coffee. "Would you send Morgan Dane back when she gets here?"

"I will." Marge turned toward the door.

As she left, Matt walked in, holding Jim Rogers's puppy in one arm.

"So, that's where you've been." Bree reached out and stroked the puppy.

"Until someone decides who gets her, she needs to be taken care of." Of course he would think of the dog.

"Have you talked to Ash yet?" Bree asked.

Matt nodded. "All done. I kept it basic."

A minute later, someone knocked on Bree's doorway. Morgan Dane peered inside.

Bree stood. "Let's get this done." Anxious to put the interview behind her, she led the way to the conference room.

"Stick to the facts," Morgan said as they walked. "If a question isn't relevant to the case or last night's incident, don't answer it."

They entered the conference room. Phillip Ash was a big, bald man. His suit slacks and dress shirt showed the wrinkles of a long night. Rolled-up sleeves highlighted Popeye forearms.

Bree introduced herself and Morgan, and then they took seats facing Ash across the table.

Morgan folded her hands. "You have Sheriff Taggert's written statement."

Ash nodded. "This is a simple debriefing."

Despite his words, Bree needed to be on her toes. Morgan clearly didn't trust him. They had that in common.

"Describe the events leading up to last night's boat chase." Ash leaned on the table.

Bree listed the highlights. "My written statement is more detailed."

"You'd passed the murder off to BCI," Ash said. "Why didn't you also hand off the search of Stephanie Crighton's house?"

"My deputy's life was in danger. Exigent circumstances." Bree would be very happy never to utter those words again.

Ash narrowed his eyes. "Would you elaborate on that statement? Did you receive any indication that your deputy was in immediate danger?"

"My deputy had been beaten and kidnapped." Bree kept her answers short, but it annoyed the hell out of her that she was being treated like anything short of a law enforcement officer. Ash's ego was in a knot because she hadn't reported to him before going after Todd.

Too bad.

A vein in Ash's temple throbbed. "It didn't occur to you that the kidnapping was tied to the double murder of Eugene Oscar and his mother?"

Bree said, "I was focused on finding my chief deputy."

"But when you deduced that Stephanie Crighton was involved with both the murders and the abduction, you still didn't see fit to notify BCI." Ash's dark brown eyes gleamed. What did he want? For her to admit she'd overstepped her authority? No fucking way. Ash wasn't her boss.

She breathed and repeated, "I was focused on finding my chief deputy." Then she added, "Alive."

"You didn't have time to make a single phone call?" Ash didn't roll his eyes, but his voice was incredulous.

"No," Bree said.

"What's the point in this line of questioning?" Morgan asked. "The sheriff pursued and apprehended the people who beat and kidnapped her deputy. Because of her immediate response, Chief Deputy Harvey is still alive. That those same people also committed other crimes is irrelevant. Also"—Morgan gestured between Bree and Ash—"you're both on the same side."

Right? Then why did Bree feel like she was being interrogated?

"I'd like to discuss the actual case," Bree said.

Ash drummed the table with his fingertips, frustration clamping his molars together. He rubbed two meaty hands down his face. Lifting his head, he sighed in resignation. "You're right. We're on the same side. Sometimes the politics of the department make us all forget that. I apologize."

Bree sat back. She hadn't expected him to own up to his missteps. "Apology accepted."

"Thank you." Ash opened his folder with a *back to business* vibe. "Some evidence came to light while you were sleeping." He shuffled papers. "The blood on Bernard Crighton's pants was his own."

"Did he know what his daughter did?" Bree asked.

Ash lifted a hand. "At this time, we have no reason to believe he had anything to do with his daughter's actions."

Bree nodded.

"As you know, the county forensics team has been searching the lake house all night." Ash continued. "In it, they found Brian Dylan's computer. On the hard drive were the working files for the pornographic deepfake video and photo-edited images of you. He also seems to have been responsible for harassing emails you've recently received, including the penis photo he sent to you. He had a copy of that picture on a burner phone. We think the photo is of himself."

Bree grimaced. "I didn't need to know the dick pic was Dylan."

"Sorry," Ash commiserated. "Your forensics department also found a second sex doll identical to the one he used to threaten you." He shook his head. "We suspect he kept it for his personal use."

Ew.

"Dylan was a busy man," Bree said.

"And he seemed determined to torment you." Ash nodded. "The gun in Stephanie's possession was registered to Eugene Oscar. We believe ballistics will confirm it was the weapon used to kill Oscar and his mother."

"Did she confess?"

"Stephanie is not talking."

"She's smart."

"She didn't get away with it." Ash closed his file and exhaled. "Because of you." He stood. "I'll be in touch. I'm sure there'll be further questions."

Unless she plea-bargained, Stephanie would be tried for murder.

"One more thing." Ash picked up his file. "Shane Bartholomew was bailed out yesterday."

Anger heated Bree's blood. "How the hell did he get bailed out?"

"He and his three pals"—Ash listed all the names that Shane had implicated in Todd's beating and kidnapping—"barely warmed the holding cells before a hotshot lawyer showed up."

"Let me guess. The Hudson Footmen sent the attorney." Bree was disgusted.

"We can't prove they sent him, but we're working on it."

"Damn it. Who knows if they'll show up for trial?"

"No need to worry about that." Ash paused. "Very early this morning, Shane's body—along with the three other men's—were found in a vehicle in the Hudson River. All four men are dead. Their vehicle went over a three-hundred-foot cliff."

Shock slashed through Bree's exhaustion. "Cause of death?"

"Don't have autopsy results yet, but that's a long drop."

"They were murdered."

"Probably," Ash agreed.

Bree considered Shane's confession and his link to the paramilitary group. "Do you suspect the Hudson Footmen were responsible?"

"It's possible they didn't approve of Shane's blabbing," Ash said.

"If he survives, Dylan will be at risk. They'll want him dead."

"He's out of surgery. He's going to make it." Ash headed for the door. "We have a guard on his door, and when he's transferred to the prison, he'll be put in solitary."

But would that be enough to keep him alive? That likely depended on how much he knew about the organization. They'd been willing to kill four men for much less.

Ash left.

Morgan stood and offered her hand. "We're working on the takedown orders. I'll keep you posted. You'll call me if you need me?"

"Yes, and thank you."

"You're welcome." Morgan picked up her briefcase. "I'll see you at the K-9 fundraiser."

"You're coming?"

"Of course. The community supports the sheriff's department. The community supports you," Morgan said.

"I hope so. We really need that dog."

Brody deserved an actual retirement.

Bree escorted Morgan to the rear exit. After closing the door behind the attorney, Bree peered down the hallway. She could see reporters gathered in the lobby. She ducked out of sight before she was spotted and hurried to her office, where Matt and the puppy waited. "The press is here. I'm sneaking home to sleep for a few hours."

They left through the back door together.

"Not making a statement?" Matt carried the puppy out.

"No. I've had enough." It felt cowardly, but Bree knew the questions would segue into a discussion about the deepfakes, and she didn't have the energy. She'd deal with them another day.

He walked her to her vehicle.

"Want to come for dinner tonight?" Bree asked.

Matt grinned. "What is Dana making?"

"Lasagna."

"Then hell yeah, I'm coming." His smile widened. He didn't kiss her in the parking lot, but she could tell he wanted to, and that was enough.

CHAPTER THIRTY-EIGHT

The next day, Matt woke to the sound of a puppy whining in Greta's crate. Greta wagged her tail and barked, eager to play with the new guest. Brody gave Matt a heavy *are you kidding me?* side-eye.

"Don't worry, Brody. She's not staying." Matt fed all three and then took them outside. The puppy was happy to bug Greta, leaving Brody to chill. After returning the older dogs to the house, he scooped the puppy into one arm and carried her out back.

Cady was in the kennel, feeding her rescues. She stopped to pet and coo over the puppy.

"Can you watch her today?" Matt asked. "I need to go to the hospital to interview Brian Dylan." His crimes crossed jurisdictional boundaries, and Ash had agreed to join forces with the sheriff's department. Ash and Bree would also be present for the interview.

"I'm headed to Todd's house as soon as I'm done here." Cady fixed her ponytail. "He's getting released this morning, and I don't think he should be alone."

"I agree." Matt lifted the puppy higher onto his chest. She bit his beard.

Staring at the puppy, Cady tilted her head. "Does Rogers's family want her?"

"He doesn't really have any family." Matt shook his head. "She's homeless."

Cady's eyes twinkled. "In that case, how about I take her with me? Maybe a puppy will cheer up Todd."

"Maybe you can talk him into keeping her." Matt thought she could talk Todd into just about anything.

"Maybe I can." Cady took the puppy. "Good luck."

"Thanks." Matt drove his Suburban to the hospital.

Bree's SUV was already in the lot when he parked. She climbed out of the vehicle. "I was waiting for you."

He told her about Cady taking the puppy to Todd's house.

Bree laughed. "Todd is totally keeping that puppy. He'll do whatever Cady wants. He has it bad for her."

Matt rubbed his palms together. "Then my devious plan worked. I found a home for the dog and fixed those two up."

"Aren't you the matchmaker?"

"Todd's a good man. Cady deserves one of those." Matt thought they deserved each other.

"They're a good match," Bree said. "Hey, you take the lead with Dylan. He'll respond better to you. He hates me."

"Do I have to be an asshole again?"

"I don't think so. Ash called. The state police and numerous federal agencies want information on the Hudson Footmen. Dylan wants to make a deal. He'll be cooperative. But he still hates me."

They took the elevator to Dylan's floor. Outside his room, a trooper was on guard duty. Ash leaned on the wall. He looked up from his phone as they approached, then pushed off the wall.

"So, what's the game plan?" Bree asked.

"I spoke with Dylan earlier, but he wasn't in any shape to answer questions." Ash addressed Matt. "I'd like you to take the lead. You're more familiar with Dylan and the case. Also, I watched the video of your interview with Shane Bartholomew. I think Dylan will respond best to you."

"I agree," Bree said. "I'll stay out of the way."

Bree walked to the far wall and leaned on it. Matt crossed to the bedside. Ash stepped up next to him. He set a digital recorder on the rolling hospital tray.

Dylan didn't look half-bad for a guy who'd been dead for a full five minutes the night before. He was pale and pasty but awake. One wrist held an IV. The other was cuffed to the bed rail.

"You're going to live," Matt said as he stepped up next to the bed. Dylan nodded.

"I hear you're cooperating?" he asked.

"I'm getting a deal." Dylan licked his lips.

"I want to ask you a few questions."

"Whatever." Dylan sighed. "Doesn't matter. I'll tell you everything."

Matt started with the least of his charges. "You made the deepfake video of Sheriff Taggert."

"Yeah. As a favor to Oscar." He glared at Bree. "He hated you."

Bree acknowledged his comment. "I know."

Dylan's mouth turned up in a sneer. "I thought the video was funny."

Matt nodded. "You also sent the harassing emails to Sheriff Taggert and set up the threatening graffiti at the farm next to hers."

Dylan shifted his gaze to Bree. His eyes glowed with sick glee. "Did you like the drawings? I enjoyed painting them."

Bree didn't respond.

Matt moved on. Dylan was almost gloating, and Matt let him. "How did you meet Stephanie?"

Dylan cocked his head. "She approached me at a bar. She was hot. She didn't tell me who she was until later. By that time, I was pissed at Oscar. He was going to rat me out in Kenny McPherson's civil lawsuit."

"Why did you and Oscar target him in the first place?"

Dylan rubbed the edge of the sheet between his fingers. "Kenny was the first dude Oscar's ex dated after their divorce. I think they only went out one time, for coffee. Oscar used to follow her. He thought it was hilarious that Kenny and his ex were oblivious to the connection."

"And after you helped him, Oscar was going to put the blame on you."

"Yeah. That's what Steph said. I was the one who planted the drugs. Oscar was making a deal with the DA. He'd get immunity, and I'd get screwed. He was always looking out for himself."

The DA was not aware of any potential deal with Oscar. Apparently, it had never occurred to Dylan—not even now that Stephanie had betrayed him—that maybe she'd lied about that to get him to help her.

"So, you killed him first," Matt said.

"I didn't do it." Dylan looked away. "That was all Steph."

"She might have pulled the trigger, but you set the whole thing up, didn't you?"

"I helped her get them tied up." Dylan swallowed. "That's it."

That was enough, thought Matt.

"She wanted to do it. Couldn't wait. Coldest bitch I've ever met." Dylan pressed his lips flat. "I was stupid. She used me. She never really wanted me. I was a means to an end. She wanted to kill Oscar and his mother, but she couldn't do it by herself."

Matt tamped down his disgust and focused on his poker face. "Take me through their deaths, step by step."

Dylan stared over Matt's shoulder. "We stopped at the farm under the guise of telling them we were dating. Then I distracted them so she could sneak upstairs and get Oscar's gun. When she came back down, she held them at gunpoint while I tied them to chairs. Once they were secured, I went outside. I knew what was going to happen, but I didn't want to watch." His pale face flushed. "I knew it was gonna be messy."

So he was squeamish, but he didn't care if people died.

Anger hardened Dylan's face. "And then the bitch shot *me* when I was a loose end." He clearly hadn't expected her to turn on him even though she'd killed members of her own family.

The irony hit Matt hard, but he pressed on in a nonjudgmental tone. "Why did she want her cousin dead?"

"She hated him. She blamed him for the brother's suicide. Her brother, Robby, was a weakling. He stuttered really bad. She said Oscar teased the hell out of Robby until the kid hung himself."

"But that happened a long time ago," Matt said. "Why kill him now?"

"Steph and her sister and father all went to the farm to ask their aunt for money. They took the sister's kids to try and win over the aunt. Oscar picked on the kids. Stephanie said he was a real dick, calling them ugly and stupid, insulting them for their father's dumbass financial mess. He made them cry. The aunt didn't care at all."

Stephanie might not be talking, but Dylan sang like he was in the choir.

"Oscar hated kids," Dylan said. "He always did."

"Oscar teasing the kids was enough for Stephanie to kill him?" Matt asked.

"Steph got weird whenever she talked about Oscar or his mother. I think her hate for them had been stewing inside her since she was a kid. Then the aunt refused to help with the money." He wet his lips. "Steph figured if she killed them, her dad would inherit the farm. They'd sell the property and bail out the family. Oscar and his mom would finally pay for Robby's death."

"Who shot Jim Rogers?" Matt asked.

"Steph. Rogers came over, all pissed off. He said he was done covering up for me. He was going to the DA." Dylan shook his head. "I wasn't all that worried. Rogers hadn't actually seen anything that night, and he's been unstable. But he saw Todd in the back of my truck, so he had to go. Couldn't trust him anymore. He got ethics or some shit lately." Dylan paused. "I was arguing with him, and Steph shot him in the back."

Matt swallowed. Keeping his emotions in check during this interview might be one of the hardest things he'd ever done. "But you kidnapped Chief Deputy Harvey."

Nodding, Dylan licked his lips. "I shouldn't have grabbed Todd. I didn't plan that. It seemed like a good idea at the time. When I was a deputy, Todd was always such a judgmental prick. I wanted to show him who was boss. Plus, I wanted to stop him from asking about the Footmen. But Steph was right. That was dumb."

Truer words had never been spoken.

"Why did you need him to stop asking about the Hudson Footmen?"

"Because that's not an organization you want to fuck with. I'll tell you more about them after I see the DA's deal. That's my leverage." Dylan clamped his lips tight.

Matt finished up the interview, and they left the room. No one commented on the interview with Dylan while he was still in earshot. Matt and Bree left Ash in the hallway. They walked down the hallway in silence and stepped onto the elevator.

Matt stabbed the button for the lobby level. The anger and frustration simmering inside him finally broke free. "I wanted to punch him in the face."

"Me too. He's complete scum."

"At least he'll be going to prison." Matt wrapped a hand around the back of his neck. "I know Rogers had his issues, but he was trying to redeem himself. Now he'll never have a chance."

Bree took his hand and squeezed it. "Stephanie will get life for his murder. She'll never see the outside of a prison again."

"That doesn't feel like enough."

"I know."

Their eyes met, and he knew she truly understood what he was feeling, and *that* made all the difference.

CHAPTER THIRTY-NINE

Two weeks later

On the night of the fundraiser, Bree swiped on some lipstick and fluffed her hair in the bathroom mirror. Dana had talked her into a girls' spa day with Kayla. The little girl, normally covered in dirt and grass stains, had loved every minute of her hairstyling and mani-pedi.

Vader sat on the vanity and gave Bree a critical once-over. He didn't seem impressed.

"Ladybug thinks I look pretty good," she said to the cat.

Lying on the bathroom rug, Ladybug wagged at the mention of her name. Vader gave the dog a disgusted look, then jumped down and sauntered away.

Bree adjusted the holster on her ankle. She'd bought a dress without a slit for a reason. She might not be able to carry her service piece, but her backup would do.

She went downstairs, the dog following so closely, she nearly tripped Bree four times on the steps.

Matt stood in the living room with Brody at his side. There was something about a well-built man in a tuxedo . . . Mm. He'd shaved, and his jaw was downright chiseled.

"Wow." He walked a circle around her.

"You clean up pretty nicely yourself, and you are very handsome, Brody." Bree leaned down to pat the dog.

"You look amazing," Matt said.

"It's not too much?" She wore a strapless gown of dark blue silk. "You don't think I should have worn my uniform?"

"Hell no—I mean, definitely not. That dress is perfect." Matt's voice was filled with just the right amount of awe.

"Of course it's perfect." Dana walked in from the kitchen, her heels clicking on the wood floor. "I picked it out." Her gown was a solid black sleeveless column with a high neck and slit to match. The lean leg that flashed as she walked attested to many hours on a spin bike.

Matt stopped next to Bree. He touched the tattoo on her shoulder. "This really is incredible." His fingers trailed along a vine and lingered on the huge dragonfly on her shoulder blade.

The heat of his hand almost made her want to skip the fundraiser.

She cleared her throat. "I decided I have no reason to be ashamed of my scars or tattoos."

"It's about time." Matt gave her a look she could only describe in a cliché: smoldering. He dropped his voice to a husky whisper. "You're totally hot. Also, that dress will put those deepfake stories to rest. Win-win."

The dress was hardly scandalous—it displayed zero cleavage—but showed more skin than usual for her. Bree didn't like that she'd been forced to put her tattoos on display. Tonight would be the first time she'd shown them in public, and she felt exposed. But she'd deal with it. Not for her job, but for the kids. For their sake, the rumors needed to be squashed. They didn't need to grow up with being teased about their aunt the porn star.

"I'm ready!" Kayla bounced down the stairs in a pale blue dress. She whirled in a circle, making the skirt spin.

At her heels, Luke toyed with his collar.

"You look very handsome." Bree straightened his black tie. "Nice tux. I thought you were wearing your suit." She did not make the kind of money that allowed for investing in a tuxedo for a young man who was still growing. It wouldn't even fit him next year.

"I wanted to surprise you. Uncle Adam bought this for me in New York. We went to a black-tie thing at the gallery." Adam and Luke had returned from the city a week ago, but Luke had been busy catching up with school. They hadn't had time to talk.

"I'm glad you had fun with Uncle Adam."

"I did. We went to museums and got pastrami sandwiches." Luke flushed and looked at the floor. "I'm sorry I've been a jerk about the camping trip. You're not the only parent who said no. Half the kids can't go."

Bree's heart stumbled. This was the first time he'd referred to her as his *parent*. Her eyes went misty. "Thanks for the apology. You're growing up into a fine man."

Luke nodded. "Uncle Adam said real men apologize when they screw up."

"That goes for women too." Bree blinked back a tear. She swiped under her eye before her mascara ran all over her face. "Look, I've given it a lot of thought, and if you still want to go camping, I could go with you and your friends." She didn't know why it hadn't occurred to her before. Camping wasn't on her list of favorite activities, but for Luke, she would do anything, even sleep in a tent with bugs.

"Aunt Bree." Luke looked pained. "I appreciate that you'd offer, but"—he lowered his voice—"it's a guys' trip."

"I understand. You don't have to explain." She held up a hand. "I can be a lot of things, but I can't be a guy." Bree couldn't be both parents, no matter how hard she tried.

"Definitely not." Matt wrapped one arm around her waist and pulled her closer. Then he turned to Luke. "How about I take you and your friends camping?" He looked down at Bree. "Would I be enough supervision for you?"

"Um. Yeah," Bree stammered, surprised. She hadn't expected him to offer, but the solution was so simple. "Definitely yes."

Matt slapped Luke on the back. "Seriously, Luke. You should have just asked. I love camping."

Adam walked in the front door. He was almost unrecognizable in a custom-fitted tuxedo. His hair was combed. He was clean shaven and not covered in paint. Ladybug rubbed on his legs. "Who's going camping?"

Matt gestured to Luke. "Me and Luke and some of his friends. Want to come?"

"Count me in." Adam brushed white dog hair off his black pants. "I'll dust off my fishing rod."

"Awesome." Luke pulled his phone from his trouser pocket. "I'm going to call the guys. I'll be outside when you're ready to go."

Bree turned to Adam. "I haven't seen you since you got back from the city. How did it go?"

"You know how I was worried that the gallery didn't like my new painting because it goes in a different direction than my other work?" Adam's latest painting had been less dark, less broody, more hopeful than his previous work.

"Yes." Bree rested a hand on his forearm. "As much as we all appreciate your support, we can manage. I don't ever want you to think you need to change your art for money. It's your passion, and you have to follow it."

"I love that you said that, but the gallery already sold the piece. The collector who bought it snapped up a few of my earlier works. He's going to loan them to the museum for an exhibition next summer." Adam's face beamed like the light in his new painting. "Seriously, Bree.

I spent this week setting up trust funds. The kids' college tuition—or whatever they want to do with their lives—is covered. I put aside money to pay the farm expenses."

"I'm speechless," Bree said.

"Good." Adam looked sad. "I didn't do enough for the kids and you before this year, but that's all in the past. We're a real family now."

Of all the things Bree had expected in her life, having her sometimes aloof and out-of-touch baby brother provide for the whole family wasn't one of them.

"I don't know what to say."

"Well, don't thank me." Adam smiled. "This is what family does. Those kids are just as much my responsibility as they are yours."

"Indeed." She kissed his cheek.

Adam moved off to talk to Dana.

Emotion overwhelmed Bree for a few seconds. She leaned her head on Matt's shoulder. "Thank you."

The hand at her waist squeezed. "You don't have to do everything yourself."

"I know. But sometimes I forget." Bree rarely remembered to ask for help. She needed to work on that.

"Are we ready?" Matt herded everyone to his Suburban. He opened the back and lifted Brody into the vehicle. The dog sat on the back seat between Luke and Kayla. Dana and Adam took the third row.

"Who's bringing Greta?" Bree asked as Matt opened the passenger door and helped her inside.

"Collins." Matt closed the door, rounded the vehicle to the driver's side, and slid behind the wheel. "I thought they should appear together."

"Good idea." Bree smoothed her dress. "If all goes well, they'll be partners."

Matt drove to the catering hall. They met Todd outside. Most of his bruises had faded, though he still favored his left side. They walked in together.

Inside, board games were set up on dozens of tables. One end of the space was devoted to the buffet. A dance floor dominated the other side. Next to it, a live band was setting up. Bree saw Cady near the entrance. She wore a stunning cobalt-blue gown. Her long hair was down and waved halfway down her back. Bree glanced at Todd, who was slack-jawed.

Cady approached them, clipboard in hand. "So far, everything is going smoothly."

Todd closed his gaping mouth but didn't say anything. His face reddened.

Cady looked down at her shoes, as if just realizing her heels made her two inches taller than Todd. "I should have worn flats."

"Why?" Todd recovered. He leaned forward to give her a quick kiss. "You look amazing."

Cady beamed.

"Can I help with anything?" he asked.

"Sure." She took his elbow and led him away.

Though Matt, Bree, and her family were early, the press already clustered at the entrance. Bree sent the kids to their table with Adam and Dana. She didn't want them near the media. Then she crossed the floor, with Matt at her side, and faced the reporters. Cameras flashed.

She pressed close to Matt, making it clear they were a couple.

In the front of the group, Paris Vickers took in Bree's dress. Her gaze stopped on the tattoo, and she seemed disappointed. The ink was intricate, extensive, and fully healed. It was the type of tattoo that took many months to complete. It clearly hadn't been done recently. "Well, I guess that's that." She shoved a mic in Bree's face. "Do you have any comments?"

"The gala has sold out." Bree pointed to Deputy Collins, entering the venue in full dress uniform. A freshly bathed and shiny Greta trotted at her side. Guests were arriving and admiring the gorgeous dog. "I expect the sheriff's department will have a K-9 team in the near future."

Paris moved on, clearly bored.

Reporter Nick West stepped forward and nodded toward Bree's tattoo. "Well played, Sheriff. Well played."

Bree gave him a nod, then crossed to a bar, where she ordered a club soda. She turned and scanned the room.

The night was a huge success. People ate, played games, and danced. As Morgan had said, everyone was there. Bree spotted her and Lance on the dance floor. Cady and Todd worked the room, selling raffle tickets and taking even more donations.

Toward the end of the evening, Bree gave a short speech, thanking everyone who'd helped and donated. Collins trotted Greta out to a huge round of applause. After laying down the mic, Bree took Matt by the hand and led him onto the dance floor.

"You're determined to flaunt our relationship?" he asked.

"Yep." She rested her hand on his shoulder. "They can accept it or not. That's on them. I won't sacrifice one bit of our happiness for public opinion. I won't sacrifice our future for anything, not even this job." Since her sister's death, Bree had continually reassessed her priorities. Seeing Matt risk death in the lake had brought that process to a swift conclusion. The future held no guarantees. She would treasure every single day with him. No exceptions.

His arm tightened around her, and he guided her around the dance floor. "Good. Because I'm here to stay."

She met his gaze. "Same."

Camera flashes blinked. Matt spun them to face the media head-on, and Bree decided that was how they would face everything from now on.

Head-on.

Together.

ACKNOWLEDGMENTS

There were days I didn't think I would finish this book, but I managed it with the support and assistance of a whole community of people. Special thanks to writer friends Rayna Vause, Kendra Elliot, and Leanne Sparks for various technical details, moral support, and plot advice. I'd also like to thank Kendra, Leanne, Toni Anderson, and Amy Gamet for the virtual happy hours that helped get me through the months of isolation. Cheers, ladies! As always, credit goes to my agent, Jill Marsal, for her continued unwavering support and solid career advice. I'm also grateful for the entire team at Montlake, especially my managing editor, Anh Schluep, and my developmental editor, Charlotte Herscher. As far as teams go, I am lucky to have the best.

About the Author

Photo © 2016 Jared Gruenwald Photography

#1 Amazon Charts and #1 *Wall Street Journal* bestselling author Melinda Leigh is a fully recovered banker. Melinda's debut novel, *She Can Run*, was nominated for Best First Novel by the International Thriller Writers, and she's garnered numerous other writing awards, including two RITA nominations. Her other books include *She Can Tell*, *She Can Scream*, *She Can Hide*, and *She Can Kill* in the She Can series; *Midnight Exposure*, *Midnight Sacrifice*, *Midnight Betrayal*, and *Midnight Obsession* in the Midnight Novels; *Hour of Need*, *Minutes to Kill*, and *Seconds to Live* in the Scarlet Falls series; *Say You're Sorry*, *Her Last Goodbye*, *Bones Don't Lie*, *What I've Done*, *Secrets Never Die*, and *Save Your Breath* in the Morgan Dane series; and *Cross Her Heart*, *See Her Die*, *Drown Her Sorrows*, and *Right Behind Her* in the Bree Taggert series. She holds a second-degree black belt in Kenpo karate, has taught women's self-defense, and lives in a messy house with her family and a small herd of rescue pets. For more information, visit www.melindaleigh.com.